Spring
TIDE

by
Robbi McCoy

Bella
BOOKS

2012

Bella Books, Inc.
P.O. Box 10543
Tallahassee, FL 32302

Printed in the United States of America on acid-free paper
First published 2012

Editor: Katherine V. Forrest
Cover Designer: Judy Fellows

ISBN-13: 978-1-59493-292-2

Other Bella Books by Robbi McCoy

For Me and My Gal
Not Every River
Something to Believe
Songs Without Words
Waltzing at Midnight
Two on the Aisle

Acknowledgments

I'm thankful to Jennifer Morehead, DVM, my old grammar school buddy, for her veterinary expertise. Likewise, Detective L.J. Reynolds for her advice on police department policy and procedures. Once again, muchas gracias Norma Serrato for your Spanish help. I'm happy to include a big thank you to my cousin Jeff, a master fisherman who's authored a few fish stories of his own.

Much appreciation to Gladys for your encouragement and for your keen reader's eye. I continue to be challenged and motivated by my editor Katherine V. Forrest, to whom I am grateful for making every book better than it was.

To my sweetheart, Dot, thank you so much for the many fun hours exploring the Delta with me in search of inspiration, and for the excellent suggestions for revision, as always.

Dedication

To my dad, for teaching me everything I know about fishing and for the long, lazy afternoons we spent on the levees of the San Joaquin Delta with bottles of Squirt and an endless supply of sunflower seeds.

About the Author

Robbi McCoy is a native Californian who lives in the Central Valley between the mountains and the sea. She is an avid hiker with a particular fondness for the deserts of the American Southwest. She also enjoys gardening, culinary adventures, travel and the theater. She works full-time as a software specialist and web designer for a major west coast distribution company.

CHAPTER ONE

A squat wooden building sat at the north edge of town just across the street from the marina. A hand-painted sign at the edge of the road read, simply, Bait Shop. Another sign above the door read Rudy's Bait and Tackle. A multitude of smaller signs announced items in the store's inventory: *Minnows, Nightcrawlers, Cold Beer, Ice, Live Crawdads, Fishing Licenses, Ghost Shrimp, Fresh Shad* and *Ida's World-Famous Beef Jerky*. In front of the shop on one side of the door was an ice locker. On the other side was a Pepsi machine. On the far side of that was an old turquoise and beige vinyl car seat bolted to the cement porch like a park bench. A stack of plastic buckets stood upside down beside the ice locker, and a row of colorful T-shirts hung from the eaves of the building. A neon orange OPEN sign glowed in the front window.

Stef had never been in a bait shop. Unlike a dozen other sports, fishing was unknown to her. She flinched at the idea of nightcrawlers and beef jerky in the same store, assuming, but not entirely sure, that the worms were for the fish and the jerky was for the humans.

She pulled her motorcycle into a parking space in front of the store and took a better look while she removed her helmet and gloves. The place was a relic, an unpretentious, cluttered, saggy, all-purpose bait shop that had obviously been here for a long time and, she guessed, hadn't changed much in all that time. Like the restaurant a half a mile away on Main Street, the Sunflower Café, unchanged in the last fifty years, she had been told, except for the occasional coat of vivid yellow paint. And the three-story brick Stillwater Bay Hotel, an even older business and the only hotel in this lazy river town.

Stillwater Bay was perched on a natural inlet of the wide, meandering Sacramento River. Stef had been in the area just over one week, but that was long enough to have seen every inch of the town. It was a short row of businesses on either side of a two-lane highway bisecting farmland—pear and cherry orchards, grazing cows, horses and sheep, fields of corn, tomatoes and melons, none of it ripe yet, but vibrant with fresh spring growth. On the country roads nearby were scattered homes, most of them sitting on a few or more acres, a metal mailbox on a wooden post sometimes the only clue somebody lived at the end of a dirt road. The area was peaceful, sparsely populated, shaded by gnarly oaks and soaring eucalyptus. It was hard to believe they were only seventy miles from the metropolitan centers of California's Bay Area where she had lived most of her life. Her turf was Hayward and Oakland, the East Bay, solidly urban and often troubled.

This town was unpretentious. It was a town people lived in. It wasn't like the quaint towns in the Sierra foothills that had turned themselves into weekend tourist traps. People didn't come here to shop in art galleries or stay at bed-and-breakfasts or sip wine or dine on the latest fad foods. People didn't seem to come here at all.

But in another few weeks, she'd learned, the town would be bursting at the seams with thousands. Every year, for one weekend in June, Stillwater Bay hosted its annual Crawdad Festival. There were banners across Main Street and posters in the windows of all the shops, including Rudy's Bait Shop. The town's claim to fame, it seemed, had something to do with crayfish, locally known as "crawdads." As you drove into town, a huge red crustacean greeted you on the side of the lone hotel. The Sunflower Café had a prominent sign in the window that said, *Crawdads Served Here.*

Stef knew nothing about crawdads, but in the images she'd seen they looked like lobsters, which, she reasoned, couldn't be all bad.

She walked up three stairs to the cluttered wooden porch. The front door was propped open with a wedge of wood. Inside, the space was dim. The aisles between the few rows of merchandise were narrow. The amount of stuff crammed into the limited space was impressive. On one side of the shop was a checkout counter with nobody behind it. Vintage signs like Coca-Cola, Pabst Blue Ribbon, Winchester Fishing Tackle, and a myriad of old metal "Gone Fishing" signs were plastered on the wall above the counter.

The store was overwhelming at first. She stood in the doorway for a moment to take some of it in: snacks, drinks, hats, vests, fishing poles, nets, sunscreen, tackle boxes, ice chests, everything you'd need for a day out fishing. There were also mysterious things like jars of bright pink balls of different sizes called Salmon Eggs, including one called Balls O' Fire with the slogan, Soft but Satisfying.

At the front of the store, under the window, stood a five-foot wide aquarium full of small lobster-like creatures, greenish and ruddy brown with long claws, antennae and fanned tails. Crawdads, she guessed. She took a closer look at the critters before turning her attention to the two men in the store, an old man with a bushy white beard and a middle-aged man with a squarish head and thick, steel-gray hair. The latter was shorter than Stef, about five six with one eye open a little wider than the other, both of them half hidden under unruly black eyebrows. In his hand was a Styrofoam carton. He was arguing with the older man, who wore a yellow short-sleeved T-shirt under dark blue coveralls, hanging loosely on his legs but stretched tightly across his rounded stomach.

Based on the conversation between them, she guessed the shorter one was the owner of the store. Her suspicion became fact when the old man called him "Rudy." As soon as she'd seen the name on the sign out front, she'd started an automatic process of classification. Rudy, Rudolf, Rudolpho…German, Italian, Portuguese. It was a byproduct of her training that she attempted to pigeonhole everybody by the slightest bit of information. Rudy could have been of Italian descent with his dark eyes and swarthy complexion, but his speech was pure American.

"If you don't want these," he told the old man, "then go with bloodworms. Always reliable for cats."

"I don't want worms," the old man countered in a grainy voice. "Best bait I ever used was chicken livers. Caught a lot of fish on chicken livers. Last month I hooked a monster on a chicken liver. He was so big he snapped my fifteen pound test line clean off."

"You sure you didn't land an old tire?" Rudy chuckled.

"It was a channel cat," the old man insisted. "He was churning up water like a paddle wheeler. That's what you get with chicken livers."

"Yeah, I know, I know," Rudy grumbled. "Chicken livers are your favorite. Been that way for sixty years."

"Turkey livers are even better, but ain't no place that sells 'em around here."

"Then go with the chicken livers," Rudy concluded, waving the carton under the old man's nose. Then he nodded at Stef to let her know he had seen her come in.

"I would, but you're charging three times what they cost in the supermarket. I can get a pint of chicken livers for a dollar fifty at Centro-Mart."

"That's because these chicken livers are all ready to go." He shook the carton again at the old man. "We've done all the work already. They're wrapped in mesh and tied off, cut just the right size for your monster cat. Just put them on the hook."

"I can cut and tie 'em myself and save three dollars if I buy 'em at Centro-Mart," the old man argued.

"Then buy the damned things at Centro-Mart!"

"I would, but that means going to Stockton, which is gonna take me an hour and three gallons of gas round trip and end up costing a whole lot more. And you know I don't like driving into the city. Why don't you sell 'em both ways instead of trying to rip off senior citizens on a fixed income? Used to be you could buy just plain chicken livers in here."

"People want convenience," Rudy said.

"People are wasteful. Next time you get a batch, just put some aside for me and don't mess with 'em. And while you're at it, why don't you sell turkey livers?"

Stef went through an arched doorway to another room containing at least a dozen large fish tanks. She peered at a school of silvery minnows swimming in unison across the front of one tank. Another had dozens of pale shrimp climbing all over one another.

"I got a solution for you," Rudy announced. "When Thanksgiving comes around and turkeys are going for ten cents a pound, buy yourself a truckload of them, take out all the livers and freeze them. You'll be set for the year. Then roast up all the turkeys and invite the whole town over for Thanksgiving."

"You're an ornery cuss, you know that, Rudy?"

Rudy shoved the carton of chicken livers at the old man. "Here. Consider that your birthday present. I'll hold some back whole for you next time. Now get outta here, Dad. I've got a real customer."

The old man grunted and left the store.

"Need some bait?" Rudy asked, walking up to Stef. "I just hope you're not looking for turkey livers, that's all I got to say."

She laughed. "No. That was your father?"

"Yeah. Rudy, Senior. He built this place. Retired now. And in all the years he ran this place, he never sold turkey livers." Rudy grinned and snorted good-naturedly, looking up at her through his turbulent eyebrows. "Now what can I get you?"

"I was told you had Fish and Game maps of the Delta."

"Yeah, sure. The whole Delta? Is that the one you want, or just this area?"

"The whole Delta, all the way to the San Francisco Bay."

He chuckled, then led her back to the front of the store where he slipped behind the counter. On one end of it was a big plastic jar labeled Ida's World-Famous Beef Jerky. Stef opened the jar and took a piece out.

Rudy put a map on the counter. "That's the one. Shows every river and all the feeders, all the navigable sloughs and cuts, location of gas pumps, pump-out stations, marinas, stores, everything you wanna know." He opened the map and spread it out between them. "Here we are right here." He pointed to the town of Stillwater Bay, situated in the middle of dozens of snaking blue lines. "Head west from here on the Sacramento River. On to Suisun Bay, then you sail right into San Francisco Bay. That's the direct route. You'll be there tomorrow."

Stef ripped off a bite of the jerky with her teeth. It was moist, tangy and peppery.

"Or you can wind your way through all these little channels," Rudy said, tracing small blue waterways with his index finger, "find some hidden fishing holes, and maybe make it to the Bay in five years."

She nodded appreciatively. "How much?"

"Six dollars. And a dollar for the jerky."

"This is good. I'll take another." She handed him the money and helped herself to another strip of jerky.

"I'll tell Ida you said so."

"Ida's local?"

"Yep. She's my wife. Makes that out of London broil. Nice and lean. The marinade, that's a secret. She won't even tell me what's in it."

Stef scanned the map, noting the vast network of waterways branching out from several rivers on their way to the Pacific Ocean, creating hundreds of islands amid the flowing tendrils. As Rudy suggested, a person could spend years exploring all those twists and turns.

"What kind of boat you got?" Rudy asked.

"Houseboat. Forty-foot Crest pontoon."

"Crest pontoon? What year?"

"Seventy-five."

Rudy whistled. "A classic! Nice. So you'll be exploring a bit. Doing any fishing?"

"I might," said Stef uncertainly.

"What'll you go for?"

"I don't know. What do you suggest?"

His face lit up at the question. "Most folks go for either stripers or catfish. If you want a surefire thing, go for cats. You can catch a cat with a bare hook around here, but I recommend bloodworms. Some people swear by chicken livers." He laughed. "If you want an adventure, you can try for sturgeon."

"Sturgeon?"

"Oh, there are some scary fish out there." His wide eye grew even wider, then he stepped over to a wall of photos and pointed at one. "Look here. That's Whitey Wilson with a three hundred pounder."

Stef peered at the photo. A bowlegged old man stood beside a hanging fish that was bigger than he was. "He caught that out here?"

"Yep. Whitey's passed on to a better place years ago now, but he used to buy his bait right here every Sunday morning. Caught that one with ghost shrimp. Nowadays, if they're bigger than six feet, you gotta put 'em back. A fish like that might be two hundred years old."

"Are you kidding?"

"Nope. Sturgeon are slow growers, but they live a long time. They come up here in spring to spawn, so that's when you can catch them."

All of the photos on the wall around Whitey Wilson and his sturgeon were of anglers with their catches. There were men, women and children, some of the children barely walking age, proudly displaying their fish. One little, dark-haired girl in a yellowed photo held a line with two fish hanging off two hooks. Must have been a memorable day for her, Stef mused, noting the girl's huge grin.

"You need a fishing license?" Rudy asked.

"Not today. I'll just take the map. Thanks for the advice."

"Any time." He folded the map and handed it to her.

She left the shop, emerging into the bright sunlight

squinting. Her boat was a long way from exploring the sloughs and rivers of the Delta, but she wanted the map to remind her of what she was working toward. It would help her imagine her future, leisurely exploring the maze of waterways, listening to frogs croaking and geese honking, enjoying the solitude, so far, far away from the crazy streets of East Bay cities and the reminders of why she no longer had a life there.

If only she could quit having nightmares, she could really leave all of that behind.

She walked to her bike, looking across the street at the rows of pleasure boats rocking gently in their berths. Each slip contained somebody's means of escape. Beyond the marina, the wide, greenish gray river lay sparkling under the hot afternoon sun, its distant bank lined with slender tule stalks.

She glanced at the map in her hand, sucked in a deep breath and thought, *This is my salvation.*

CHAPTER TWO

Wind decorated the surface of the water with a regular pattern of inch-high ripples that sparkled in the early evening sunshine. Jackie paddled steadily, matching Gail's pace, moving her kayak unhurriedly upstream. Like always, Jackie had her eye out for wildlife, a muskrat or river otter if she was lucky, but more likely a great blue heron would appear in the shallows near the shore, its slender head cocked to keep one eye on the water, waiting for a meal.

At a fork, Gail's bright yellow craft veered right into Duggan Creek and Jackie followed. They entered a narrower waterway shaded by large overhanging trees where the sunshine didn't penetrate. Jackie had been here plenty of times before and knew the likelihood of seeing herons was high, but fishermen, so plentiful on the banks of larger sloughs, were rare. This stream off of Georgiana Slough cut through acres of grazing grassland with few inhabitants other than cattle. She saw cows now and then, wading down to the shore to take a drink or cool off. But at this time of the evening, she didn't expect any cows. They would have headed back to the dairy by now to be milked and fed.

It was quiet except for the sound of their paddles cutting the surface of the water and the occasional croaking frog that always went silent as they approached. Duggan Creek was narrow but deep, so it flowed slow and smooth-surfaced. It was still swollen with spring rains, though it was late May and there had been no rain at all since April.

Plowing the way ahead, Gail wore a red baseball cap over her curly blonde hair and a sleeveless blouse that revealed her pale upper arms and the distinct line where the short sleeves of her Fish and Game uniform fell. Below that line, her arms were already thoroughly tanned from working outside much of the time. By mid-summer her face and arms would be dark brown. At forty-two, she was lean and sinewy, shaped like an athlete, a long-distance runner, not a wrestler, straight up and down with no curves. But Gail wasn't a runner. She was just naturally skinny, blessed with an efficient metabolism. Her wife Pat complained bitterly on a regular basis that she and Gail ate the same diet, yet she kept getting fatter and Gail got even thinner.

Gail and Pat were Jackie's best friends, the three of them making up the core of Stillwater's lesbian community. Gail had been in town five years, since she started working for Fish and Game, but Jackie had known Pat all her life. Their families were neighbors. The Wongs had been in Stillwater Bay since the beginning. They were one of the families who had settled here when the Chinese arrived in the 1800s to build the vast levee system.

Recalling Pat as a child, Jackie remembered the thin, willowy girl who gave the appearance of extreme fragility, an impression enhanced by her pale skin and petite build. Despite the look, Jackie knew Pat as anything but fragile. She was quiet and docile most of the time, but messing with her was a bad idea. She could turn ruthless in a second, as more than one playground bully had learned. Jackie herself had made the mistake of pulling her hair once when they were little and had ended up on her back on the ground with the wind knocked out of her and her nose bleeding. That was the last time she'd even considered tangling with tiny Patricia Wong.

Despite their long-term acquaintance, Jackie had never guessed Pat might be gay. Pat claimed she had never guessed it either…until Gail showed up. Gail was her first lesbian romance and, by all appearances, would also be her last. They were a solid, well-matched couple.

"How was your day?" Gail asked without turning around.

"The kind I dread," Jackie replied. "I had to put a cat down."

"Oh, that's lousy."

"It was. A little girl and her mother brought in their orange tabby. He'd been hit by a car and there was nothing I could do. The girl looked at me with big round watery eyes like she was expecting a miracle." Jackie sighed.

"Sorry about that."

"Yeah. Not what you want to see come in…ever. That's why I called you tonight. So you could make me laugh."

"Oh! I'm the comic relief, am I?" Gail laughed her deep, carefree chortle, scaring up a pair of ducks. They lifted off from the water and circled above, looking for a less crowded place to roost.

"But I do have some good news," Jackie said. "You remember that shepherd we rescued last month?"

"Sure. The one that was nearly starved to death. Stupid bastards." Gail was referring to the previous owners of the dog who had been evicted from their rental and had left their pets behind. The cats had fared better, being free to roam and find food, but the dog had been confined to the backyard with nothing to eat but grass. Fortunately, a neighbor had finally noticed that the vacant house was not entirely uninhabited and had brought the dog to Jackie. Her veterinary hospital wasn't officially a rescue center, but it wasn't unusual for people to "donate" ailing animals they found. Jackie didn't ever turn them away and most of the time the story had a happy ending. She had a knack for finding the right home for the right pet. Once in a while, the right home turned out to be her own. She thought briefly of her menagerie. At least this dog would not be joining them. She didn't expect to have any trouble finding a new family for him.

"He's recovered," she said. "Physically, at least. And is coming around otherwise. Much less timid now."

"Poor thing."

"We named him Mortimer. I think I can start looking for a home for him soon. You interested?"

Gail spun around to furrow her brow at Jackie. "Oh, no you don't!"

"All he needs is some love and patience. He'll be a great pet once he learns to trust again."

"One dog is enough," Gail said firmly. She and Pat had adopted a dog from Jackie a year ago, a boxer mix, Bosco, whom they were very happy with. And, equally important, he was as happy with them.

Jackie smiled to let Gail know she was teasing. "What about you?" she asked. "How was your day?"

"Pretty routine for me." Gail stopped paddling and let the paddle rest across her boat. It drifted sideways until they were facing one another, Gail's craft floating backwards. "I wish some things weren't so routine. I stopped out at Whiskey Slough this morning. Some greenhorn. He'd caught a large-mouth that had swallowed the hook. He'd practically tore the fish up trying to get it out. Damn fool was planning on throwing it back. As if he thought it would live."

Jackie shook her head.

"I told him the fish was too injured to survive. It was legal size. He could keep it. He said he didn't want to eat it. Didn't like fish."

"What'd you do?"

"I put it out of its misery. It was practically dead already anyway from being out of the water while he shoved a pair of needlenose pliers down its throat. I suggested he use it for cut bait."

"People think fish are incredibly resilient," Jackie added. "That they can handle a huge amount of misuse."

Gail shoved her paddle in the water and pushed her kayak face forward again. "They're actually not that tough."

"But they're not mammals. They don't smile or look sad, so people don't think they suffer."

"Right. That's why we use the smiling cartoon fish with the kids, to show they can be happy or sad just like them, and hope they grow up to be sensitive anglers."

"You're doing your part, Gail. The kids get a kick out of those lectures. My nephew Adam was so excited that day you came to his class. He said you brought mudpuppies."

"Yeah. Kids like salamanders, especially mudpuppies because of their name. I'll tell you what, though. When I set out to be a wildlife biologist, I had this idea I'd be protecting deer and other furry forest animals from poachers, forest fires and that sort of thing." She shook her head. "Turns out it's all about fish."

"Especially around here," Jackie noted.

They went around a bend and the creek narrowed again. None of this territory was new to Jackie. She knew every curve, the names of all the waterways and their characters in every season. It was late spring now and the occasional patch of wildflowers poked up through the bordering grasses. The bank was lined with willow, scrub oak and thorny wild blackberry vines with their clusters of light green berries promising a summer bounty of sweet purple fruit.

"What's that?" Gail asked, pointing to the east bank.

A large animal moved through the brush on shore. They lifted their paddles and watched, letting the boats drift. As they neared, Jackie saw it was a dog with a beautiful amber-colored coat and red collar, rutting through the grass.

"A golden retriever," she said.

As they watched, the dog started digging at the ground with its forepaws. Unusual to see a dog here, Jackie thought. He must have come from one of the farmhouses.

At the sound of a short whistle, the dog looked up. Jackie followed the direction of his nose to see a woman thirty feet further on. She stood under an oak tree, wearing camouflage cargo pants and an open, long-sleeved shirt over a black form-fitting top. Her hair was dark brown, wavy and shoulder length.

She was tall with a shapely body, but her face was in shadow and Jackie couldn't make out any detail.

"Deuce!" called the woman, her voice echoing across the waterway.

The dog left the hole he was digging and bounded to her side as the kayaks drew nearer.

Gail turned around to raise her eyebrows at Jackie, then turned back to give the woman a wave.

The woman on shore reached up a hand to push her hair back. As she looked their way, a ray of light through the tree branches briefly illuminated her, revealing a pale, youthful face. Her eyebrows were arched and her eyes narrowed in an attempt to see them clearly through the glare of the sun. She waved back tentatively before turning and walking away from the water, the dog running ahead of her. She had disappeared beyond the horizon of the bank before they reached her location.

"Oh, mama!" Gail exclaimed. "Who was *that*?"

"Don't know. Never saw her before."

"I thought you knew everybody around here?"

"Not anymore. The town's growing. There's that new development on the north side. Or she could just be visiting somebody."

"Miss Tall, Dark and Delicious can visit me anytime," Gail declared with enthusiasm.

Gail was a self-acknowledged flirt and sometimes got downright crude in her suggestive remarks, but she was devoted to her wife Pat, and it was all in fun for her. Especially since in a town the size of Stillwater Bay, lesbians were rare and Gail's flirty behavior was almost always directed at straight women. Single lesbians were rarer yet. Single lesbians you hadn't already dated were nonexistent. Or if they did exist, they were so far in the closet you'd need superpower gaydar to detect them. If they were that far in the closet, no point to it anyway. *Slim pickin's in these parts*, Jackie thought, not for the first time.

It was unusual to see someone on this particular stretch of the creek, so she was mildly curious. It was true, she knew almost everybody in town. Not hard to do with a population under a thousand. Stillwater Bay was a town of merchants supporting the farming, fishing, boating and tourist trade. Jackie's family, her paternal grandparents, had moved into town in 1947 after her grandfather had gotten out of the army and bought a small, affordable house in the heart of the California Delta. It was that house they were now paddling toward with its weathered wooden dock. It was Jackie's house now. Her grandparents had sold it to her and moved "downtown" two years ago, feeling suddenly that the five miles into town was too far to drive on a regular basis.

As they edged the kayaks up to shore and stepped out into shallow water, Jackie asked, "What time does Pat get home tonight?"

"Ten. She's got her night class. I'll be ecstatic when she gets enough seniority to have regular, daytime hours."

Pat was a teacher at a vocational school. Because she hadn't been there long, she'd been saddled with night and weekend classes, leaving Gail to fend for herself more often than she would like.

"You don't sound like you care for my company," Jackie pouted, grabbing the rope on the front of her kayak. She hauled it up on the bank, sliding it easily across the grass.

"I adore your company, Jacks!" Gail laughed. "What would I do without you? But I'd like to spend a whole weekend with my woman once in a while. Besides, one of these days you're going to have your own significant other and no time for me."

Jackie sighed, then smiled, knowing there was no need to comment. Gail was well acquainted with Jackie's romantic prospects, or lack thereof.

Gail pulled the other kayak up on the bank as Rooster, Jackie's one-eyed dachshund, came running toward them, tongue out, tail zipping back and forth like hummingbird wings. Gail scratched his head as he happily greeted her.

"So we've got hours to kill," Jackie said. "How about a movie?"

"Okay. What're you in the mood for?"

Jackie picked up Rooster and gave his wriggling body a squeeze. "There's a new lesbian romance that just came out."

Gail laughed shortly. "Are you kidding? You think I'm going to waste a hot lesbo flick on you?"

Jackie conceded her stupidity with a sigh. "What then?"

"Crime drama. Adventure. Something with cars blowing up."

With Gail following, Jackie carried Rooster through her backyard to the cozy two-bedroom house she shared with the little dog, three cats, a gerbil, four chickens and a freshwater aquarium full of an ever-changing array of aquatic life.

"Maybe we should play Scrabble," Jackie suggested, pulling open the back door.

"No, thank you. You always win. I know I'm not your dream date, Jacks, but until she shows up you can put up with a mindless blood-and-guts movie now and then. You make some popcorn and I'll see if I can find something both of us might like."

Jackie put Rooster down on the back porch, then went to the kitchen while Gail headed to the family room. Gail would never be Jackie's dream date, but she was a good friend and Jackie was grateful for her. She took the popcorn kernels out of the cupboard, flashing back to Miss Tall, Dark and Delicious on the shore of Duggan Creek. Now somebody like that, she thought wistfully, could definitely qualify as her dream date.

CHAPTER THREE

Needham turned a sharp corner, sliding out of his stride, nearly losing his balance. A shot rang out from Molina's gun. A clean miss. Molina rounded the corner two seconds behind Needham, his department-issued boots hitting asphalt as sharp slaps that echoed down the street. Stef lagged behind. She was having trouble breathing, gasping to take in each breath. She didn't know why. She was in great shape. They hadn't run far. Something was wrong with her. Heart attack? she wondered, as she labored to catch up.

She heard a siren somewhere in the distance. *Was that their backup?*

As she turned the corner into an alley between concrete apartment buildings, she saw Needham running up ahead. Molina fired again, aiming low. The bullet grazed Needham's leg. He went down with a cry of pain and Molina was on him fast, slamming him face down in the street, a knee in his back. Stef stood back with her gun trained on Needham as Molina cuffed him.

No longer running, Stef still couldn't catch her breath. She felt like she was drowning.

Out of nowhere, somebody jumped her, knocking her sideways and grabbing for her gun. As she lost her balance, her body went into slow motion. She took her left hand off the gun to fight off the attacker, catching him under the chin and pushing his face back as hard as she could.

Why hadn't she heard him coming? The sirens in the distance? The hum of an air conditioner in a nearby window? Her own labored breathing? There was another sound too. The familiar ring of a cell phone.

Fighting against her assailant in slow motion, she realized she was holding her breath. All of a sudden their struggle was taking place underwater. She kicked at the man and clawed at the water, trying to get to the surface so she could breathe. For some reason she could still hear a phone ringing. Finally, slapping at the water and kicking as hard as she could, her lungs desperate to suck in air, she broke the surface of the water and opened her mouth.

Gulping in oxygen, she looked around, taking in her surroundings. She was sitting up in bed in her tiny bedroom. She looked around at the familiar space, grasping its details. Her queen-sized bed nearly filled it with just a two-foot wide area on one side between the wall and mattress. Her bedroom television was mounted on the wall across from the headboard. Next to the bed was a small table wedged into the corner. On it was a clock radio. A swing-arm lamp was mounted over that. She focused on the wood grain of the paneled walls and gradually her breathing slowed to normal.

Deuce, her golden retriever, jumped on the bed and pushed his cold nose against her bare arm. She absentmindedly petted him while gazing out the window at the dry grass that stretched toward a line of green vegetation a quarter mile away. Between the houseboat and the creek, there was nothing but a bare brown field of weeds and hard dirt. Still, that was better than her old city view—the wall of the neighboring building just a few feet away.

It was almost nine o'clock. She'd had trouble getting to sleep the night before, as she often did. The miracle of sleep had occurred somewhere around three o'clock. Though she wasn't on a schedule, this was late to be just waking. She rolled out of bed and pulled on an oversized T-shirt, slipped her feet into the rubber flip-flops beside her bed. Remembering the ringing phone from her dream, she went to the living room to check her messages. Normally, there was no ringing phone in this nightmare. That had to be what woke her up. The message was from her mother, not surprisingly. Stef had avoided calling her for the last two weeks, not ready to tell her about the new plan. She knew her mother would disapprove of the houseboat. She'd think it was rash and shortsighted. She'd view it in entirely pragmatic terms, as in, was it a good investment? Stef laughed shortly at the thought. Her mother was a sensible woman whose advice was often sound, but this was one situation where her experience was of little value. The houseboat was not an investment, at least not a financial one. But just so it didn't seem entirely nuts, Stef wanted to wait until it was seaworthy to tell her mother. Then it would be a boat that actually cruised the rivers and not just a strange little house in the country.

She tossed her phone back on the shelf where it bounced off the edge of a picture frame, a five-by-seven of herself and Molina standing side by side in uniform, leaning into one another so their shoulders touched. They were the same height, five eight. His hair was thick, almost black, cut short. He had a thin mustache, a feature Stef had never seen him without. Even in photos from his younger days, before he was a cop, he'd still had that same little mustache.

He'd signed the photo near the bottom: *Next time, Hot Stuff!*

This had been taken five months ago, just after the famous pepper-eating contest. One of their many impromptu competitions and one of the loonier ones. She smiled to herself, remembering, then pulled a stool out from under the shelf and sat down. She touched the picture frame tentatively. She loved this photo. It captured the two of them so perfectly, how they were then, their swagger and vitality, their affection and playful antagonism. He had been a brother to her in every way but blood. She especially loved the expression on her own face, so carefree and confident, like she had the world in the palm of her hand. Maybe because in hindsight she had.

Was that only five months ago? she marveled, counting the months back to a mild winter day on a patch of lawn behind the police department building.

One of those much-loved Friday cookouts was underway. A big barrel barbecue was loaded with hunks of tri-tip. They were carving it up for sandwiches and tacos. One of the guys, Womack, had brought a tub of pepper spread, his special mix of roasted jalapeños, serranos and habaneros. The usual taunting and posturing was going on, but there weren't too many who would venture more than a dab of that fiery condiment.

"No problem," boasted Molina, spreading a brave portion of it in his taco. "Peppers are like mama's milk to me."

"Hey, Byers," called Womack as Stef put two tacos on her plate. "You wanna try some of this pepper mania?"

"Sure," she said. "Why not? Peppers don't scare me. But put it on the side. I want to taste the meat."

"Put it on the side!" Molina croaked. "So she can pretend she ate it." He raised his eyebrows at her in that way he had, a challenging look in his eye.

"I'll eat it," she assured her colleagues, then faced Molina, who was still grinning. "You think I can't?"

He shrugged. "Maybe you can eat that much. If you're trying to prove something."

"You think you have an advantage because you're Mexican?" Stef glanced around at the mostly male complement of police officers. "Or because you're a man?"

As she expected, that comment elicited a round of groans and whistles. Then, predictably, someone yelled, "Throw down!"

A few others chimed in. Molina held up a calming hand. "Now, come on, fellas. Don't egg her on. She has no chance against me eating peppers. Nothing she can do about it. It's just genetic. You set us both down with a pile of spaghetti and she'd have a fair chance. She'd still lose, but at least it'd be a contest."

Everybody went quiet then as Stef stood facing Molina's self-satisfied grin. There was probably no one present who thought she would back down, but the moment was tense anyway as they waited for her response. It was a perpetual struggle for dominance between them, two alpha dog personalities who were constantly trying to get the upper hand in any situation.

It was never easy being a woman on the force. Guys expected you to be weaker, to cry or succumb to emotional stress. To lose your cool under pressure. All those jokes about female officers on the rag. So you overcompensated a little. Most of the women did. Tried to be like one of the guys. Man up! Don't let anything get to you. Be even tougher than they are. If you break, you break only on the inside. If you cry, you cry only when you're alone. You don't let them know you're hurt. You don't ask for help. You can take it as well as they can and sometimes better. That's the person Stef had learned to be around these guys. She didn't make any distinction between an ugly situation on the street and an off-duty pepper-eating contest. In some ways, she was always on duty.

"Bring it on!" she shouted.

Everybody cheered. Molina laughed, casting her an admiring glance. Two places were set on either side of a picnic table with plates, glasses of water, bottles of beer, a pan full of tacos, and two equal containers of pepper spread, two full cups apiece. Anybody who had tasted the stuff knew there was no chance of anyone finishing anywhere near that much of it. Molina and Stef sat down facing one another. Everyone else crowded around to watch.

"You're going down, Byers!" Molina snarled, playing his role well.

"In your dreams, Molina."

They each spooned a heap of peppers into a taco. With her first bite, Stef tasted a nice, spicy flavor, perfectly edible with a hint of burn on the tip of her tongue, and wondered what the fuss was about. A few seconds after she swallowed, the heat began to spread through her mouth like a wildfire, gaining in intensity. *Oh, shit!* she thought. *This is crazy!*

"Whooeee!" breathed Molina. "Fire in the hole!"

Stef glanced around at her co-workers, catching sight of Womack's long, horse-like face, full of concern. As the mother of this stuff, he knew how dangerous it was. She took another bite and swallowed fast. Then she drank a mouthful of beer as a burn spread through her stomach. Molina was chomping through his taco like he was enjoying it. By the fourth bite, Stef couldn't taste the taco shell or the beef. Just pain.

"Come on, Byers," someone shouted.

Molina finished his first taco and drank some beer. Stef noticed the sweat on his upper lip, making his mustache sparkle.

"Don't kill yourself," he advised quietly. "I'll be a gracious victor. Just walk away and nobody will think any less of you."

She shoved the rest of the taco in her mouth and finished it, chewing defiantly at him. They each piled peppers onto another taco. As Molina ate this one, he made crazy faces, bulging his eyes out, wagging his head, baring his teeth. Finally, Stef had to stop eating to laugh.

"What the hell?" she complained. "Are you trying to make me choke?"

He stopped with the faces and they both grew quiet. Stef's eyes teared up and her nose ran. Somebody gave them both a towel. She stopped eating to catch her breath and blow her nose. Three-quarters of the second taco lay in her plate, taunting her. Molina's face was flushed and covered in sweat. His mouth hung open as if he were trying to leave an escape route for the heat.

"Can somebody get me one of those sandwich rolls?" he asked, his voice elevated slightly.

Stef took this as encouragement and quickly finished the second taco. She couldn't taste anything and her entire lower face was numb. Molina tore hunks off the piece of bread and stuffed them in his mouth, trying to soak up the pain.

"You got him, Byers!" said somebody behind her.

She secretly cursed whoever it was, knowing that would give renewed determination to Molina. He picked up the rest of his taco and shoved it in his mouth, swallowing it practically without chewing.

They had both eaten two tacos. They had finished the same

amount of the hellish pepper spread. They sat looking at one another, both of them waiting for the other to make a move. Clearly, neither of them wanted to concede and neither wanted to go on.

Finally, Molina asked, "How are you doing?"

"Okay," she said as the sweat from her forehead mingled with the tears running down the side of her nose. "How about you?"

"Okay." He wiped his face again with the towel. "You had enough?"

"Have you?"

"We're dead even. It'd be a tie if we stop now."

Stef stared across the table at him. He appeared to be suffering. No sign of arrogance on his face now.

"I've had enough of these tacos," she said, pushing the pan aside.

Molina's poker face melted into a tableau of relief.

Stef reached for her pepper jar, picked it up, dipped in a spoon and took out a big spoonful. She shoved it in her mouth. Several people watching burst into hoots of appreciation. She watched Molina defiantly as she swallowed.

With renewed resolve, he grabbed his own jar, stuck his spoon in and pulled out a heaping tablespoon, which he held in front of his face for a few seconds before eating it, his eyes full of fear. The crowd was going wild now as they both ate directly out of their jars. Unexpectedly, Molina abruptly put his down, grabbed his stomach and cried out in agony, then rolled off the bench onto the grass, belching loudly.

Stef put her jar down as someone lifted her arm in victory. Then she took a beer in each hand and crawled to a shady spot under a tree, feeling like she wanted to die. Molina joined her there a few minutes later and they lay under the tree together, nursing their distress for the next hour while the rest of the crew continued their party.

The undesirable effects of that contest had stayed with them both for two days afterward. But it had been worth it, she decided. Everybody had loved it, and every time hot peppers showed up in their midst after that, they'd both laughed themselves silly.

Stef looked again at the photo in front of her. Molina sported his characteristic grin on a mischievous, handsome face. On his left cheek, a prominent scar testified to his violent youth. He'd been cut, shot and beaten by the time he was an adult. Even before his troubled teenage years, his childhood had been the sort that would have turned most kids hard. That he had survived to adulthood was an accomplishment in itself. He had no father. His mother was a prostitute and drug addict. His home was a squalid apartment he, his brother and his mother shared with others who came and went, sleeping on mattresses on the floors, eating whenever someone bothered to bring food into the place. In that apartment, night and day blurred. There were no set hours for meals or sleeping, but the landlady, a strange ogre of a woman who scared Joe nearly to death, came up to the apartment each weekday morning and dragged him and his brother, Roberto, downstairs and put them on a school bus. At the time, he said, he thought of her as a hideous old monster he didn't dare disobey, but as he got older, he realized she was the only person in that building who had cared what happened to him. Her name was Mrs. Avila. The tenants, including Molina's mother, never referred to her in any other way than "Bitch!" That he had hated and feared her through several years of his childhood had preyed on his conscience in recent years. According to his memory, she was neither kind nor honest, but she had played a critical role in saving him.

It had become a more and more common refrain of his in the last year that he "should look her up." He had wanted to thank her and let her know she did some good. "Wouldn't she be surprised," he had said, "that I became a cop? A worthless little shit like me."

Deuce came up and let his head rest heavily on her thigh. She put a hand on him and turned from the photo, but the image remained in her mind.

Next time, Hot Stuff! Those two young police officers with their brash grins had had no idea there would be no next time for Joe Molina.

Stef leaned over and pressed herself against the dog's body, closing her eyes and whispering close to his ear. "You miss him too, don't you, boy?"

CHAPTER FOUR

"A woman walks into a vet's office," Niko started, appearing in the doorway of Jackie's office.

She put down her pen and swiveled her desk chair to face him where he stood with his face full of anticipation, feet firmly planted, knees flexed, both hands out in front of him like a basketball player waiting for a pass. A skinny basketball player. A stunted, skinny basketball player wearing a long-sleeved plaid shirt unbuttoned over a plain white T-shirt. Okay, Jackie thought, he looks nothing like a basketball player. He looks like a goofy kid about to tell a joke he expects will make her fall out of her chair.

Once he had her full attention, he began again. "A woman walks into a vet's office. She sits down next to a man with a dog at his feet. 'Does your dog bite?' she asks. 'No,' he says. A few minutes later the dog bites her leg. 'I thought you said your dog doesn't bite!' the woman complains. 'He doesn't,' the man says. 'That's not my dog.'"

Niko, her receptionist and assistant, fancied himself the Henny Youngman of the veterinary world, though Jackie doubted he knew who Henny Youngman was. Jackie herself only knew because he was one of Granny's all-time favorite entertainers. Niko took every old joke he could find and transformed it into a veterinary setting, even going so far as to mangle Youngman's signature line into, "Take my dog...please!" It was a peculiar type of humor from a twenty-year-old male, but he kept her customers entertained. The old women especially liked it. Every once in a while, even Jackie had to admit, he came up with a hit. This time, the joke was so well-worn that she mouthed the punch line along with him.

His face fell. "You know it."

She stood and put a hand on his shoulder. "Everybody knows it. It's like this one." She faced him, commanding his attention. "A guy walks into a bar. 'Ouch!' he says."

Niko burst out laughing, slapped his thigh, and stumbled down the hallway. She followed him to the reception area, at the moment empty of customers. Bud the parakeet perched on a wooden dowel in his cage, singing quietly to himself.

"Have you looked in on Max lately?" she asked.

Niko fell into his chair at the reception desk. "He's starting to wake up. I checked on him a minute ago." He opened a Styrofoam box and picked up a huge, luscious looking hamburger and took a bite so big his face filled out when he closed his mouth around it. A trail of juice ran down his chin.

"Where'd you get that?" she demanded. "Did you go out? Did you get me one?"

He shook his head, unable to speak, and rapidly chewed until he could say, "I didn't go out." He swallowed, then wiped his chin with a napkin. "Mrs. Peterson brought this in a half hour ago."

While Jackie stared at him, uncomprehending, he took another bite even more juicy than the last, so much so he had to hold the burger over its box so it wouldn't drip all over the counter.

"You mean to tell me Mrs. Peterson, our old Mrs. Peterson with the walker, brought you lunch? Why would she do that? I'm the one who operated on Max. What gives?"

"She didn't bring it for me. She brought it for Max. She felt sorry for him, having the operation."

"But Max can't eat something like that today. He may not be able to eat anything at all until tomorrow."

"I know that, but what was I gonna do? She said, 'This is Max's favorite meal, a double cheeseburger with the works. You give it to him when he wakes up.' And I said, 'Okay, Mrs. Peterson, I'll do that. Don't you worry. He'll love it.'"

Jackie stood speechless, watching him eat. He shrugged.

"You could have at least cut it in half and shared it. When you're done with that, give Spooky her bath. Mike's coming in to get her this afternoon."

Niko winced. "She'll skin me alive."

Jackie shrugged in imitation of Niko's recent gesture, then went back toward her office just as the phone rang.

"You should take this," Niko called from the front. "Mrs. Chen."

Jackie slid into her desk chair and took the call. "Hello, Mrs. Chen, how are you?"

Mrs. Chen was frantic. Her dog, Mr. Wiggles, was listless and vomiting. She was afraid he was dying.

Fifteen minutes later, Mrs. Chen arrived, her wide face constricted into a field of worry, and Jackie took her and her dog into an examining room.

Mr. Wiggles, an adorable white bulldog with one black ear, had an elevated temperature and appeared weak and wobbly. That he wasn't his usual perky self was evident.

"It was that horrible Anthony Agnolotti that did this," Mrs. Chen said. "He's poisoned Mr. Wiggles, I know it."

Anthony Agnolotti was Mrs. Chen's neighbor and the owner of three exquisite Abyssinian cats: Huey, Dewey and Louie. Although Agnolotti wasn't a dog guy, Jackie couldn't imagine him doing anything so evil as poisoning someone's pet. "Why do you think that?" she asked.

"Because Mr. Wiggles digs under the fence. He's warned me

before to keep him out of his yard because of the cats. I try, but it's not easy. Besides, Mr. Wiggles wouldn't hurt those cats. And they're not afraid of him. They parade along the top of the fence, taunting him." Mrs. Chen frowned. "They're temptresses, those cats."

Jackie decided to sidestep the issue of Anthony Agnolotti's cats. "When did the symptoms begin?"

"Sometime last night. This morning I saw he'd thrown up. Then he threw up again about eight o'clock. After that, he just curled up in his bed and didn't move."

"Any chance he could have eaten something unusual? Some medicine left lying about? Do you have any new houseplants?"

Mrs. Chen shook her head thoughtfully.

"What have you been feeding him?"

"Just dog food." She looked strangely defiant, her eyebrows arched and her chin tilted up, as if someone had accused her of an impropriety.

Jackie was used to this routine. "Good. That's the best thing, but a little treat now and then won't hurt, as long as he doesn't get anything dangerous, like chocolate."

"Oh, no! I would never give him chocolate. That can kill a dog, I know."

Jackie nodded, laying a hand on the sad-looking Mr. Wiggles. "He's such a sweet little guy. What's his favorite food?"

Mrs. Chen brightened. "He loves tacos! Whenever we have them, we give him one of his own, but no hot sauce. He gobbles them up like..." She stopped suddenly, looking contrite as she realized she'd given herself away.

"Did you have tacos last night?" Jackie asked.

"No." She was past holding back now. "But I did give him a cookie. They were so good. Mr. Wiggles loved it, didn't you, Mr. Wiggles?" She took his face between her hands and kissed his nose.

"What kind of cookies?" Jackie asked.

"No chocolate. Just regular sugar cookies with macadamia nuts."

Jackie drew in a sharp breath. "Macadamia nuts are toxic to dogs."

"They are?" Mrs. Chen's eyes widened.

"Yes. How many nuts would you say he had?"

"I don't know." Mrs. Chen looked alarmed. "One cookie's worth."

Jackie told Mrs. Chen she'd keep Mr. Wiggles for observation for the rest of the day, to make sure he didn't show any signs of nervous system disorders.

"Don't worry," Jackie said. "He'll be fine. It just has to work itself out of his system."

Mrs. Chen went away in tears, understandably distraught that she, not her neighbor, had been the agent of harm to her dog.

"Let's find you a quiet spot to rest," Jackie said to Mr. Wiggles, tucking his compact body under her arm. "It's that cute little mug of yours, isn't it? Who could resist giving you a treat?"

By three o'clock, Mr. Wiggles was much livelier, running around the back room playing with a ball. His temperature had returned to normal. Jackie gave him a little food, which he kept down.

"I'm going to take Mr. Wiggles home," she told Niko around four. "We can lock up a little early today."

"Do you have plans?" he asked.

"Nothing special. Maybe I'll take the kayak out. You can leave whenever you're done."

"Thanks. But before you go, there's something super important I have to tell you."

About to leave the room, Jackie stopped and faced Niko. "Oh? What?"

"A dog wearing a cowboy hat, spurs and chaps limps into a vet's office with his leg wrapped in bandages. He sidles up to the counter and says, 'I'm lookin' for the man that shot my paw.'"

CHAPTER FIVE

Remembering the woman and golden retriever from a few days earlier, Jackie headed to Duggan Creek after taking Mr. Wiggles home, this time by herself, paddling down the center of the waterway under a late afternoon sun. She didn't expect to see the woman again, but had been thinking about her, wondering who she was.

As she approached the spot she'd first seen the dog, she could hear a steady banging, like someone hammering on wood. She stopped paddling and listened. The noise was coming from some distance back from the creek. She paddled over to the edge and stepped out of the kayak into shallow water. She pulled her boat up on shore, then scrambled up the bank and emerged in what was clearly a cow pasture, evidenced by a heavy pattern of hoofprints in dried mud. There were no cows in sight, just a field of straw-colored grass with a barbed wire fence marking a boundary to the north. Beyond that, a couple of horses grazed in the neighboring field.

She walked to the top of the rise toward the hammering noise. As the view opened up and the noise got louder, she saw something she would never have anticipated: a houseboat. She stopped walking and stared. Definitely a houseboat. It was a rectangular white box with pale blue trim, a flat, railed-in viewing deck up top and two torpedo-shaped pontoons underneath. It had a flat deck that extended a couple feet on either side of the main cabin and several feet fore and aft, altogether about forty feet long. The fore deck was covered with a permanent metal awning and had two folding chairs on it. The boat looked old, beat up, in need of a good paint job and probably a lot more. It sat atop heavy wooden blocks, the pontoons clearing the ground by several inches. There was no one in sight.

The hammering stopped.

Overcoming her surprise, Jackie started moving again, walking toward the vessel as the buzz of a power tool ensued. As she neared the boat, she noticed there was a road nearby, a small country lane, and an unpaved driveway leading right up to the boat like any driveway to any house. Parked in the driveway was a silver and black motorcycle.

As she cleared the bow, the power tool went silent, but she could now see the source of the noise. A woman stood next to a pair of sawhorses, positioning a sheet of wood paneling across them. It was the same woman, Jackie realized, that she and Gail had seen the other day: Miss Tall, Dark and Delicious. She wore olive green shorts and a black tank top. Her smooth, muscular arms were bare, biceps flexing as she put the panel into position. Her wavy brown hair fell across the side of her face, obscuring her eyes from view. A circular saw lay on the ground beside her feet, an orange extension cord connecting it to some unseen power source behind the boat.

Jackie was about to say hello when the golden retriever burst out from behind the woman, barking. The dog rushed at her, but stopped six feet away, standing between Jackie and his owner. Startled, Jackie stumbled backward just as something whizzed past her head. She reeled, tripped over her own feet and fell to the ground, butt first.

The dog barked again, but didn't appear menacing. In fact, a couple of whimpers interspersed between barks told Jackie he wasn't sure how to respond.

"Deuce!" the woman called sharply. "Sit!"

He obeyed her and went silent, looking anxiously back and forth between the two women. Still on her butt, Jackie got her first good look at the stranger's face. Wow! she thought. She's gorgeous! In contrast to her dark hair, her eyes were light, bluish-hazel and wary. Her face was angular with pronounced cheekbones. Her lips were so full and pouty she looked a little like she was sulking. She seemed about the same age as Jackie, somewhere around thirty, give or take. She held herself with an air of confidence and vigilance, as if she were just shy of snapping to attention. Remembering the camouflage pants from the other day, Jackie wondered if Miss Tall, Dark and Delicious had a military background.

She walked over to where Jackie sat in the dirt, raised an eyebrow with an expression of curiosity, then stepped past her to yank a dagger-like knife out of the trunk of a tree. Jackie realized that was what had gone singing past her head a moment ago. The woman held the knife firmly in one hand. Then she reached the other out to Jackie, who hesitated before taking it. She felt the strength of the arm that pulled her to her feet.

"You could have killed me with that," Jackie accused, indicating the knife.

"I could have," agreed the woman matter-of-factly, "if I'd been aiming at you."

They stood facing one another. The expression on the woman's face was passive, her eyes calm and unrevealing. Her forehead was beaded with sweat, a few strands of hair pasted in place across it.

"A girl's gotta defend herself," she said in a breezy voice that seemed to mock the whole idea of a girl needing to defend herself. "You shouldn't sneak up on people."

"I wasn't sneaking. I didn't have a chance to say anything before your dog came after me."

"Deuce," the woman said, snapping her fingers toward the dog. He trotted over to her side. "This is Deuce. And I'm Stef."

"Stef? Short for Stepha—"

"Just Stef."

"I'm Jackie. Golden retrievers are usually pretty mild-mannered. Deuce seems kind of high-strung."

Stef shook her head. "He's not. You scared him. He's actually really gentle."

As if to prove it, Deuce wagged his tail and came over to sniff Jackie's hand. She patted his head and began to feel more relaxed. "Personally, I prefer a gun for self-defense," she said. "More control."

Stef looked amused, curling up one side of her mouth as if in a reluctant smile.

"See the light spot on the trunk of that oak over there?" she asked, pointing to a tree forty feet away. A five-inch circle of bark was missing from the tree trunk, revealing the lighter wood beneath. Stef pulled the knife behind her head, then threw it hard, one foot coming off the ground behind her like a pitcher releasing a fast ball. The knife flew so fast Jackie barely saw it before she heard a sharp crack of wood and it stood embedded in the dead center of the target.

"More control than that?" Stef asked coolly.

Jackie stared with disbelief at the knife, then at Stef, who smiled condescendingly, her expression one of haughtiness. She thinks she's all that, Jackie realized, and then decided maybe she was, at least when it came to knife throwing.

"If I tried that," Jackie admitted, "I'd slice my hand off."

"You don't actually touch the blade. You're thinking of the spinning method. This knife's better for straight throwing." Stef walked over and retrieved her knife, then returned with it lying across her palm. "It's a World War II combat knife. Fairbairn-Sykes. It belonged to my grandfather. He was an Army Ranger."

"Nice souvenir. And your skill is scary cool."

"Just a matter of practice."

"Same with a gun," Jackie pointed out.

"You have a gun?"

"A shotgun."

"Do you hunt?"

"I do some target shooting now and then. I don't get any pleasure out of killing animals. How about you?"

"I'm not into guns," Stef said flatly.

"Have you ever shot one?"

"Yeah."

A woman of few words, Jackie noted. "What about fishing? Do you fish?"

"Never tried it."

"You don't hunt or fish. You might not like it here much. Everybody's into hunting and fishing around here. Other sports too. Water sports, mostly. Skiing, parasailing. I like kayaking myself. I saw you the other day when I was out with my friend Gail. Maybe you remember." Jackie waited, but Stef didn't seem inclined to respond. "Do you kayak?"

Stef narrowed her eyes at Jackie, her expression solemn, and shoved her knife into a tree stump. "What are you doing here, Jackie?"

Jackie shrugged. "Just curious. I didn't know anybody lived here. I thought this was all grazing land, this side of Duggan Creek. I haven't been down this road in a long time, but there were never any houses along this stretch."

They both glanced at the houseboat.

"Or boats," Jackie quipped.

"Then you haven't been here in a while. This boat's been here three years."

"It has?"

"That's what I was told. I bought it from an old guy who used to live on the river. This was his idea of settling down, I guess. Actually, he didn't have much choice. The condition she's in, if you tried to put her on the water, she'd sink." Stef laid a hand on the side of the boat and patted it like a pet. "I got a good deal on this tub."

"I'm not surprised," Jackie said. "Does this tub have a name?"

"He called it Compton's Castle. That's not going to work for me. Still working on its new name."

"How long have you been here?"

"Three weeks."

"I figured you must be new. The town's so small, everybody knows everybody and I know I've never seen you." Jackie let her gaze drop momentarily to Stef's chest where the skin just under her collarbone sparkled with perspiration. "I would have remembered," she added.

Stef tilted her head and regarded Jackie coolly. "I won't be staying long. The plan is to get her back in the water in a few weeks."

"Really?" Jackie glanced at the boat, astonished. "Is that possible?"

"Don't see why not. Obviously, it's going to take some work. The engine's dead. Propeller's broken. There's some wood rot. That's what I'm working on now. Replacing ceiling panels in the main cabin. I guess it had a few leaks up top, but I've put on some of that rubberized roof coating, so it should be good now. It'll all come together."

Stef smiled. She had a pretty face, lean and smooth like the rest of her. Her luxurious brown hair was beautiful. Her multi-hued eyes were serious, solemn even, a trait that appealed to Jackie. She didn't like frivolous women. You could tell right away there was nothing frivolous about Stef.

"You're going to live on the river?" asked Jackie.

"Yep. They say there's almost a thousand miles of navigable water here in the Delta. Plenty of room to explore."

Or get lost, Jackie thought, remembering that Stef had never been fishing, so didn't likely have a boating background. "What made you decide to do that?"

Stef looked momentarily thoughtful, then said, "I'm pretty busy here. I need to get back to this."

"Oh. Sorry. I could help. I know how to handle tools."

Stef smiled half-heartedly. "No, thanks. I'd just as soon do it myself."

"But it would go faster if—"

"No," Stef said more firmly, "thanks." Her expression was tense and unwelcoming.

"Okay," Jackie relented. "Good luck, then."

Stef nodded tersely and turned back to her paneling. Jackie realized there was nothing to do but leave, so she walked back across the pasture to the line of trees marking the edge of the creek, then launched her kayak and went on her way. As she paddled, she went over the encounter in her mind. Stef had asked her nothing about herself, had shown absolutely no interest. Nor had she attempted to be friendly as you might expect from a new resident. But then she wasn't planning on staying, as she had made clear. Still, she didn't have to be so indifferent. If you counted the knife-throwing, it was worse than indifferent. More like hostile.

What kind of woman goes off to live on a houseboat on her own? Jackie asked herself as she headed home.

***

Stef dug through the musty hold looking for a slotted screwdriver. Old man Compton had been thoughtful enough to leave his tools behind. Fishing equipment too. Most of it. He'd taken one fishing pole and a tackle box in case he wanted to do a little fishing from the bank. He'd pronounced himself done with boats. She could have the rest.

She wasn't sure she wanted the rest. There were rods, reels, lures, spools of fishing line, packages of hooks and sinkers and a lot of rust. She'd decided to hang onto this stuff for a while. Living on the river would be a whole new sort of life. Fishing might be fun, a good way to pass the time and relax. But at the moment the fishing gear was just in the way.

Once she found the screwdriver, she walked to the stern of the boat, passing by her knife sticking out of a tree stump. That reminded her of her visitor from earlier: Jackie. Cute girl. Late twenties with a trim body. Short brown hair. Intelligent, thoughtful brown eyes. Big, eager smile. Except when that knife flew past her head. She might have thought it was a close shave, but it wasn't. Stef had given her a three-foot berth, easy. She just didn't want her to feel too welcome. Even if she was nice to look at, Stef had no time for or interest in making friends. Stillwater Bay was just a place she was trying to get out of.

She pulled the knife from the stump and slid it into the leather holster on her belt. Then smiled to herself, remembering Jackie's wide-eyed disbelief when she'd realized what had sailed past her head. Screwdriver in hand, Stef positioned herself above the open engine.

Gay or straight? she asked herself as she removed the flywheel to get to the points and coils. Hard to say. Nothing stood out. Probably straight. Most people were. Law of averages. Stef thought she herself gave off a definite lesbian vibe, so if Jackie were gay, she'd have picked up on that and given some indication they had that in common. Which she didn't.

Didn't matter anyway, Stef reminded herself, since they weren't going to be friends...or anything at all to one another.

Thinking of friends "or anything at all," Stef's mind drifted to thoughts of Erin. It had never been truly serious between them, though Erin had been spending nights at Stef's apartment for a while. But they both seemed to be taking things lightly, enjoying one another's company, not making any demands, not talking about the future. Everything had been cool until...

The old coils in the engine were visibly cracked. She removed them and opened the package containing the new ones, wishing every train of thought didn't lead to the same place. It was like there was a meaningful life before that day three months ago and then something else after it—a kind of purgatory she was trapped in.

CHAPTER SIX

Over the years, Jackie's mother's passion for gossip had been a frequent embarrassment to her daughter. In a town where everybody knew everybody, Ida Townsend knew everything about everybody. At least that was her goal and she spent endless hours engaged in the social networking that kept her in the know. Owning a local business helped, as it kept her in touch with everybody in town, with no more than two or three degrees of separation. Jackie hadn't inherited the interest or skill for invading people's privacy, but tonight she was counting on her mother's resources to inform her about Stef. Surely Ida would know something about the mysterious young woman in the houseboat. And if she knew something, she'd be happy to tell it.

Jackie hadn't been able to get Stef out of her mind. There was something about her, a look in her eye that undermined all the bravado and derision she demonstrated with her words and behavior. Jackie knew that look. It was the look of an injured animal that disguises its infirmity with a show of exaggerated aggression. It was a posture of desperation. That's what Jackie saw in Stef and it called out to her.

When she arrived at her parents' house, she found it empty. This time of the evening, she knew she'd find them sitting outside by the slough. They used their private dock like a patio most evenings, sitting on lawn chairs and watching fish jump for mosquitoes.

It was still light out when Jackie walked through the backyard and up a steep flight of wooden stairs to the top of the levee and the dock. Her parents sat in their usual places, her father on the left, her mother on the right, only the tops of their heads visible above the railing of the deck. They sat in sturdy redwood chairs facing the water, its murky green surface calm and unbroken. Dad was drinking a beer, which rested in a cup holder fastened to the arm of his chair. Mom had a can of mixed nuts open on the little table beside her and her bare feet were propped up on a wooden stool. Her sneakers had been placed side by side under her chair. Adam, Jackie's five-year-old nephew, sat at the edge of the dock with his bare legs dangling over, a blue baseball cap on his head, a fringe of straw-colored hair protruding beneath it. It must be a school night for her sister Becca, Jackie realized, if her parents were babysitting.

The slough was running high up on the levee banks. It had been a year of heavy rains and all the waterways were swollen, but as summer approached, they were subsiding at last and the danger of ruptured levees receded as hot weather rolled in. Up and down the road bordering the levee, newer homes were built on metal frameworks, lifted up to the level of the slough where they were safe from flood damage. Under these houses, between the metal girders, residents parked their cars and boats. But the older homes, like the Townsends', were built on the ground in the reclaimed marshes below the water level.

All of the land on all of the islands in the Delta was kept dry and arable by the levees, six thousand miles of them funneling water in a controlled pattern toward the Pacific Ocean. If not for the levees, all this land would turn into a huge marsh. The levees defined the landscape and anybody living here knew their worth. They also knew how precarious their houses were on the dry side of those snaking mounds of rock and dirt. When a levee broke, it was usually without warning and the result was almost always vast and devastating. The last major break had been eight years ago. The result: twelve thousand acres of crops under water, homes destroyed, livestock drowned. Jackie remembered it well. Her mother and father talked sometimes, especially when something like that happened, of having their house raised up, but it was an expensive procedure. When the danger had passed, they relaxed again and forgot about it for a while. They'd lived here in the same house for thirty years, since before Jackie was born, and it seemed unlikely anything would happen to change that.

"Hi," she called, and all three of them turned to look.

"Hi, Jackie," Adam yelped, jumping up and running to her for a hug.

She squeezed him tight, then he ran back to his place at the edge of the dock. Jackie pulled an empty chair up beside her mother, noting with mild alarm the black and white striped shorts she wore. Like an umpire's uniform, but Jackie was sure no umpire had ever worn such a pair of shorts. She was also sure nobody anywhere had ever worn such a pair of shorts with a green, blue and purple paisley blouse. Her mother shopped routinely at the thrift store and based her choices strictly on price, regardless of appearance, quality or even fit. The Townsends weren't poor; they could afford decent clothes, but Ida got tremendous pleasure out of snagging a "deal." It was entertainment for her, like hitting a jackpot in Vegas. Apparently she had recently gone shopping for her summer wardrobe. Jackie was grateful this extreme thriftiness hadn't manifested itself sooner, when she was a child, or she might have had to go to school in a shirt like that. That was the good news, that Ida was the only victim of her clothing disasters.

"Mack's liquor store got robbed last night," Ida announced, reaching into the can of nuts. "At gunpoint. There were two of them. A couple of young punks."

"Oh, that's awful!" Jackie said. "Was anyone hurt?"

"No. They took cash and a few bottles of whiskey. Scared Mack near to death, though."

"That's the third robbery in two months. I'm really starting to worry about you two at the shop."

"Same guys," her father speculated.

"You don't know that," Ida returned.

"Sounds like the same guys," he insisted. "Chief Schuller thinks so too. In a town this small, chances are it's somebody we know. Somebody's rotten kids."

"What a thing to say about your neighbors," her mother objected. "It's some thugs from the city. From Sacramento. Lots of thugs over there."

Jackie's father turned to frown at his wife. "Now why the hell would thugs from Sacramento drive all the way over here to knock off our little liquor store? Does that make sense to you?" He turned to his daughter. "Jackie, does that make sense to you?"

She gave her mother a sympathetic look. "It doesn't seem likely."

Ida grunted and tossed some nuts in her mouth.

"I saw one!" cried Adam, pointing at the water where several concentric circles spread outward, confirming his report of a jumping fish. His grandfather nodded indulgently.

"Mom," Jackie asked, "what do you know about a houseboat off of Baylor Road?"

Her mother's eyes opened wide with sudden interest. "Barry Compton." She nodded. "He lived out there on the river for years. He'd pull in every once in a while and come into the shop for clams. That's all he ever bought. Clams and Mountain Dew."

"Crazy old hermit," Rudy muttered, then took a drink from his beer bottle.

"You remember him, Jackie," Ida said. "He had a brother named John Paul and everybody used to call him The Pope."

Jackie shook her head uncertainly.

"He had a dog, a little white mutt named Jack Daniels."

"Oh!" Jackie said with recognition. "I remember that dog!"

"I knew you'd remember the dog!" Ida laughed. "Anyway,

a few years back Compton ran into one of the World War II tugboats they've got anchored over at Rough and Ready Island. You know those rusty old tugs that've been sitting there for decades?"

"Yeah, I know."

"Plowed right into one of 'em. Ripped a hole clean through one of the pontoons. Left side of the houseboat went in, under water about a foot." Ida leaned sideways to demonstrate, looking like she was enjoying her tale. "That wasn't his first accident. He ran aground a few times before that."

"Too old to be driving," Rudy added. "On land or water."

"They pulled him out," Ida continued. "He parked it over there on his cousin's land. I haven't seen him much since then."

Jackie reached into the nut can and picked out a cashew. "He doesn't live there anymore."

"No, no," Ida agreed emphatically. "He couldn't live alone anymore. His heart's weak. He's gone to live with his daughter, I think. Some female relative. I heard he sold that old houseboat a few weeks ago."

"Some damned fool got ripped off!" Rudy sputtered.

Ida turned to him. "A young woman."

"Young woman?" he asked, knitting his wild eyebrows together. "Why the hell would a young woman buy an old broken-down houseboat?"

"What do you know about her?" Jackie asked her mother, taking a couple more nuts.

"Not much. I heard she was from somewhere in the East Bay. She's on her own. That's all I know. She's gonna fix that boat, she says, and put it back in the water."

"No chance of that!" Rudy declared, snorting out a laugh.

"How do you know?" Jackie asked.

Her father's beer stopped halfway to his mouth as he turned to look at her. "Boat's a wreck. That's what I heard."

"Most things can be fixed," Jackie pointed out.

"Yeah," he relented, "I guess that's true if you want to sink a fortune into it."

"Maybe she can do the work herself." Jackie recalled Stef's lovely, competent arms lifting paneling.

He nodded, looking skeptical. "Good luck to her, then." He swallowed a mouthful of beer. "What kind of boat is it?"

"Forty-foot pontoon," Jackie said. "Crest, I think."

Her father looked thoughtful. "I think I met her."

"You did?" Jackie turned in her chair to face him.

"You did?" Ida asked with obvious envy.

"Yeah. Forty-foot Crest pontoon. She didn't say it was grounded. Came into the shop for a map."

"What's she like?" Ida asked.

Rudy shrugged. "Tall, good-looking. She rode in on a motorcycle. Kind of gritty like she could slit somebody's throat without blinking."

Jackie thought of Stef's penchant for knife throwing.

"What makes you say that?" Ida exclaimed. "Is she covered with tattoos or something? A nose ring? Talks rough?"

"No nose ring and no tattoos that I saw. No, nothing rough about her that way. She was nice and friendly."

"She was?" Jackie asked, trying to imagine that.

"Yeah. Talked about exploring the Delta. I just got the feeling you didn't want to pick a fight with her, that's all. Just a feeling, like she could take care of herself."

"What else did she say?" Jackie asked.

"Not much. She wasn't very talkative."

That was easy to imagine, Jackie thought, reaching into the nut can for another cashew.

"If you're hungry," said her mother, "there's a peanut butter sandwich on the kitchen counter. I made it for Adam, but he didn't want it."

Hearing his name, Adam turned to squint at them, the setting sun in his eyes. Then he suddenly slapped his forearm, hollering, "'squito!" He brushed the dead bug off with a look of disgust.

"Light those citronellas," Ida commanded.

Rudy lifted himself from his chair and went to all four corners of the dock to light the citronella candles against the mosquitoes. The candles sat atop four by four posts and burned with a distinctive lemony smell, emitting yarn-like black smoke.

"Why are you asking about that woman in Compton's houseboat?" her mother asked.

"Just curious. I met her yesterday. Her name's Stef."

Ida looked indignant. "I can't believe everybody's met her but me. And you even know her name. What else?"

Jackie shook her head. "Nothing. Except she has a golden retriever named Deuce. Like Dad said, she's not very talkative."

"But she likes your jerky," Rudy added, settling back in his chair.

"Well, then," Ida said with satisfaction, "she can't be all bad."

"I wanna go fishing," Adam announced, hopping to his feet.

"He's not using my pole," Rudy declared.

"Not using mine either," Ida said. "Last time he threw it in the mud and gunked up the reel."

Adam stuck out his bottom lip in a surly pout.

"You don't need a pole," Jackie told him.

"I don't?"

"Nope. Go find a nice long stick about this big around." She held her thumb and forefinger in an inch-wide circle. "And one of those oak balls. You know what I mean? Those round things that grow on oak trees. Check under that oak right over there. Not too small. And while you're at it, run into the house and bring that peanut butter sandwich back for me."

Rudy chuckled and gave Jackie a knowing look as Adam took off running to fulfill his quest. They watched him rooting around under the oak tree for a few minutes until he turned and held up his hand triumphantly. Then he was off in search of a stick.

"Do you remember my friend Connie Herbert from Sacramento?" her mother asked.

"No, I don't think so."

"I ran into her the other day and she told me her daughter is a lesbian. What a coincidence, I told her. Connie's daughter is just a year younger than you. Her name is Martha. Martha Herbert. Do you know her?"

Jackie rolled her eyes. "No, Mom. I've told you before we don't all know each other. There are a lot of lesbians in Sacramento. I know maybe four of them. It's not like we're all in this club that meets once a month."

"I know that, Jackie," her mother said with irritation. "But Martha was in the veterinary program at UC Davis. I thought you might know her because of that."

"Oh." Jackie felt contrite. "No, sorry. She must have been after me."

Ten minutes later Adam returned with the oak ball, a crooked but sturdy tree branch, and a paper plate containing a peanut butter sandwich. Jackie picked up the sandwich and tore a bite off while Adam stood expectantly beside her chair. She reached into her back pocket and pulled out her wallet. She unzipped a pouch in it, producing a coil of fishing line with a hook on the end and a single split shot fastened six inches above that. She held it in her palm to show Adam. "This is all you need. If you have this, wherever you go in the world you'll never starve. You can always catch fish."

"Except maybe in the Sahara Desert," muttered her father.

Jackie picked up an ink pen from the table and forced it through the oak ball, making a hole through the middle.

"This'll be your bobber," she said, threading the fishing line through it.

"Grandpa's got real bobbers in his tackle box," Adam offered.

"No tackle box. Remember, we're lost in the wilderness and living by our wits."

Adam's eyes lit up with that thought, and he watched her patiently as she tied off the bobber, then tied the end of the line to the stick.

"There you go," she said, handing him the makeshift pole. "Ready to catch a fish."

She sat back and took another bite of the sandwich.

Adam looked confused. "What about bait?"

"Your grandpa's always telling people you can catch a catfish around here with a bare hook."

Ida laughed shortly and declared, "He is!"

Adam looked skeptical.

"Okay," Jackie relented. "Just to be on the safe side, let's use bait."

"I can dig up a worm," Adam offered.

Jackie wrinkled her nose in exaggerated disgust and pinched a piece of her sandwich out of the center. She rolled it between her palms until it was a tough little ball. Then she slid it over the hook.

Adam's mouth fell open in speechless wonder. He turned toward his grandfather to show him the dough ball on his hook. Rudy held up his thumb and nodded encouragingly.

Adam went to the edge of the dock, sat down and dropped his line in the water, holding the pole between his knees in a classic posture of boys and fishing poles throughout the ages. He turned to smile at Jackie when the bobber floated as intended.

The light faded as twilight descended and the fish started jumping with regularity. Jackie finished her sandwich, her mother finished her nuts, and her father finished his beer in silence as they all relished the cool breeze that had come up, wafting curls of black smoke from the candles into the evening air.

A fishing boat went by, breaking the calm and leaving a series of waves behind that washed Adam's bobber to shore. When the waves subsided, he tossed his line out again.

This was how Jackie's parents spent most evenings. They didn't seem to have much to say to one another, but she never questioned their contentment. Sometimes Jackie thought the definition of happiness was simply knowing what was going to happen from day to day, like the three of them knowing that on Sunday afternoon their family would gather here for dinner like they had every Sunday for years. When they'd failed to do that, it was usually because something was wrong. Somebody was sick or some unforeseen disaster had occurred, like the time Grandpa had backed out of his garage without opening the door, and they'd spent Sunday repairing the damage. Or the time Mom had fallen and broken her wrist. But if all was well, Grandma, Grandpa, Mom, Dad, Ben and Rosa and the baby, Becca and Sean, Adam and Jackie would be here on Sunday for fried chicken, pot roast or some other familiar meal.

People don't like change. It makes them nervous and fearful. Most changes are unwelcome disruptions to the lazy bliss of routine. If people are looking for change, they're trying to fix something that's wrong. Jackie's own life was good. There wasn't much she'd want to change. Except that she'd like someone to share it with, someone who would eventually sit on the dock with her in her old age, comfortably, not feeling compelled to say anything, but feeling content.

Her thoughts were shattered by a boisterous cry from Adam. He jumped to his feet, gripping the stick tightly in both hands. Jackie sprang from her chair and put her hands on his shoulders to calm him.

"Don't yank it," she cautioned, watching the bobber duck partially underwater, then resurface, then duck again, weakly, indicating a small prize on the hook.

"Let me hold the pole," Jackie said. "Then you pull the line up."

He handed her his stick and took hold of the line, pulling hand over hand the few feet up from the water. A small yellow perch thrashed on the end of line.

"You got him!" Jackie hollered. "Whoo hoo!"

Adam looked from his fish to his aunt, beaming with joy and pride.

"You got one?" asked Rudy. He and Ida got up and stood at the edge, looking over at the fish.

Adam pulled the line up the rest of the way.

"Way to go!" Rudy said.

"You want to eat it or throw it back?" Jackie asked.

"Eat it!" Adam said without hesitation, startling her.

"You sure? You hooked him on the lip." Jackie took hold of the fish and eased out the hook. "We could put him back and he could live a long happy life."

"Eat it!" Adam declared again.

"Gosh sakes, Jackie," her mother said. "Let the boy eat his fish."

She handed the fish to Adam. He held it securely between his hands and beamed a broad smile at his family members. "Can I catch another one?"

"That's enough," Ida said. "Your dad'll be here in a few minutes to pick you up. Besides, it's getting dark."

"Let's go clean that fish," Rudy said, putting his hand on Adam's back. "You can take it home to your mother and have her fry it up for you. That's a heck of a lot better than a peanut butter sandwich, now, isn't it?"

Adam nodded enthusiastically. Jackie sat back down in her chair, smiled at her mother and stared absentmindedly across the water, thinking about a lovely woman and a dog in a broken-down houseboat.

CHAPTER SEVEN

Jackie could hear Stef's dog barking from inside as she drove up to the boat. The same black and silver motorcycle stood directly in front of the vessel. She took her offering up the creaky wooden steps. At the top, a brass bell hung at the edge of the deck, so Jackie rang it. Deuce appeared at the sliding glass door, looking anxiously out at her. A few seconds later, Stef appeared and slid open the door, her feet bare, wearing shorts and a tank top as before, and a yellow towel around her neck. Her hair was wet. The expression on her face was a mixture of confusion and annoyance. *Not happy to see me*, Jackie realized with dismay.

"Hi," she said, more cheerfully than she ordinarily would have, her response to Stef's less than welcoming demeanor. She held up the basket. "I brought you a few things. Some local produce."

Stef stared and said nothing.

"Invite me in?" Jackie asked, pretending to be undaunted, but remembering her father's assessment of Stef as somebody who could easily slit your throat. She didn't strike Jackie that way, but the gritty part, yeah, she could see that.

Stef shrugged and withdrew into the cabin. Jackie followed into a wood-paneled interior with scant light. The pressboard furniture was all built-in, well-organized and simple. No extravagance. This room was twelve feet across and about the same lengthwise. A long bench lined one wall. A table, bolted to the floor, stood in front of that. A dark, narrow passage led from the back of the room and a steep staircase led up to the top deck. Along the other wall were rows of closed cupboards. On one plain section of paneling, a map of the Delta was pinned up. On the other side of the room was the galley, an efficient space with several cupboards, a midsized refrigerator, a sink, three-burner gas cooktop, oven below that, a microwave oven mounted under a cupboard, a short counter with a toaster and coffeemaker, and an under-cabinet row of hooks holding mismatched mugs. The layout was typical of older houseboats of this size. The carpet, Jackie noticed, was worn and stained. In contrast, the ceiling looked bright and clean, testifying to Stef's recent repairs.

Jackie put the basket on the table as Deuce came up and invited her to pet him. "It looks like it has everything you need," she said.

"Uh-huh. Seems to. I don't see any problem with full-time living here. There are a few things I want to change. Maybe get some new furniture and replace a couple light fixtures. And take down some of this dark paneling, eventually, and update it with light colored walls."

"That'll brighten it up."

"That's the idea."

"This is nice," Jackie said, petting Deuce. "Nicer than I expected."

"All the comforts of home," Stef said, rubbing her hair with the towel. "Hot water, heat, air-conditioning, fully-equipped kitchen. The guy who owns this land wants to build a house here. He got as far as bringing in utilities and sinking a well a few years ago, then he ran out of money, but he wants to start up again."

"So you have to move the boat one way or another."

Stef smiled, a brief, ironic smile. "Right. One way or another."

"That's your bike out front, right?"

Stef nodded, her mouth hinting that was a stupid question.

"Do you have a car?" Jackie asked.

"No, that's it."

"Does Deuce ride on that?"

"I have a pet trailer."

"Good. Those are nice. And a lot safer. There's a dude around here who rides with a Maltese on the seat between his legs. A chopper. He puts this contraption on the dog's head, a homemade type of dog helmet and goggles, like some old World War I pilot type of thing. It's funny to see, but I always cringe, imagining that dog jumping off into traffic."

Stef smiled and her face looked dazzling. Jackie noticed an acoustic guitar propped against the living room wall. "Do you play?"

Stef nodded.

"Me too. I can play guitar, but it isn't my main instrument. I play the banjo, mainly."

"Banjo?" Stef looked taken aback.

"I know, it's an unusual instrument, but not for bluegrass."

"Bluegrass," Stef stated with a flicker of interest. "So you're into hillbilly music?"

Jackie was used to this sort of reaction from people who were unfamiliar with bluegrass, thinking it was a simple and haphazard barn dance phenomenon or, even worse, the same as country western. "Bluegrass is a legitimate music style," she objected, "and not just a bunch of yahoos banging on a wash basin."

Stef started to speak, but Jackie, having started, cut her off. Stef seemed to resign herself to Jackie's impassioned defense of bluegrass by leaning casually against a wall and giving her complete attention.

"It's just as important and varied as jazz," Jackie continued, "an entirely American style of music with roots in the traditions of the Scots and Irish immigrants, with some African-American influences, gospel and blues. It has very specific elements, a truly unique character, and is appreciated all over the world. To call it hillbilly music is to completely dismiss it as trivial."

Stef regarded Jackie with a look of wry appreciation. She leaned over, picked up her guitar, put the strap over her shoulder and produced a pick. She held it between her thumb and forefinger to show Jackie before launching into a thoroughly bluegrass version of "Rocky Top." She played through the first chorus, flatpicking in true bluegrass style, looking up once to grin and wink at Jackie, then finished with a short, improvisational breakdown.

Realizing Stef had been teasing with the hillbilly music remark, Jackie nodded apologetically and said, "That was great."

"I'm more of a classic rock fan," Stef said, "but I like a good hillbilly stomp now and then." She put the guitar down and pointed to the basket. "What'd you bring me?"

"I thought you might like a taste of Stillwater Bay. You can really get to know a place through its produce, the local specialties."

"Who says I want to get to know the place?" Stef asked.

"It can't hurt." Undaunted, Jackie pulled a bundle of asparagus from the basket. "This grows all around here. One of our major crops. And these strawberries, I picked these myself." She put a box of berries on the table.

Stef approached and picked up one of the berries, putting it between her lips to take a bite. She ate slowly, her eyes locked on Jackie's. Stef said a lot with her eyes. Or maybe it just felt that way because she said so little with her mouth, so you were forced to read her some other way.

"That's good," she said. "Really good."

Jackie pulled a plastic bag full of ice out of the basket. "I also brought you some crawdads. Our claim to fame. You can't live here and not eat an occasional crawdad."

"Crawdads? They seem to be like a local mascot or something."

"Have you ever eaten one?"

"I don't think so."

"Just grill or boil them and eat the tail meat like a lobster."

"Did you catch those too?" Stef smiled, creating dimples in her cheeks.

"No. I've caught them plenty of times, but I got these from a local guy who supplies the restaurants."

Jackie felt quivery all over just standing in the same room with Stef. She did her best to appear casual, to keep her flustered thoughts to herself, but the way Stef cocked her head to the side, regarding Jackie with cool amusement, took her completely off her game and left her defenseless. The woman was projecting "come here" and "get lost" all at the same time. In her experience, some lesbians had a way of looking at other women, directly into their eyes with a merciless penetration. That was Stef. For that reason, and a few other subtle indicators, Jackie was certain she was gay. At the moment, she didn't know if she was glad or sorry about that.

Stef tossed her towel on the bench. "It's nice of you to bring me this stuff, but what are you doing? Why do you keep showing up here?"

"Just trying to be friendly."

Stef hesitated, then frowned. "You're one of those annoying, perpetually cheerful types, aren't you?"

"And you're one of those moody, sarcastic types," Jackie shot back, defensively.

This wasn't going as planned. Jackie had been hoping to improve on their first meeting. Instead, she was now trading insults.

Standing with her shoulders slack, her hair unruly, looking smug and impudent, Stef looked incredibly hot. Her sulking lips were parted slightly, asking for trouble. Jackie tried to ignore all the signals going off in her brain: ping-ping-pinging like a pinball machine.

"I was just trying to make you feel welcome," she said. "Since you're new around here and don't know anybody."

"So you're the self-appointed Welcome Wagon? Should I make a pot of coffee and we can sit down and have a nice chat?"

Being mocked rankled Jackie. "Look, I just thought you might be lonely out here by yourself all the time."

"I've got Deuce."

Jackie glanced at the dog lying on a throw rug. "You know, so far I haven't heard enough out of him to get what a fascinating conversationalist he is."

"What I really like about his company is how little he has to say," countered Stef. "And how little he expects me to say in return. We're very casual and undemanding here, and that's the way I like it."

"People have things to offer that dogs just can't. Essential things."

"Like crawdads?" Stef chuckled.

"Like humor," Jackie returned. "Like culture. Understanding. Humans are a highly social species. We need each other."

Stef took a step closer, her gaze making the rounds of Jackie's face. "I'll admit there are needs only another human can satisfy." Stef's voice was soft and deep, incredibly alluring. "Is that why you're here?" she taunted. "To satisfy my needs?"

Excited and nervous, Jackie took a step backward, backing up against the table. Stef came closer, her eyes full of amusement. She's teasing me, Jackie decided. Though that realization angered her, she still wanted Stef to touch her.

"I was just trying to be friendly," Jackie whispered, acutely aware of Stef's body so close to hers. Their mouths were only inches apart.

"Okay, then" said Stef quietly, raising her hand to Jackie's face, letting the backs of her fingers graze her temple. "Be friendly."

Stef's hand slid to the base of Jackie's skull, holding her head stationary as she leaned in to press her lips to Jackie's, briefly. She pulled a couple of inches away and Jackie saw a cloud of uncertainty pass through her eyes before she kissed her again, lingering, urging Jackie's lips apart. As her kiss deepened, their bodies moved closer, solidly against one another, overwhelming Jackie with the sensation of heat and pressure and a delicate smell of shampoo or shower gel. Her arms went around Stef's neck, letting her deeper into her mouth. Stef's arms circled her waist and pulled her in tighter as her mouth grew hungrier. Desire sprang up in waves in Jackie's body, rising and falling as the tabletop pressed into the back of her thighs. Stef's mouth moved to her neck and Jackie let her head fall back, melting, as Stef planted breathy kisses in a line down to the base of her collarbone.

The grip around her waist unexpectedly relaxed.

"You'd better get outta here," Stef whispered, "before your Welcome Wagon makes an unscheduled delivery."

Stef released her and stepped away. Her eyes were smoldering, but her expression was disdainful. She shook her head in a mildly disapproving way, as if disappointed.

Jackie recovered her footing, feeling foolish. Stef was playing with her. Like a cat with a bird. Everybody knows a cat loses interest in the bird when it stops struggling. Had Stef been expecting, hoping for, a struggle?

"You're right," Jackie said with as much composure and dignity as she could manage. "I should go. I'm sure you and Deuce have a lot to talk about."

She swept past Stef and out the door, stumbling on the deck before skipping down the stairs and out to her pickup. She was sure Stef was laughing at her, if not aloud, then at least in her mind. How humiliating! Why had she been so compliant? She didn't usually go around letting strange women kiss her. At least not without going on a couple of dates, having a few conversations, getting to know her and finding out if there was the promise of some genuine feeling between them. This was so primal. The way she'd felt, so helpless, overcome by physical desire. The woman touched her and she collapsed, devoid of will and embarrassingly passive. Like an old-fashioned heroine in a romantic movie, swooning and breathless.

Jackie slammed the door of her pickup and spun out of the driveway in a cloud of dust.

CHAPTER EIGHT

Molina rounded the corner two seconds behind Needham, his shoes hitting asphalt as sharp slaps that echoed down the street. Stef lagged behind. She was having trouble breathing, gasping to take in each breath. She didn't know why. Something was wrong with her. Heart attack? she wondered, as she labored to catch up.

As she rounded the corner, she saw Molina slam Needham face down onto the road, a knee in his back. She stopped and trained her gun on Needham as Molina cuffed him.

No longer running, Stef still couldn't catch her breath. She felt like she was drowning.

Out of nowhere, somebody jumped her, knocking her sideways and grabbing for her gun. As she lost her balance, her body went into slow motion. She took her left hand off her gun to fight off the attacker, catching him under the chin and pushing his face back as hard as she could.

Why hadn't she heard him coming?

She fell to the ground under the weight of her assailant, desperately trying to hold onto her gun as he tried to wrench it from her. She managed to get her finger on the trigger, and fought to turn the barrel toward her attacker. His face, now directly beside hers, was sweaty, his teeth were bared, his breath was hot on her cheek. The gun barrel was facing his body. All she had to do was squeeze the trigger and it would be over. Just one muscle contracting. That's all that was required to kill a man.

He grabbed her wrist and slammed her hand down hard on the pavement, trying to knock the gun loose.

As her index finger pulled the trigger, she knew it was too late. He'd deflected her in time and now had her pinned down. She wouldn't have another chance.

She looked toward Molina to see if he was coming to her aid. He was! He was on his feet, running her way, but his boots made no sound on the road.

Then she saw the bullet sailing toward him, sailing straight and slow, the bullet from her gun, misfired and heading for her partner. Molina, still coming, didn't see it. She tried to yell a warning, but her tongue was like stone. She tried to stop the bullet with her mind. She could call it back if she tried. *Try harder*, she urged herself. This time she would stop it. She had to stop it!

But once again, like every time before, the bullet continued determinedly on its way. As it struck Molina in the forehead, time returned to normal. Blood poured down his face. He looked confused, reeled backward. His gun slipped from his grasp. He fell to his knees.

Stef's attacker was momentarily distracted by Molina. She took the opportunity to shove the barrel of her gun into his gut. She squeezed the trigger. The gun jerked. The man jerked. She squeezed again and he went limp. She shoved him off. Blood covered her hands and stomach. She stared at her hands until she heard the sound of shoes clicking out a rhythm on the asphalt. Looking up, she saw that Needham was on his feet and running away, his hands still cuffed behind him. She could hear again, she realized, as the screaming of sirens overwhelmed her.

Molina lay on his side in the alley, his eyes staring unblinking at her.

"You're not dead," she asserted forcefully. "You're not dead! You're not dead!"

Suddenly he lifted his head, then got up and walked over to her. He reached down to help her up, his forehead smooth and unmarred. He smiled his cocky smile, his thin mustache stretched out straight across his upper lip.

"Course I'm not dead," he said. "How many times have I told you, I'm indestructible?"

She threw her arms around him, holding tightly and squeezing with all her strength. But she couldn't hold him up. He slid from her grasp and fell at her feet like a car crash dummy, limp and lifeless.

Again she couldn't breathe. Then she knew, suddenly, that she was awake, gasping for air, her body covered in sweat.

The room was dark. She looked at the glowing red numbers on the clock: 4:00 a.m. She swung her legs over the edge of the bed and sat up. Deuce appeared at her side. She put her arm around him and patted him reassuringly, as if he were the one needing comforting.

There was no point trying to go back to sleep. Besides, there was plenty of work to do, so an early start to the day wouldn't go to waste. She got up and washed her face with cold water in the cramped bathroom, with its white molded plastic shower stall and two square feet of open floor between the toilet, sink and the wall. She stood with her hands on either side of the sink, looking at herself in the mirror. Her thin face looked tired. She tried to smile reassuringly at herself, but it came out false.

Three months and she was still having this nightmare several times a week. At first she hadn't been able to sleep at all and the department shrink had given her sleeping pills. Erin had said they made her snore and she felt drugged in the morning, so she quit taking them. Erin didn't mind the snoring, she said, if Stef was able to sleep. But Stef didn't like drugs, not even painkillers. They always cost you something. In addition to side effects, they cost you strength and independence. She'd flatly refused the antidepressants she was offered. It was better to find other ways to cope with illness or pain or sorrow...if you could. In the long run, it was better to rely on your own mind and body to heal themselves. That was her opinion, but she realized there were times your mind and body weren't up to the task. She hadn't decided yet if that was true in this case. She still had hope that she could get her life back. Not the same life, obviously, but some kind of life that didn't hurt so much so often.

That's what all this was about, after all. This houseboat scheme. She was used to sailing on the San Francisco Bay and knew how calm she always felt on the water. To live on water, she had decided, would be a way, perhaps, to find some peace of mind.

CHAPTER NINE

Pouring herself another glass of wine, Jackie glanced at the wall clock. She and Gail had another hour before Pat came by to take her home. They were playing cards at Jackie's dining room table, listening to a contemporary pop music station on the stereo. From the living room, the fish tank gave off gurgles at irregular intervals. Rooster was asleep under the table, curled up next to Hobo, Jackie's old white cat who was easygoing enough to sleep with any of the other animals, including guinea pigs or hamsters, and whom Gail often called "Ho" because she shared her bed indiscriminately.

Jackie examined the cards in her hand, then said, "Do you have any threes?"

"Go fish," Gail replied. "Speaking of fish, somebody called me a 'fish cop' today."

"Who?"

"Some drunk I gave a ticket to for taking too many bass. He was an asshole. He asked me, 'What kind of gun is that? Hasbro or Mattel?'"

"You could have shot him with it and showed him."

Gail shrieked with delight at that idea. "You got any kings?"

Jackie frowned and handed over her two kings.

"People don't take us seriously," Gail complained. "They don't realize we do more than give tickets to disobedient fishermen. We arrest people. We run undercover operations. There are some dangerous situations out there, like that abalone poaching ring over on the coast. Don't think those guys wouldn't have killed a couple wardens if they'd had the chance. And we have the same training as regular cops."

"I know." Jackie had heard these complaints before.

"But the pay sucks. Combine that with the public perception and it's no wonder we're always hurting for people. Anytime we get a good warden, he's off to join some police department as soon as there's an opening."

"But not you."

"No." Gail held out her glass for a refill. "I love my job. Fish cop or not."

Jackie poured more wine into both their glasses.

"I've been meaning to tell you," Gail said, "I saw that chick again the other day. She was at the hardware store. Pat and I were there getting a new flapper for our toilet. Flushing great now, by the way."

"What chick?"

"That chick we saw when we were kayaking last week. The hot mama with the dog. She was buying a cartload of stuff. I said hi, but I don't think she recognized me."

"Even if she did, she wouldn't have been friendly."

"Why not?"

"She's arrogant as hell!" Jackie realized that had come out a lot more forcefully than intended.

A small, suspicious smile appeared on Gail's face. "Jacks?" She laid her cards down. "What do you know about sexy dog lady?"

"I paid her a visit," Jackie admitted.

"No!"

Jackie nodded. "I did."

"You're a sneaky one, aren't you?"

"Just being neighborly."

"Uh-huh, sure. So tell me all about it. What's she like? What's she doing here? Is there a husband? Wife?" Gail's eyes bugged out with the possibility. "Is she gay?"

Jackie laid her cards down and considered her answers as Gail leaned in with an anxious, almost comical look on her face.

"She may be gay," Jackie said noncommittally, remembering the incredibly luxurious kisses they had shared. Despite what it felt like at the time, it had turned into a shameful memory. She didn't want to share her humiliation with Gail. "She didn't have much to say about herself. Her name is Stef. Just Stef. Not Stephanie or she'll bite your head off."

"Stef, yeah, that's kinda butch. What else?"

"She's living in Compton's houseboat on Baylor Road, trying to get it fixed up to get back on the water. She's planning to sail away into the sunset."

"By herself?"

"Just her and the dog."

Gail looked impressed. "Nice reconnaissance, Jacks. What makes you think she's gay?"

Jackie balked, unprepared for the question. "Uh, you know, the usual things that add up. She's got the lesbian lope, for instance."

"Lesbian lope?"

"You know. That gait that when you see it, you just know."

Gail pressed her lips together thoughtfully. "Hmm. Do I have that?"

Jackie hesitated, considering. "Yeah, you do."

"Do you?"

"I don't think so. But it's not something you can see in yourself. You have to be observing. So you'd have to tell me if I did."

"I didn't even know there was such a thing as a lesbian lope. Sounds funny. Lesbian lope." Gail pronounced the phrase with an exaggeratedly low tone, making it sound like something cowboys might do in a rodeo. "Can you demonstrate so I'll recognize it when I see it?"

"I'm not sure I can. Why don't you have Pat videotape you walking normally and play it back?"

"If I walked normally, there'd be no lesbian lope now, would there?" She laughed.

"Very funny."

Gail leaned back in her chair, smiling. "You must be ecstatic."

"Why?"

"A single gay woman with a luscious body, passable face. Yours for the taking."

"Passable face?" Jackie was incredulous. "She's gorgeous!"

Gail laughed, and Jackie realized she'd been tricked.

"But don't get ideas. I admit I was...intrigued."

"Intrigued? You're so cool, Jacks. Anybody else would say they were drooling."

"Whatever. But after talking to her a couple of times—"

"Oh! A couple of times?" Gail slapped the table with both palms and stared in amazement.

"Yeah, yeah, a couple of times, briefly."

"Now the truth comes out. You went back for more."

"She's not for me," Jackie stated flatly.

Gail's grin faded. "Why not?"

"She's extremely conceited and rude. She's a loner. She made fun of me just for trying to be welcoming."

"No kidding? She didn't go for Stillwater's best and most respected veterinarian? *Only* vet, actually, but still the best."

"She doesn't care who I am. She practically threw me out."

"Maybe you need to put a little more wiggle in your waddle." Gail blinked coquettishly.

Jackie sighed.

"A livelier worm on your hook?" suggested Gail.

"She's not going to bite, regardless of what I dangle in front of her. She doesn't want to be friends, even, let alone..."

"Lovers," Gail pronounced in a sultry voice, making bedroom eyes.

"Yes. Definitely not. I can't even imagine going there."

"Well, I can."

"That's because she hasn't spoken to you. I think she may be nuts. She actually threw a knife at me."

"For real?"

"For real." Jackie realized she wasn't giving a completely accurate picture of her encounters with Stef or her feelings about her, but this version of events was the one that suited her current opinion, that Stef deserved to be left alone, just like she wanted. "Barely missed my head."

"Wow."

"She's a menace."

"Maybe I should go out there and arrest her." Gail nodded thoughtfully. "Yeah, that's what I'll do. I'll go arrest her, cuff her to her bed and teach her to be polite...and obedient...and ladylike."

Jackie giggled. "Fantasize all you want. The real thing isn't worth the effort."

"Okay, then, if you're serious. Too bad. For you, I mean. You know I want you to be happy."

"I am happy," Jackie protested.

"I mean really happy. Like clothes in a wad on the floor, skin covered in sweat happy."

"My God, Gail, all you think about is sex."

"And I suppose you don't think about it?" She took a drink, looking over the rim of her glass skeptically.

Despite her anger at Stef, Jackie's own fantasies had been progressing nonstop ever since that day, becoming increasingly graphic and salacious and often starting where the real-life incident had abruptly ended. Instead of stopping, Stef's kisses had become more intense, turning Jackie into a quivering mass of sexually-charged protoplasm. In several of these daydreams, Stef had been unable to control herself and had torn off Jackie's clothes and taken her right there on the sofa or the little table or the floor. In another version, instead of stomping out indignantly when Stef pulled away from her, Jackie had said, "Oh, no, you don't. You're going to finish what you started. Down on your knees, woman." Stef obediently did as she was told and it just got better from there.

Jackie glanced across the table to see Gail watching her suspiciously. She felt flushed and hoped the look on her face had no resemblance to her thoughts. She picked up her cards and said, "Do you have any twos?"

In a challenging voice, Gail drawled, "Go fish."

CHAPTER TEN

"Not bad, huh?" Stef asked Deuce after tossing him a bite of grilled crawdad.

Deuce licked his chops, looking expectantly at her in case any more treats were forthcoming. But she reserved the rest of the shellfish for herself, shaking a couple drops of Tabasco sauce on each bite. She sat in her picnic area beside the boat, relaxing after a frustrating morning. Nothing was going right today. Having no luck getting the engine running, she'd moved on to the broken propeller, but hadn't been able to remove it. The nut was fused onto the bolt with rust. WD-40 hadn't helped. She didn't have a big enough wrench to apply the kind of torque necessary to break the nut free. She'd been running into complications from the beginning with this craft. It was fighting her all the way.

She turned her grandfather's knife over in her hand

absentmindedly, trying to decide what to tackle next. At least everything on the inside worked. When she'd moved in, there'd been no hot water, but that was now fixed. Hot showers never felt so good. Thankfully, the cold showers of that first week coincided with warm spring days. The interior was in good shape, considering. Now that the leaks were patched and the rotted wood replaced, everything left to do inside was cosmetic, and all of that could wait.

Thinking back over the last month, she could see she'd made some progress, but now she was wondering how likely it was that she'd ever get this bucket floating again. She was beginning to have doubts.

She remembered Jackie's offer to help. Help would be good, especially from somebody who knew something, like a boat mechanic. But Jackie wasn't one of those and hiring one would be a last resort. She had practically run out of money. She'd spent her savings on the boat and the new pontoon had cost a bundle. She had one more paycheck coming, then she wasn't sure what she was going to do. At least her expenses would be small once she got on the water. No rent, just gas and groceries, which she figured she could supplement with fish. And maybe a few crawdads. She stabbed the last piece with the tip of her knife and ate it. Then she sat back in her lawn chair, leaned her head back and watched some fluffy clouds drift across the sky.

Her mind returned to Jackie. She recalled the sensation of kissing her, of holding her close, of how good that had felt. She'd been completely surprised at Jackie's reaction. She'd expected protestations, shock and recoiling. Cursing, maybe, like, "What the fuck do you think you're doing?" or whatever Jackie's equivalent was. She had never expected to get as far as their lips touching. But once they had, it had been a tremendous challenge to stop.

Stef kept asking herself why she'd done that, why she'd kissed that woman. Just trying to shake her up? Mess with her assumptions? Scare her off? All of the above? But the move had backfired. Stef's own assumptions, one being that Jackie was straight, had apparently been wrong. She hadn't expected Jackie to kiss her back. She hadn't expected the inviting pressure of her body and the eagerness of her arms. It wasn't Jackie who'd been shaken up after all. Stef still wasn't sure what all that added up to...if anything.

Though Jackie had seemed very eager to be friends, when she had stomped off the other day, she was steamed. She wouldn't turn up here again anytime soon. Which was fine, Stef thought. That was the idea, to chase her away. So everything was great. Just quit thinking about her.

She sat up straighter in her chair, aimed at a shadow on a nearby tree, and threw her knife. It hit the target and stuck. She stood and stretched, reluctant to go back to work.

"I wonder if we could catch some of those tasty critters," she said to Deuce. "There's probably some here in our creek, don't you think?"

Deuce lifted one ear and tilted his head, as though perplexed.

She decided she'd had enough frustration for one day, so she rummaged through the hold looking for a long-handled net she recalled seeing, and after several minutes of digging, she pulled it out. After locating a plastic bucket plenty big for a mess of crawdads, she whistled for Deuce and they walked through the rutted field to the creek.

Walking along the bank for a short distance, she found a good perch on a tree root at the edge of the water where she could look directly down into the shallows and watch for any crawdad activity. Deuce went poking around the grass and leaves nearby, exploring. Every so often, he would run through the water at the edge of the creek, gleefully sending up a spray. He was a happy dog with a puppy-like disposition, innocent, playful and sometimes dopey. He was easy to love.

Once Stef got accustomed to the look of things in the water, she could see the muddy bottom two feet below and a school of minnows swimming back and forth through the filtered sunlight. She sat peering at the mud for as long as she could stand it and saw nothing other than minnows. Maybe crawdads weren't as ubiquitous as the town's obsession with them implied. Or maybe they'd been fished out in preparation for the crawdad festival.

After a fruitless half hour, she stood up and looked around for

Deuce. Not seeing him, she listened, but the only sound was the rustling of tree leaves. She climbed up the bank to look around the field. As she reached level ground, she heard him barking and followed the sound, scanning the landscape for a sight of him. The barks were the sort that suggested he had cornered a toad or something—joyfully excited.

As she reached a barbed wire fence, she caught sight of him hunkered down beside two beautiful brown horses methodically eating dry grass. He lunged toward one of them and barked at its back legs, then tore around in a circle and came back to his original position. He was trying to play. The horse tossed its head and swished its tail, then returned to pulling up grass. Stef didn't know much about horses, but she didn't think it was likely they'd feel like playing with a dog. Deuce had probably never seen a horse before, but assumed, as he did with all animals, they were potential friends. Despite their size, he didn't seem the least bit frightened of them.

"Deuce!" she hollered, standing next to the fence. "Come here, boy!"

He looked her way, his tongue hanging out, his eyes gleaming with excitement, and ignored her, then ran at the horse again.

"Deuce!" she yelled in a firmer tone, then realized he wasn't about to obey her. This was just too much fun. She'd have to go after him. She examined the fence to see how to pass through it. Going under seemed to be the safest bet. She put down the net and bucket and got down on the ground, on her back. She held the lowest row of wire up with her hand and wriggled under and clear of it.

As she got to her feet, she located Deuce barking at the heels of one of the horses. Then her heart leapt into her throat as the horse's leg shot out behind it. Its hoof connected with its target. Deuce let out a terrifying yelp and tumbled backward in a cloud of dirt. Stef took off running. The angry horse turned to face Deuce, rearing up over him. He lay in the dirt, immobile. Dead or alive, Stef didn't know. She knew she couldn't reach them in time to prevent the horse from mauling her dog if that's what he was planning. She reached for her knife, but let go of it immediately, realizing that was no option. The horse came down, its front hooves inches from Deuce's head. As the horse reared again, Deuce shook himself and attempted to stand. He was alive! Stef yelled loudly to get the horse's attention, then she picked up a large dirt clod and hurled it at the horse, hitting him on the flank. He turned and ran. The other horse followed.

Yelping in rhythm with his footfalls, Deuce came running, seriously limping, one side of his head covered in blood. Stef knelt down to receive him, holding him tight against her, feeling the shivering of his shoulders in her arms. He whimpered quietly, his bloody head buried against her chest.

"I'm so sorry," she said. "So, so sorry. It'll be okay. You'll be okay. You're safe now."

CHAPTER ELEVEN

Jackie had finished giving Precious, a well-loved and well-fed Persian cat, her shots when she heard a commotion from the reception area, the muffled sound of tense conversation. She finished with Precious and scratched behind her ears, fearing the scene out front. By now she knew that excited voices like that usually heralded an emergency. "Please, not another pet to put down," she whispered with eyes closed.

She picked up Precious and held her against her white smock, then hurried to the waiting area to find Niko speaking in his calmative tone to a woman with a golden retriever on a leash. The dog had dried blood on his snout, around his mouth, and on the fur of his neck. He also had mud caked on his flanks. The woman, whom Jackie instantly recognized as Stef, was in a similar condition, dirt all over her clothes and blood across the front of her shirt. The two of them presented an alarming scene.

"He needs to see a vet right away," Stef insisted.

"No problem," Niko said. "Just let me get some information."

Stef was clearly distraught, looking completely different without all the attitude. At first glance, Deuce didn't appear to be hurt too badly. He was alert and standing, tail swishing slowly from side to side.

"What happened?" Jackie asked, stepping out from the hallway.

Stef glanced at her and did a double take. "You?"

"What happened?" Jackie repeated firmly.

Looking impatient, Stef said, "He got kicked by a horse."

Jackie handed Precious to Niko, then knelt before Deuce to observe his wounds. He had a cut across the top of his snout and a deep gash in his lower jaw which was open and raw, but no longer bleeding.

Speaking to Niko, Stef said, "Look, when can we see the vet?"

Jackie glanced up at Niko, who knit his eyebrows together in confusion. Then he jerked his head toward Jackie with a look of "Duh!"

Stef stared at Jackie, clearly stunned into silence.

Jackie turned her attention back to Deuce, keeping her smile to herself. "Hey, there, boy," she said gently, visually examining his eyes. She looked up to ask Stef, "How many times was he kicked?"

"Uh," Stef said haltingly, but much calmer than before, "once, I think, but things got a little crazy there. I'm not sure. He was limping, so there's something else wrong. He could have internal injuries. He seems to be in pain when he walks."

"How long ago did this happen?" Jackie asked.

"Maybe an hour."

Jackie patted Deuce's head and stood to face Stef. She seemed to have gotten over her surprise at finding Jackie here and searched her face for information. "He'll need some stitches. Any drug allergies? I'd like to give him Telazol."

"What's that?"

"It's a sedative and will help with the pain. He'll be woozy after, for an hour or two."

"As far as I know, he has no drug allergies."

"What about you? Are you okay?"

Stef looked momentarily confused, then glanced down at her bloody shirt. "Oh, yeah, I'm fine. This is his." She seemed significantly calmer than she had a moment ago.

"How did it happen?"

"He was trying to play with some horses. Pissed them off, I guess. I should have been watching him better."

Jackie took the leash from Stef's hand. "Niko will do the paperwork while I take care of Deuce."

"I'd like to come in," Stef said.

"I'd prefer you didn't. I've got a full schedule of appointments this afternoon and need this to run as smoothly as possible. He seems calm. Don't worry. We'll take good care of him. You can wait out here or come back later to get him."

Stef's body slumped in resignation. "I'll wait."

Jackie realized her manner was cool, but foremost in her mind was how Stef had rejected her attempts at friendship and made a fool of her.

She led Deuce into the back, to an exam room where she checked him over thoroughly. He remained passive throughout, licking her hand once when she reached in to press the stethoscope to his chest.

"Gave your owner quite a scare, didn't you?" she asked quietly. "She doesn't seem nearly so tough and sure of herself today. Nothing like a pet in trouble to unhinge somebody, is there?"

**

Stef sat in the reception room and filled out a form giving her name and address and some details of Deuce's history. She didn't know everything. She wasn't sure of his age, but she guessed as close as she could. The letterhead at the top of the form read Delta Veterinary Hospital, Jacqueline Townsend, DVM, Stillwater Bay, CA.

A woman sat near her holding a cat crate in her lap. Inside was a white ball of fur with two green eyes peeking through the wire grate. A birdcage stood near the reception desk with a blue parakeet inside, clinging to the side of the cage and pecking at a tiny bell.

There was no one at the reception desk. Jackie had asked for Niko's help with Deuce. Before leaving, he had put a placard on the counter that said, "Back in a few minutes. Sit! Stay!"

After ten minutes, he returned and removed the sign. Niko was a pale young man of about twenty, slight and thin with black hair parted in the middle and falling down to his shoulders, and a long, straight nose. Stef got up to hand him her completed form across a counter containing pamphlets about heartworm and feline gingivitis. At one end of the counter sat a plastic jar full of jerky strips. Ida's World-Famous Beef Jerky.

"How's it going?" she asked Niko.

"Fine. Don't worry. Dr. Townsend's the best."

He smiled that smile that meant, "Just sit down and be patient and don't ask any more questions because I'm not going to tell you anything anyway."

She went to the restroom where she cleaned the dirt and blood off her face, hands and arms. The rest could wait until later. She looked at herself in the mirror and ran her hand through her hair, moving it away from her face. Her eyes, she thought, looked haunted. She closed them briefly and tried to shake off the feeling of impending doom. He'll be okay, she told herself. Jackie didn't seem too worried. But maybe she was trying not to alarm Stef. This was her job, after all.

Stef had called her landlord in a panic and asked for the nearest vet, and, surprise, the vet had turned out to be Jackie. It was shocking and embarrassing after the way she'd treated her.

She waited impatiently, watching the clock on the wall as Niko carried the green-eyed cat to the back, then returned without it. For forty minutes there was no sign of Jackie until she finally emerged from the hallway with the cat in its crate and set it on the counter.

"All ready to go, Michelle," she said to the cat's owner.

Stef stood up in anticipation of some news. Jackie approached, her expression passive, her manner professional and distant.

"It's not too bad," she reported. "No broken bones. Some bruises. Nothing serious. I closed the wound on his lip. You'll want to give him soft food for a few days. I'll send an antibiotic home with you to prevent infection. Give him five hundred milligrams every day for ten days, till it's gone. Any sign of oozing or swelling, bring him in. You can take a cone home in case he tries to scratch the wound. Niko will show you how to put it on. If he leaves the sutures alone, he doesn't have to wear it."

Stef nodded at each instruction.

"Niko will make you an appointment to remove the sutures." Jackie held her gaze, her expression noncommittal, making Stef uncomfortable.

"I didn't know you were a vet," she blurted.

"You didn't ask," Jackie said evenly, "anything."

Jackie was so different today. So impersonal. During their earlier meetings, Stef would have described her as nearly "perky." Certainly eager and friendly. Nothing even close to that today. The best that could be said for her manner was that she was courteous. Was it just the setting? Or was she still angry? She certainly had every right to be, after the way she'd been treated.

"Thank you…doctor," Stef said as humbly and sincerely as she could.

She thought she detected a tiny smile before Jackie left the waiting room.

CHAPTER TWELVE

As usual on Saturdays, Rosa's Brazilian Churrascaria sat parked on the edge of the lot in front of the bait shop. The familiar food truck was painted in brilliant colors with parrots, palm trees, a profusion of tropical ferns and flowers and a buxom Latina woman in a low-cut blouse. She had voluminous blue-black hair decorated with an oversized magenta orchid, large, alluring eyes, extravagant eyelashes, scarlet, shimmering lips, and a look that suggested she was selling more than *arroz com feijão*. Jackie's brother Ben, Rosa's husband, had painted the truck. The spicy Rosa on the truck resembled to some extent his wife, though the real woman was less like a professional samba dancer and more like the young working woman and new mother that she was. Jackie had never seen her wearing such a blouse or a flower in her hair. If she ever did put on such a costume, Jackie imagined, it was possible she'd look like the Rosa Ben had created with his paintbrush.

The food truck was highly successful, so much so that Ben no longer worked another job, but worked full time in support of the restaurant. The food served on the truck was all authentic Brazilian cuisine, all cooked by Rosa as taught to her by her Brazilian-born mother and aunt. The churrascaria had become a popular fixture in Stillwater Bay, and it didn't bother the locals a bit that it was the only restaurant in town that didn't serve crawdads in one form or another. Even during the crawdad festival, Rosa's truck delivered the same menu as always: grilled meats with Brazilian spices and sides, as authentic as any served in a home in Rio De Janeiro, Rosa claimed.

Jackie parked and walked over to the truck counter where Ben greeted her with a familiar smile. His round, clean-shaven face was red from the heat inside the truck, his brown hair slicked back from his forehead like a forties gangster. He leaned his bare arms on the stainless steel counter and said, "Looking for lunch?"

"You bet. How about the churrasco sampler? And a couple of fried plantains."

He nodded and ducked back through the window. "Rosa," he called, "give me a sampler. And make it spicy. It's for Jackie." He popped back through the window.

"Dad said he's making homemade ice cream for Grandpa's birthday tomorrow."

"Really? What kind?"

"Strawberry."

"Great." His smile drooped. "If we go."

"Why wouldn't you? Is the baby sick?"

"No. It's just Mom. She's constantly bugging us to put a jar of her jerky in the truck. She won't give it up and I'm tired of hearing about it. I've told her a hundred times Rosa has this thing about nothing goes on the truck but her own cooking. No exceptions."

"You know how Mom is about her jerky."

"Yeah. Impossible!"

Their mother had launched her jerky-making enterprise

less than a year ago, and had done so with immense energy and enthusiasm. It wasn't her first business venture. Most of the others had fallen flat, but this one actually seemed to be working out. Ida had approached it seriously, getting the proper permits, keeping accurate books, aggressively marketing her product. As a result, there was a jar of Ida's World-Famous Beef Jerky on the counters of restaurants, bars, drugstores, grocery stores, the hair salon, the feed store and just about every other establishment within a twenty-mile radius, including the Delta Veterinary Hospital where Jackie's clients sometimes purchased the jerky as treats for their pets. Jackie kept that fact to herself, as she thought it might make Ida indignant.

One thing Ida was good at was bullying people into doing what she wanted. Jackie sometimes wondered if she hadn't also blackmailed a few people into selling her product, knowing everyone's secrets as she did. Apparently she had no secrets to hold over Rosa because she had so far failed to win her over.

"Now she's implying that if I was a good son," Ben said, "if I loved my mother, I wouldn't turn down such a small request." He lowered his voice. "If it was up to me, I'd do it. Just to keep the peace. But Rosa won't budge. Both of those two, they're stubborn as hell."

Rosa appeared beside him with a paper plate. "Who's stubborn as hell?" she asked in her mild Latin accent. The look she gave him with her dark, languorous eyes made it clear she knew he was talking about her. She handed the plate to Jackie with a smile. "Here you go, Jackie."

After leaving the truck, Jackie walked into the bait shop, pulling a chunk of spicy grilled beef off a wooden skewer with her teeth. Her mother sat behind the checkout counter reading a gossip magazine. She looked up as the door chime rang.

"Hi, Mom," Jackie said. "Where's Dad?"

"He's gone to town to get some turkey livers. He wants to surprise Grandpa for his birthday. He spent all morning phoning all over creation looking for a store that carries them and finally found this little Asian grocery in Walnut Grove."

"Turkey livers?" Jackie made a face.

"He's not gonna eat 'em! It's for bait."

"I know. Still, you're going to ruin my lunch."

"What are you eating?"

Jackie held up a meat skewer. "Charrusco. Want a bite?"

Ida sat up straight on her stool with a sudden look of interest. "Are they out there?"

Before Jackie could answer, her mother was on her feet and coming around the counter. Jackie nearly gasped out loud when she saw her mother's shorts, black with a skeleton design in white—tailbone, pelvis, hip bones and femurs cut off at the bottom hem of the shorts.

Ida ran to look out the window, let out an excited grunt and scurried back to the counter where she scooped up the jar of Ida's World-Famous Beef Jerky. Then she was out the door in a flash.

Jackie stole one more bite before putting down her plate to follow. Her mother stood at the window of the truck, her chin just reaching the ledge. Ben and Rosa crowded each other at the window, leaning out to observe her. Ida placed the jar of jerky on the edge of their counter with both hands and held it there.

"You can put it right here," she was saying. "It won't bother anybody."

"No!" Rosa shrieked, shoving Ben out of the way as she leaned out the window and tried to push the jar off the ledge with one hand. But Ida had a firm grip on it, so it stayed where it was.

Jackie stopped on the porch steps of the bait shop, debating her next move. She didn't want to get involved in this family feud, but it was starting to look like it might get carried away and someone had to be the voice of reason. Ben, she knew, would have a hard time coming between his wife and mother.

Rosa gave up trying to push the jar off the ledge and disappeared from the window only to reappear from the side of the truck, stomping toward Ida in her white apron. Ida clutched her jar protectively to her chest.

"I've told you before," Rosa said angrily, "only food authentic to the *República Federativa do Brasil* goes on my truck. Only food I cook myself goes on my truck. Why don't you understand that?"

"What harm could it do?" Ida asked. "It might even bring

in some new customers. Maybe not everybody likes Brazilian food."

"What?" Rosa stood with her hands on her hips, her face scrunched into an intimidating scowl. "Are you kidding me? If they don't like Brazilian food, they're not going to come to Rosa's Churrascaria. Are they?"

Ida shrugged. "They might come for the jerky."

Rosa let out a cry of frustration and glanced at her husband, who was still hanging out the service window, looking worried. He offered nothing.

"This is my truck," Rosa declared. "I make the rules. No beef jerky! No jerky of any kind."

Ida sputtered defiantly. "And this is my parking lot," she countered.

Uh-oh, Jackie thought. This was heading in a bad direction. She started toward them.

"No jerky," Ida proclaimed, "no taco truck on my property."

"Mom," Ben protested, "we've been parking here every Saturday for three years."

"Taco truck?" Rosa looked like she was about to blow. Her eyes bulged out and her lips were set into a thin, hard line. "Does this look like a taco truck to you? Do you see a taco anywhere?"

"Move it!" Ida ordered.

"Mom, calm down," Ben suggested gently.

"Me? You tell your wife to calm down. All I'm asking is that you put your mother's little jar of jerky right here." She reached up and put the jar on the ledge again.

Just as Rosa moved to knock it off, Jackie interceded and grabbed it. "Maybe you should go back in the shop, Mom," she suggested.

"I'm not budging until these people move their truck off my property."

"Fine!" Rosa proclaimed, then stomped around to the cab of the truck and started the engine.

Hanging out the window, Ben threw up his hands, looking distraught and apologetic as the truck tore out of the parking lot, flinging up gravel.

Ida's look of defiance remained intact as the truck headed down the highway into town. She turned to Jackie and said, "And you aren't allowed to eat at that taco truck anymore!"

Jackie opened her mouth to argue, but thought the better of it.

Ida pulled the jerky jar roughly from her hands, then marched into the bait shop, the little pelvic bones on her rear end swishing fiercely to and fro.

CHAPTER THIRTEEN

"Captain Shoemaker wants to see you Monday, Byers," Sergeant Miller told Stef over the phone. "Nine a.m. sharp."

There was nothing in his voice to tell her whether this was good or bad news.

"What's it about?" she asked, though she was positive she knew.

"IA has finished their investigation," he reported.

"And?" she prompted.

"That's what the captain wants to talk to you about. See you Monday."

After he hung up, Stef called her mother. As the phone rang, Deuce tramped in, head hanging down, his gloomy, bandaged face peering out from a white cone. He couldn't have looked more dejected. After having discovered that normal movement around the house was dangerous because the cone kept banging into things, he now walked plodding and tentatively everywhere he went. Both of them couldn't wait for the day they could remove what Deuce most certainly thought of as a punishment.

When her mother answered the phone, she explained about her Monday morning appointment.

"Okay if I spend the night Sunday?" she asked.

"Of course," her mother replied. "I can make lasagna."

"You know I love your lasagna."

"Are you nervous, Stephanie? What do you think they're going to say?"

"I'm expecting to be exonerated. I can't think of any reason I wouldn't be. It was obviously an accident."

"No, I'm sure you will be. I don't even see why they had to go through all this. You didn't do anything wrong."

"It's routine, Mom. Anytime an officer shoots a firearm, there's an investigation. In this case, a man was killed. Two men were killed. Very serious."

"Yes, it was very serious. I know, but why do they treat you like a criminal? Interrogating you. Putting you on suspension."

"It's not suspension. It's paid administrative leave. And nobody's treating me like a criminal. It's just routine."

"I'll be so glad when this nightmare is over and things get back to normal. You can get back to work, get on with your life. I know you'll feel so much better when you're back on the job and not just sitting around brooding."

"Mom, about that—" Stef hesitated. "We can talk about it when I see you Sunday."

"Okay." Her voice revealed concern. "How are you doing, Stephanie? Feeling better? Was vacationing out in the boondocks a good idea?"

"Yeah. It was. It's kind of a strange place, like it's a million miles away from home. It's quiet here. That's what I was looking for."

"I still don't know why you gave up your apartment. You knew you wouldn't be on leave for more than a few months. Now you're going to have to find a new place just as you're starting back to work. But you know you can stay here as long as you need to. We can move those boxes out of your old room. It's no problem."

Her mother, like everyone, had been treating her with special care. Even if she didn't understand exactly what Stef was going through, she did understand it was traumatic and painful. Her mother thought she was staying with a friend. Just getting away for a while to clear her head. Stef hadn't told her the bigger plan because she didn't want to disappoint her. Her mother had always been so proud of her daughter the police officer. And no matter how old she got, she always felt like she was in big trouble when she disappointed her mother. She suspected it had something to do with the fact that her mother was the only person who ever used her full name: Stephanie. Even her brothers had adapted to "Stef." But her mother had refused to use the nickname. That old gripe went way back.

"Stephanie's such a pretty name," she'd complain. Stef had given up "Stephanie" by the age of eleven. Photos of herself at that age depicted a skinny, knobby-kneed girl in shorts and T-shirt, wearing a cowboy hat and holster, spinning a toy six-shooter on her finger. "Sheriff Stef," she'd introduce herself in a growling voice. Her brother, Bruce, who was older and therefore in charge, would correct her. "You're not Sheriff Stef. You're Deputy Stef. I'm the sheriff. You can't have two sheriffs."

"Why not?" she'd whine.

"You just can't."

Their younger brother, Jay, by virtue of being the youngest and therefore weakest, would usually have to be the crook and end up tied to a chair.

She'd let them call her Deputy Stef to appease Bruce, but in her mind, she was still Sheriff Stef. She would have thought it impossible to be Sheriff Stephanie. Why not? she wondered now. Too girly? A girl could be a sheriff. But maybe she didn't realize that then. Or maybe it wasn't too girly. Maybe it just sounded too fragile, more like a victim than a heroine. Like Sheriff Annabelle. Wrong image.

"Have you heard from Erin?" her mother asked.

"No. Not since she left. I don't expect to hear from her."

"I think it was so cruel of her to break up with you at a time like this."

"I don't blame her. I wasn't easy to be with."

"That's the point, isn't it? She left you in your hour of need. She should have stood by you."

"That's for committed couples, Mom," Stef said with irritation. "Erin and I were just dating. It wasn't that serious. I was a bitch, so she moved on."

"You shouldn't blame yourself. Of course you weren't yourself under the circumstances. A person who cared about you would be patient and understanding."

"Mom, please, let's not talk about Erin. It doesn't matter."

"I just don't want you to be alone."

"I know, but Erin was never going to be that woman for me anyway, to have and to hold, in sickness and health, till death do you part."

She heard her mother sigh. "I wish you could find somebody like that."

"And I wish *you* could find somebody like that too."

"Oh, Stephanie," her mother laughed. "I'm glad to see you still have a sense of humor."

"Love you, Mom," Stef concluded. "I'll see you Sunday."

She hung up and glanced at the photograph of herself and Molina, thinking about her mother's desire for this nightmare to be over. Which she apparently thought would happen on Monday. But it wasn't that easy. The nightmare haunted her every day and every night and would continue to do so no matter what she was told on Monday. She didn't know how long that would be true. At the moment, she felt it would always be true.

She felt grief returning as Molina's grin in the photo reminded her of how she would never see that expression again in real life. Another of his expressions was seared much more brutally into her memory—the last one, as he dropped to his knees and his gun clattered on the asphalt. It had been a look of disbelief. It had happened so fast. Neither of them realized what had happened in that moment. It was only later, as she replayed the scene over and over in her mind, that she fully understood what she'd done. How one muscle contracting in one split second had caused so much devastation.

"Dammit, Molina!" she whispered, then opened a drawer and put the photo inside, slamming it shut.

How could her mother expect Erin, who had known her only a few weeks when all this went down, to put herself through this ordeal? Stef wasn't acceptable company for any woman. They had never been about that anyway, the whole building a future together scene. When Erin had said she couldn't take it, that she hadn't signed up for this, Stef had let her go without reproach. She didn't want anybody near her now anyway. She didn't want anybody to see her coming apart at the seams.

CHAPTER FOURTEEN

"Are Ben and Rosa here yet?" Jackie asked her mother, hoping she'd beaten her brother to the house so she'd have a chance to smooth ruffled feathers over the food truck incident. She knew they were coming. She'd been afraid they might not, but when Jackie called her brother earlier, he said, "We'll be there. For Grandpa's sake, Rosa says, but don't be surprised if she doesn't have much to say to Mom."

Ida stood at the sink snapping the ends off a colander full of green beans. She wore an absurd pair of pink shorts with yellow ducklings on them. A huge pot of potatoes simmered on the stove.

"Not yet," her mother reported. "You want to finish these beans for me? I've got to put the chicken on the grill."

A platter of raw, marinated chicken parts rested on the

counter, three chickens worth, easily enough to feed their family of ten. The baby didn't count, as she was still on a bottle. On the other counter, a pink bakery box beckoned intriguingly. Jackie lifted the lid to observe a sheet cake decorated with white frosting and an image of a man in a rowboat fishing under a smiling sun. At the end of the fishing line was a green fish leaping out of the water in a vain effort to escape. *Happy 75th birthday, Grandpa!* was written in red gel script over the scene.

"Nice, huh?" Ida said, digging a pair of tongs out of the utensil drawer.

"Uh-huh. Cute." Jackie closed the cake box and stepped up to the sink. "Before you go, Mom, I want to talk to you about Rosa."

"What about her?"

"About yesterday." Jackie picked up a green bean and pulled the string off in one motion. "The argument you had over the jerky."

"Can you believe that woman?" Ida shook her head. "Stubborn as hell!" She picked up the chicken platter. "I've got to get these on or dinner will be late."

"But, Mom—" Jackie called as her mother opened the back door. It was no use. Ida waved her off and hurried outside to the grill.

Standing in front of the kitchen window, Jackie watched her mother on the patio. Smoke rose and hung over the backyard as she put the chicken over the fire. Her father was on the lawn playing catch with Adam with a plastic wiffle ball. Adam wore a T-Rex T-shirt and a baseball mitt too large for his hand. He turned it awkwardly to allow the ball to fall into it. Becca and her husband Sean watched from lawn chairs in the shade of an old willow Jackie used to play under as a child. Becca laughed when the wiffle ball fell into the glove and Adam looked at it with astonishment. Grandpa, bare-headed and wearing the same denim coveralls he always wore, wandered between the tomato rows in the garden beyond the lawn, gingerly stooping now and then to pull a weed. She didn't see Granny. Maybe she was out on the dock. She liked to be close to water. So everybody was here already but Ben and Rosa.

Jackie stringed and broke the beans into pieces, waiting for her mother to come back inside. Her anxiety was mounting, fearing the potentially loud confrontation that might erupt between Rosa and Ida. If she could just get her mother to apologize for running them out of the parking lot, she was sure that would be enough to let the whole thing blow over.

As Ida returned with her empty platter, letting the screen door slam behind her, they heard the front door open. Almost immediately, the sound of a screaming baby rang through the house.

"What a racket!" Ida declared and started toward the hallway.

"Wait, Mom!" Jackie cried, grabbing a towel to dry her hands.

Her mother ignored her and kept going, on her way to greet her son and daughter-in-law. Jackie dashed out of the kitchen after her, realizing she'd squandered her opportunity to be the voice of reason, and it was too late to prevent the clash of the Titans.

Rosa and Ben were just inside the front door. Rosa held little Lena, swathed in a pink onesie. No longer crying, she sucked on a pacifier, her eyes half closed. Ben had the diaper bag slung over his shoulder. With his free arm, he hugged his mother and kissed her cheek. Rosa stood stiffly, unsmiling, then turned to Jackie and said, "Hi, Jackie. How are you?"

"Good. Let me take Lena to the bedroom."

Rosa handed the baby over. As soon as she was out of Rosa's arms, Ida reached for her.

"Let me see that little darling!" she cried, lifting Lena from Jackie's grasp. Ida cradled her gently, putting her head close to Lena's and making a face at her.

"She's so sweet!" said Ida, addressing herself to Ben. "And growing so fast. I swear she's bigger than she was last Sunday."

Lena's face was scrunched into a series of wrinkles from chin to forehead, her version of a smile, and both her hands were in the air reaching toward Ida's face.

Ida cooed at her, then said, "You two go outside and say happy birthday to Grandpa."

"I hope there's cake," Ben said, turning the diaper bag over to Jackie.

"Of course there's cake!" Ida affirmed.

Rosa gave one cool glance at Ida before following Ben through the house to the backyard. Jackie followed her mother to the bedroom where a crib for the baby was kept, along with a baby monitor with a direct line to the kitchen and patio. Lena's pink face peered over Ida's shoulder, swaying mildly from side to side as they walked. Jackie made a face at her and touched her index finger to her tiny button nose and was rewarded with another scrunchy smile.

"You and Rosa are just going to ignore one other?" Jackie asked. "Is that how you're going to handle this?"

"How do you think we should handle it?" Ida asked distractedly, settling Lena in the crib.

"You can sit down and talk about it. It needs to be resolved. If you apologized, I'm sure it would be all over in a minute."

"I have nothing to apologize for." Ida faced Jackie solemnly. "Do you think it's right that my own son should be kept from doing his mother this tiny favor?"

"It's not a tiny thing to Rosa."

"So you're on her side?"

"No, I'm not on anybody's side," Jackie objected. "I just don't want a rift in the family over something so easy to resolve."

"My point exactly. All she has to do is put my jerky on her truck, and everything's hunky-dory. Until she agrees to do that, I have nothing to say to her."

"But, Mom, it's Grandpa's birthday."

"All the more reason for us not to discuss business today. Don't worry, nobody will notice anything, least of all Grandpa. Now run into the kitchen and make sure the potatoes aren't boiling over."

Jackie left her mother talking baby talk to Lena and returned to the kitchen, checking the potatoes before resuming her bean chore. Maybe her mother was right. Maybe the whole jerky battle was merely a business issue and had no place here at a family gathering. She was also right that Grandpa wouldn't notice a little cooling of affections between Rosa and Ida. He would be too distracted by everything else going on and would likely be asleep as soon as dinner was over.

The game of catch in the back yard, she noticed, was now a three-way affair between Dad, Rosa and Adam. Ben tended the grill, turning the chicken over. Granny had appeared and taken a chair on the lawn. Sean came over and gave her a kiss before putting a stool under her feet. Despite the unresolved conflict between Rosa and Ida, peace and harmony reigned over the Townsend household. It was a Sunday afternoon like any other Sunday afternoon.

Jackie didn't blame anyone for the feeling of loneliness that swept over her sometimes on days like this. In fact, she felt guilty for having that feeling, surrounded as she was by loving family members. But there were few situations that highlighted her singleness so starkly as this one. She was the only one without a mate. The last time she'd come to Sunday dinner with someone had been two years ago. She'd been dating a woman for a few weeks and had decided it was time to have her meet the family. It hadn't worked out. They didn't like her and she didn't like them. In fact, it was that Sunday that had informed Jackie that she didn't much like the woman herself, not enough for a real relationship. She'd broken up with her a few days later, justifying herself with the idea that the woman had failed the Townsend family test.

She could see, in her memory, her mother's almost imperceptible left eye twitch, along with a tiny droop on the right side of her mouth that gave away her disapproval, despite the apparent look of congeniality she conveyed to the stranger in their midst. Without her saying a word, it was obvious that Ida didn't like Jackie's date. Neither did her father, but Ida's opinion was the one that mattered more, the one that would determine the course of the family as a whole, whether they would embrace someone or not.

Jackie couldn't remember what it was exactly that had irritated Ida about the woman, but she did remember them cutting one another off during dinner conversation. They were two people competing for the center of attention, not talking to one another, but talking over one another so the rest of them hadn't known who to listen to.

Jackie drained the potatoes in the colander, holding her head clear of the burst of steam rising from the sink. Through the window she saw her mother run over to the grill and grab the tongs from Ben's hand, making shooing motions at him.

Mom would love Stef, Jackie thought with a small chuckle. *You can hardly get a word out of her.* Then she shook her head, wondering why that thought had come to her. There was no reason her mother and Stef would ever even meet one another. There was no reason to consider whether or not her mother would like Stef. Besides, if that was the only thing in her favor, that she didn't have much to say, her mother wouldn't like her at all. She'd probably think, *What a gosh-awful unpleasant woman, Jackie! What the hell did you drag her over here for?*

Jackie shook her head again, realizing her thoughts were going in circles. Realizing too that she was still trying to imagine what her mother would think of Stef. Which could be helpful to know because for some reason she couldn't explain, she herself still wanted to like Stef.

CHAPTER FIFTEEN

The station felt both familiar and foreign to Stef as she walked through it Monday morning on her way to the captain's office. She felt the eyes of her colleagues on her and told herself it was probably her imagination. She'd had no serious conversations with any of them since it happened and wondered what they really thought. She'd gotten plenty of pats on the back afterward, pats that said, *I'm sorry this happened to you, but I'm so grateful it didn't happen to me*. And a lot of silent looks of pain which she wasn't sure were for her or Molina.

The atmosphere around her in the first couple of weeks after it happened had been funereal. When she walked into a room, it immediately went silent. Nobody knew how to act or what to say, which was partly her fault, she knew, because she routinely deflected any genuine attempts at consolation, and to act as if nothing was wrong would have been ridiculously insensitive. So her co-workers were left with wordless expressions of sympathy. She had dreaded coming to the station the few times she had. But it had been over three months now since the shooting. Everybody else had been going about business as usual during all those weeks. Today, things were easier. A few of the guys greeted her with a wave, a smile, lighthearted acknowledgments.

"Hey, Byers!" someone called. She looked to see Terry Langley hailing her with a friendly smile. "Are you back? You owe me a beer, remember, for that bocce ball win."

She jerked her chin up in a quick nod. "Like I could forget the one time I let you beat me!"

He chuckled. "Nice to see you."

She was relieved at the friendly welcome, but she knew nobody had forgotten what had happened.

Once she was inside the captain's office, he shut the door behind her.

Captain Shoemaker was a fleshy-faced man with a coarse gray mustache and an undisguisable gut concealing the wide belt holding up his uniform trousers. He was a good commander and fought hard for his officers when they needed his support. As she had these past several months. He'd done everything he could to keep her away from the official proceedings. He'd been the one to suggest she should get out of town and take a long vacation while the investigation was ongoing.

He eased into his oversized leather desk chair and smiled at her with obvious pride and joy, like a father. He felt that much responsibility for his officers. Stef appreciated his paternal attitude, but it made her a little uncomfortable. Her mother and father had divorced when she was five. Once her father had left her mother, he'd left his kids too. He didn't visit, didn't write. He'd gone on to start another family and his new kids absorbed his attention. They became his real family. Stef's mother blamed his new wife, claimed she didn't want him to have anything to do with his first family. Stef wasn't sure what the reason was, but she knew there was bitterness between the adults. She didn't really care. Just as her father had forgotten her, she'd forgotten him. Maybe her older brother had sometimes missed his father, but she had not. She was just fine without a father. So Shoemaker, sitting there with his moist blue eyes exuding parental affection, left her feeling grateful and embarrassed at the same time.

"IA has finished their investigation," he announced.

"I figured."

He handed an envelope across his desk. "This is the final report."

She took it, searching his face for some clue to its contents.

"Go ahead," he urged. "Read it. No surprises."

Inside the envelope was a letter addressed to her. She scanned it quickly to assure herself it was the result she expected. Like she had told everyone else, she knew she'd be exonerated. She knew the investigation was just routine. Still, when it came right down to it, you couldn't be a hundred percent sure of anything. There was still that nagging doubt, spurred on perhaps by her own personal feelings of guilt. Once she got the gist of the letter, that it was good news, she focused on the critical paragraph:

Based on the investigation surrounding your use of deadly force, your actions are exonerated. This finding means that the incident occurred but your actions were lawful and consistent with department policy.

She looked up to meet Shoemaker's eyes.

"Welcome back, Byers!" he pronounced joyfully.

"Whoa!" She sucked in a deep breath. "So it's over?"

"Completely over. The DA found no grounds to file charges. You're cleared. Free to start back on the job tomorrow if you want."

"It feels good," she said. "I didn't realize I was so nervous."

"I myself was under investigation a couple times," he said. "It makes you feel guilty of something just being asked all those questions."

She nodded her agreement.

"So, no hurry, but when do you think you'll be ready to come back?"

Stef shook her head slowly, her joy rapidly dissipating in the face of what she knew would be disappointing news to Shoemaker. "I'm not coming back."

"What do you mean?" A scowl of confusion came over his face.

She pulled an envelope out of her bag. "I've got my letter of resignation right here." She put it on the desk and pushed it toward him."

He glanced at the envelope, then leaned back, his expression serious. "Talk to me."

She shrugged, uncomfortable in this setting. "I can't do this anymore."

"Maybe you just need more time. That's not a problem. And more time with the shrink, on us, if you want. That's what he's there for."

"I don't think that'll help. It's not my thing."

He frowned. "Look, Byers, things happen. It's lousy, but that's just the way it is in this business. You'll get over it, in time. You decide how much time. Whatever you need."

She shook her head. "The problem is, I can't do my job because…"

He waited, watching her gravely.

"I wouldn't be able to shoot a gun," she said. "I don't even think I could touch a gun. I start sweating every time I see one or even think about them. It wouldn't be fair to the other guys to have me out there. If the time came to use deadly force, I'd choke."

"Okay, I get it. The shrink can help you with that. You just gotta give him a chance."

"A chance to do what exactly?"

"To get you over the hump, so you'll be comfortable using a firearm. It'll be second nature again."

"I don't think I want to be like that again. What's the point?"

"You know what the point is. If we're not out there, good, innocent people get hurt. Not everybody can do what we do, Byers. Those people depend on us. They respect us and they're grateful to us. You've got a job to do. You've got the training, the right skills and the right attitude. You're a good cop, and you owe it to me, to them and to yourself to get back on the streets. You can do it. I know you can. You're tough."

"Maybe I'm not as tough as you think." Stef nervously rearranged herself in the chair.

Shoemaker gazed thoughtfully at her for a moment before asking, "How about you ease into it? You can have a non-patrol assignment for now."

"You mean a desk job?"

"Right."

"I can't see myself doing that. I really appreciate what you're trying to do for me, but I've given this a lot of thought and I've just gotta do something else now."

"What kinda something else?"

"Not real sure. I've never done anything else. I've wanted to be a cop since I was a little kid. But I'll figure something out. For now, I've got a little place out in the Delta. Quiet. Relaxing. Just me and my dog." She sucked a breath between her teeth. "*His* dog, I mean."

Shoemaker gave her a look of sympathy. "Byers, you didn't do anything wrong. It was an accident. Nobody blames you except you."

"Are you sure?"

"Why do you ask?" He looked concerned.

"That day, at the funeral, all those cops staring at me." She shook her head, remembering.

"It was compassion, Byers. They were all standing there thinking about how it could happen to any one of them, and feeling for you. They weren't accusing."

She nodded uncertainly, thinking he was probably right.

"If you don't have anything else lined up, you may as well stay on admin leave for a while until you find another job."

"You've already paid me three months for nothing. I don't feel right doing that when I know I'm not coming back."

"Stef," he said in exasperation, "I'm trying to help you."

She looked away to avoid his eyes, noting his unusual use of her first name.

"I've seen this before," he said. "You've suffered a terrible blow. It's knocked you down and it feels like you'll never get up. Some guys never do. But you're not one of those guys. You're just impatient. You're not giving yourself a chance. You're too fucking hard on yourself and you won't let anybody help you." He looked seriously upset. "And you're worrying me."

"I'll be okay." She smiled to reassure him. "I'm not planning on jumping off any bridges."

"Good!"

"Nothing like that," she said lightly. "I'm going fishing."

"Fishing?"

"That's right. I bought a boat. I'm going to float around the rivers and catch some fish."

He looked suspicious. "You ever fished before, Byers?"

"No, but it seems a lot of people get something out of it."

He shook his head, then sighed. "Okay. I can see you've made up your mind. I'll quit giving you a hard time. Go do what you need to do, but when you're ready to come back, give me a call."

"Thanks." She picked up the letter that declared her innocent of any wrongdoing, tucking it into her bag. No matter how many reports said, "your actions are exonerated," those words faded into a faint, near silence behind the prominent noise of Stef's own haunting thoughts and memories. Still, this was the official verdict and it felt damn good.

***

"You bought a what?" Stef's mother lowered herself into a kitchen chair, looking stricken, her face full of incomprehension.

Stef had anticipated this reaction, so she'd timed her announcement to follow on the terrific news she had just gotten from Internal Affairs, hoping some of her mother's relief and joy over that would cushion the blow of her other news, the worst of which she had not yet delivered.

Kate Byers was fifty-three, a solidly built woman who stood five ten without shoes. She was a big woman, proportionately large all over, carrying a healthy weight for her age and frame. She had always considered herself unattractive, or more accurately, scary to most men who seemed to prefer women to be smaller than they are. "Men are afraid of me," she would say with regularity, whenever some situation didn't go well with a man, whether it was a date or a job interview or a conflict with a store clerk.

Stef and her brothers had taken their mother's assessment

at face value. As a result, Stef had always admired any man who dated her mother, concluding that he had overcome his fright to see Kate's inner beauty. As she got older, Stef began to realize her mother was overly self-conscious about her size and wasn't such a freak of nature after all. She was an attractive woman, becoming more attractive as she aged, as some women do, taking on a regal elegance and stark beauty in a face characterized by a broad chin, wide-open eyes and high cheekbones. There were certainly men who would be intimidated by her height, but she wasn't quite the misfit of her imagination.

"A houseboat," Stef repeated.

Her mother looked no more enlightened than before.

"Uh," Stef began uncomfortably, "when I was in Sacramento a few weeks ago, I took the scenic route home and I saw this sign on the road. Houseboat For Sale. I stopped and took a look. There it was sitting in a...well, a cow pasture, actually."

Her mother shook her head. "A houseboat in a cow pasture. And you suddenly lost your mind and bought it?"

"I didn't buy it right then. I thought about it for a while. The more I thought about it, the more I liked the idea."

"The idea of a houseboat in a cow pasture?"

"No. The idea of a houseboat on the water. Of living on a houseboat."

"You mean full time?"

"Right. There are a lot of advantages to living on a houseboat. People do it."

"People do—" her mother sputtered. "Crazy old hermits who never shower or cut their hair do it."

"There's a shower."

Deuce appeared in the kitchen, a white cone surrounding his head. He banged it against the leg of a chair as he made his way over to Stef and dropped dejectedly to the floor at her feet.

"Stephanie," her mother persisted, "what were you thinking?"

"It's not that crazy. As soon as I get it seaworthy, I'll bring it up the river and take you for a cruise."

"You mean you can't take it on the water?"

"Not yet."

Her mother stared hard at her, a look of grim concern on her face. "Where is this boat?"

"Off of Highway One-Sixty in Stillwater Bay."

"So you're going to commute all the way in from there every day until you get it seaworthy? That's like a two-hour drive? And then you're going to bring it up here and park it in some marina and pay hundreds of dollars a month for a slip? I just don't see how that makes sense. Your apartment was nice and affordable and only ten minutes from the police station."

Her mother was, as usual, boiling everything down to the practical matter of money.

"It wouldn't make a lot of sense," Stef agreed, "if I was still going to be working for Oakland PD."

They'd come to the place in the conversation where Stef had to tell her the real news. As mystified as her mother was about the houseboat, it was nothing compared to how distressed she would be by Stef's larger plan. They were in for a difficult evening. Stef didn't know how she would explain what she barely comprehended herself, that she needed to get away, far away, and try to forget, and that she believed the gentle lapping of water against the hull of her boat would somehow allow that to happen. And if it didn't, at least out there, lost and alone, she wouldn't be a threat or concern to anyone.

"I won't be commuting, Mom," she said, steeling herself. "I resigned from the force today."

CHAPTER SIXTEEN

Tuesdays were Jackie's late nights, the day of the week they kept the office open until eight so people could come in after work. It was always busy Tuesday nights and she was usually exhausted by the time it was over. This night was no exception. After hanging up her smock in her office, she came out front to find Niko locking the door.

"Let's get outta here," she said.

He smiled and nodded. "Just gotta feed Bud." He opened the parakeet's cage and took out the plastic feed dish, saying, "A canary walks into a vet's office and asks for a bag of bird seed. The vet hands it over and says, 'That'll be twenty dollars.' The canary pays and the vet adds, 'We don't get many canaries in here buying their own bird seed.' 'At those prices,' said the canary, 'I'm not surprised.'"

Jackie chuckled. Niko replaced the dish full of seed, and Bud immediately hopped over to it and started eating.

Jackie covered her mouth as she launched into a sizable yawn. Thinking over the hectic day, she realized it was about time for Deuce to come back to have his sutures removed.

"Can you check and see when the follow-up appointment is for Stef Byers and Deuce?" she asked.

"The appointment was for Monday. Yesterday. She canceled."

"Canceled? Did she reschedule?"

"No. I asked, but she said she'd get back to me."

"What was the reason?"

"She didn't say." He puckered his lips at Bud and made a kissy sound as he closed the cage. Bud's head bobbed rapidly up and down in response.

"Give me her phone number. I'll give her a call tomorrow. Those sutures need to come out."

Niko called up the record on the computer and scanned the screen. "No phone number here. Let me check the form."

He went to the records room to consult the original form Stef had filled out.

"She didn't put a phone number," he reported when he returned. "Left it blank. Sorry. I didn't notice at the time."

Jackie sighed. "Okay. Thanks."

"A guy walks into a vet's office," Niko began, so Jackie paused at the door, knowing that all his jokes were mercifully short. "The guy has a parrot on his head. The vet says, 'What's the trouble?' and the parrot says, 'You gotta get this guy off my ass.'"

She patted his shoulder, as if in sympathy, said good night, then left the clinic, debating her next move with Stef. She knew she'd been brusque that day, so much so that she felt guilty about it almost immediately afterward. She had been looking forward to the follow-up appointment, planning on a friendlier encounter this time. Maybe Stef had gone to another vet. Who could blame her?

Her car was sucking fumes, so she pulled into the gas station on Main Street and hooked the hose into her tank while she went into the Quickie-Mart for a chili dog. This was an indulgence she allowed herself only occasionally, usually on these late Tuesday nights when she could justify it with the claim of raging hunger and no time to cook.

"Hey, Jackie," called Mona from behind the counter. "Working late?"

"Just got off," Jackie replied.

Mona was a single mother with difficult challenges. She had never finished high school. She was in her early twenties, thin, with thick black eyebrows starkly contrasting her long butter-yellow hair. She and Jackie had gone to the same high school, but their experiences there and afterward were remarkably dissimilar. Jackie didn't know why. She thought it was just the way things fell out. You can make plans for yourself, but things happen every day you didn't count on. Mona had had plans too. She'd wanted to be a nurse. She still did. But one night in her junior year of high school she went to a football game with a boy and things got hot under the bleachers. Everything changed for Mona in that moment. At eighteen, she became a single mother. Jackie knew it could have been her. Or she could have ended up in an accident like the one that had killed one of her classmates and permanently disabled another. Things happen you don't expect. All the time. Life changes in an instant. She was acutely aware of that.

Jackie had been lucky. Most of her plans had worked out. She'd gone to veterinary school and eventually opened her own practice, fulfilling her professional dreams. But she had had other plans that didn't work out. Like the ones about getting married and having a family. When she was nineteen, in college, she was engaged to a nice math major, a guy who wanted to give her everything, make her happy, set out on a fairy tale life with her. She had wanted that so badly, to be normal and safe, to leave behind the part of herself that made her different and kept her running scared.

How she had loved showing off her engagement ring, being his fiancée, announcing to the world that she was like everyone else, a woman about to be a man's wife. She'd loved being the boy's fiancée more than she'd loved the boy. At the time, she was in love with a girl and had been for a while. Leslie. Fortunately for both of them, though her fiancé didn't appreciate it then, she realized in time she was meant for a different kind of life and let him go. She then began the more difficult journey of embracing her true identity. Whenever she thought about her nineteen-year-old self, she was grateful to her, grateful she'd made the right decision and had been brave enough to give up the default path.

Even though Jackie hadn't yet found someone to spend her life with, she was optimistic that she would, eventually, meet the right woman.

"I put a couple hot dogs on the roller grill just a while ago," Mona informed her with a smile.

Jackie smiled back. She and Mona were the only people who knew about her dirty little hot dog secret. She went to the back of the store where the wieners were riding on a metal rack inside a warm Plexiglas cube under a fluorescent tube light. Their taut skins sparkled with beads of fat, a testament to their salty, porky goodness. This was wrong in so many ways. Jackie knew, but she didn't care.

She put a wiener in a bun and piled on a dipper of chili, then a hefty dollop of melted cheese. Anticipating her first bite, she wondered if this was a benefit or detriment of being single. If someone were waiting at home for her, saving her a healthy plate of food, there'd be no chili dog. On the other hand, there'd be someone waiting at home for her, joyfully anticipating her arrival, kissing her affectionately at the door. She did like chili dogs, but on late Tuesday nights, perhaps more than any other time, the empty house seemed emptier than ever. The chili dog was a tiny bit of compensation for that.

Jackie returned to the checkout counter to pay, noting the big jar of Ida's World-Famous Beef Jerky at her elbow. "How's Ashley? Still playing the violin?"

"Yes," Mona declared proudly. "She's getting really good. The grammar school's going to give a mini-concert later this month at the crawdad festival, so they're practicing for that."

"I'll try to catch that, but I'll be working the festival all weekend myself so I may not see much of the other entertainment. Our band is playing."

"I'll bring Ashley by. She'll be blown away by your Granny and her fiddle."

"Granny's a wonder, isn't she?"

"All of you are. Maybe you can sneak out for a few minutes to check out the rest of the festival. They've got to give you a food break so you can get your annual fix of crawdads." Mona laughed. "Ashley used to be afraid of them, but now she thinks they're yummy."

Jackie bit into her hot dog, snapping through the wiener casing with an audible pop. "I'll tell you what's yummy," she said after swallowing. "This!"

Mona laughed. "Oh, Jackie, you're funny. Everybody thinks you're a vegetarian. You know that, right?"

"No clue where they got that idea."

"Maybe they got it from my Ashley. Remember a couple years ago when we brought in that miserable little runt of a puppy I thought for sure was going to die?"

"The chocolate Lab."

"After you saved that puppy, for a year at least, whenever anybody asked Ashley what she wanted to be when she grew up, she said she wanted to be a vegetarian like Dr. Townsend."

Jackie laughed. "That's cute. For some reason, people do expect an animal doctor to be a vegetarian. That doesn't seem all that logical to me. Sort of like expecting a farmer to eat only meat." Jackie shrugged and took another bite of her hot dog. "I'm not altogether sure this is meat, but it's really good, whatever it is."

Mona opened her mouth to speak and Jackie raised one hand. "No, I don't want to know."

CHAPTER SEVENTEEN

With no phone number for Stef, Jackie decided to make a house call Wednesday after work. Could be a rotten idea, she knew. She might even get a knife between the eyes, but she felt compelled to do it, if only to make it clear there were no hard feelings on her part. Yes, Stef had been rude and had mocked her and tried to humiliate her, but at their last meeting at the clinic, she had been a totally different woman. She'd been humble, contrite and clearly distressed by her dog's injuries. A woman in distress, that's the last image Jackie had of Stef, and it moved her. She found that image much more attractive than the other sarcastic, disdainful one. She had a hard time resisting a woman in distress.

Stef was working at the back of her boat. She stopped what she was doing and stood up, peering at Jackie's vehicle as it pulled into the driveway. Deuce ran over to greet her, no longer wearing bandages or a cone. Stef walked over, an adjustable wrench in hand.

"Hi," Jackie called cheerfully, stepping out of the car.

"Hi," Stef replied.

"How's Deuce doing?" She knelt down to get a closer look at his mouth.

"Great. He's his old self. He's just a little tender."

"Niko told me you canceled your appointment. I was concerned."

"Nothing to be concerned about. Something came up, so I was out of town."

"We should get those stitches out."

"I was going to bring him in tomorrow."

"Oh." Jackie nodded, aware that there was nothing of the woman in distress about Stef today. "Since I'm here, why don't I do it now. Save you a trip. I brought my scissors."

Stef hesitated, her lips pressed tightly together, her eyes vaguely antagonistic. Damn, she was a sexy woman! Jackie thought. Sexy in an aloof way. A tough, sultry kind of way. In a way that just made you want to grab her and kiss that pout right off her mouth.

"Why don't you give me a hand here first," Stef suggested, indicating the rear of the boat.

"Okay. Sure," she said, taken by surprise.

"I finally got the old propeller off," she explained, pointing to the broken part in the dirt. "If you hold this one in place, I can get it attached." She lifted up the propeller and slid it over the shaft. "Just hold it on there like that."

Jackie squatted down to take hold of the propeller blades, pushing the unit flush against its mount. Stef stood behind her, leaning into her while she slid on a washer, then screwed a nut in place. She hand-tightened it, her thigh against Jackie's shoulder. Jackie allowed herself to indulge in the pleasure of that sensation for the few seconds it lasted.

"Okay," Stef said, stepping back. "You can let go."

Jackie moved out of the way while Stef snugged up the nut with the wrench.

"Thanks. That was a three-handed job." Stef wiped her forehead with the back of her hand, leaving a smear of dirt. A rare smile of triumph appeared on her face. "Progress, at last!"

"You think she'll be on the water soon?" Jackie asked.

"I don't know. There are still some sticky problems. The engine, for instance. I haven't figured out what's wrong with it yet. And the bad pontoon. I'll have to replace the pontoon, which is on order, but I can't afford a new engine. I have to fix it somehow. I'm not a mechanic, but thank God for YouTube, you know! Everything's on there. How to replace coils and the water pump impeller. Been a lifesaver so far."

"YouTube!" Jackie laughed. "Is that what you're relying on?"

"Partly. I know a little. I have an older brother who was always tinkering with cars. He taught me a few things."

"That brother might come in handy right now."

"He might, but he lives in Florida."

"Do you have other siblings?"

"Another brother, Jay. He's younger. Haven't seen him in a while. My family's not all that close." Stef laid her wrench on the deck. "Let's take care of Deuce."

While Jackie took the stitches out, Stef held the anxious Deuce still. The wound was healing at a good pace with no visible complications.

"Looking good." Jackie gave Deuce a pat on the head and stood, pulling off her gloves. "Pretty soon he'll have forgotten all about that horse."

"I hope he remembers a little bit about it, so he won't mess with one again."

"Good point."

"Thanks," Stef said. "Considering all the trouble that little excursion caused us, you'd think we'd at least have gotten ourselves a few crawdads."

"Crawdads?"

"That's what I was doing that afternoon, hunting crawdads. I thought I could scoop them up with a net. No luck. I didn't see a single one."

"They're nocturnal. You might see them now and then in the day, but they come out to eat at night. If you go out at dusk, you can catch them, usually, with a net. The official way to catch them is with a baited trap. You put it in the water overnight. It'll be full of mudbugs the next day."

"Mudbugs?"

"Another name for crawdads," Jackie explained. "Sort of a pet name, I guess."

"Oh. Sounds like they're easy to catch if you know how."

"They are. There are a lot of methods that work. Kids catch them any way they can. I used to catch them with my bare hands sometimes...very carefully. Or we'd make these funky scoops by cutting a milk carton in half and shoving a long stick through it. Then rustle around in the shallows." Jackie saw that Stef was smiling, so she continued with her crawdad reminiscences. "We'd sneak hot dogs out of the house, my sister and I. We'd cut them into chunks, then tie them on a string and lower the string into the water. When the crawdad comes to eat it, you just pull up and there he is, nibbling away."

"You must have really liked crawdads."

Jackie laughed. "We liked catching them. Back then, you could sell them directly to restaurants. They paid kids a dollar a dozen, a terrific deal for the restaurant. They'd turn around and sell them to tourists for ten times that. But we would have done it for even less because it was just a fun thing to do. You'll think this is silly, but as a child I even kept them as pets."

Stef looked askance at her.

"My mother doesn't like animals around the house," Jackie explained. "I wasn't allowed to have traditional pets like a dog or cat. So I had a fish tank in my bedroom with a few crawdads in it. I even tried to teach them tricks. I had one where they climbed up a little plastic ladder that came on a toy fire truck. Like circus dogs. They got very good at that, but I'm pretty sure they were just trying to escape."

Stef laughed. "That's funny!"

Jackie shrugged.

"If you can catch them with a milk carton on a stick, I ought to be able to catch some in a fishing net. Maybe I'll try again."

"You need a fishing license for that, you know. I wouldn't want you to get fined."

"Oh. Thanks. I didn't realize."

"I guess you must have liked them if you want to catch some more."

"No, not really," Stef replied. "I was thinking of turning them into a circus act and going on the road with them."

Jackie laughed, trying to keep her eyes off Stef's mouth.

"Seriously," said Stef, "I did like them. The berries and asparagus were good too. It was nice of you to bring them. I'm sorry I was such an ass that day."

"Apology accepted."

Jackie was happy to see Stef's change of attitude, though she wasn't sure exactly what parts Stef was sorry for. Did that include kissing her? She hoped not. She hoped that was just an awkward beginning to a thrilling romantic adventure. She hoped Stef was genuinely attracted to her. Because she really wanted to kiss her again. But Stef was aloof as well as repentant today, seeming not the least bit inclined toward romance.

"Thanks for your help," she said, moving toward the door, clearly signaling that it was time for Jackie to go.

"I've got a couple crawdad traps at home. I can take you out to a foolproof spot and show you how it's done."

Stef nodded uncertainly, as if she were carefully considering her answer. "I should keep working on this thing. There's still a lot to do."

"You need to take a break sometime. How about Saturday? You want to explore the Delta, right? I can show you around. I know some sweet out-of-the-way spots."

Stef looked ambivalent.

"Come on," Jackie urged. "It'll be fun."

"Okay," Stef relented.

Jackie felt a huge sense of relief, as if she'd just won a major battle. "Great!"

CHAPTER EIGHTEEN

What am I doing? Stef asked herself as she rode her bike to Jackie's house Saturday morning. She had been so clear on the plan when she came here. Fix the boat, shove it in the water and get lost in the labyrinth of waterways between here and the ocean. Don't get involved with people. Definitely don't make friends. She wasn't a part of this town and wasn't planning on being a part of it. But it was hard to remain indifferent to Jackie. She was so adorable and so enthusiastically friendly. She also had a warmth about her that had a soothing effect. Deuce responded to it too. He had become noticeably calmed under Jackie's hands, despite the fact that she must have been distressing him by pulling out those stitches. She was gentle but confident, giving you the feeling that everything would be all right. She was a healer, a disposition and persona that apparently extended beyond animals.

Stef tried to relax and give herself permission to enjoy the day. How much harm could it do, anyway, to have a little fun?

She pulled off the road at the address Jackie had given her, hand painted on the side of a metal mailbox on a post. "J. Townsend" was the name on the box, and next to that was painted a small brown dog and white cat. She recognized Jackie's pickup in the driveway.

Stef rode up to a small, older house surrounded by ancient oak trees and an unbroken stretch of mown grass tying the front, sides and back yards together. The house was painted white with forest-green trim and had an enclosed front porch. A calico cat sat on the railing licking its paw. Window boxes on the porch contained blooming geraniums.

The nearest neighbor was a quarter mile away, separated by a brown field enclosed in a barbed wire fence. Behind the house, a relaxed slope led down to a wide creek. On the bank rested two kayaks, one yellow, one red. Creekwise, Jackie had said, she and Stef were less than a mile apart. The roads were less direct. Stef removed her helmet and stepped off the bike as a rooster crowed somewhere nearby.

Jackie emerged from the house, all smiles as she approached, wearing shorts and a T-shirt, looking unabashedly happy. One thing about her that had impressed Stef from the first was how open and honest she was. Stef had the feeling she could take everything about Jackie, including what she said, at face value. If she was happy, like now, you'd know it. If she was angry, you'd know that too. That was unusual in Stef's experience, but refreshing.

"The trap's in my truck," Jackie said, shoving her hands in her front pockets. "Are you ready to go crawdad fishing?"

Stef nodded, noticing a big, white three-legged tom cat that limped up and rubbed against Jackie's leg.

"Your cat?" Stef asked.

"One of three. This is Tri-Tip."

Stef let out an involuntary hoot of laughter. "Oh, that's a good one! Did you name him?"

"Yes. Before I got hold of him, his name was Snowball. I'm the one who took off his leg."

"He doesn't seem to hold it against you."

Jackie walked toward her truck with Stef following. "Animals don't often hold a grudge. They live more in the present than we do."

"He belonged to somebody before you?" Stef asked. "The people who called him Snowball?"

"Yes. When I told them I'd have to remove his leg or he'd die, they decided to put him down. He was only two years old and sweet as could be. I decided to keep him. He's been here a year now. A three-legged cat can live a perfectly normal life. His previous family didn't want an imperfect pet. They thought it would be creepy." Jackie leaned down to pet the cat, then scratched briefly under his chin.

"So," Stef said, "Jackie the Vet to the rescue!"

Jackie straightened up, looking at Stef with mild displeasure. Stef could see that her sarcastic humor might work well among her usual crowd, but Jackie didn't appreciate it.

"You said you have three cats?" Stef asked.

"Right. Hobo—that's her on the porch—was a fire victim. She lived in a homeless camp that burnt down. The guy who had her ended up in a burn unit and Hobo was brought to me. She's okay now, minus a couple patches of fur. My other cat, Stinky, has a feline version of irritable bowel syndrome and lives outside out of necessity, if you know what I mean." Jackie wrinkled up her nose. "All of my cats, and my dog Rooster, are rescued from some mess or another."

"Your dog Rooster?"

"Only one eye."

Stef nodded, starting to appreciate Jackie's sense of humor. "I heard a rooster crow a few minutes ago. That wasn't your dog, was it?"

Jackie laughed. "Actually, that was Dog, my rooster. I have three hens and one rooster. I got him after my dog and the name was irresistible."

Stef shook her head, amused. "You don't get confused?"

"Nope."

"Do they?"

"Maybe. What about Deuce? How'd you get him?"

Stef was taken off guard by the question. She hesitated, considering her answer. "He belonged to a friend who couldn't keep him anymore," she said vaguely.

Hearing a honking horn, they turned to see a white van pull off the road and come directly toward them.

"That's Gail and Pat," Jackie said, looking puzzled.

As soon as the van stopped, one of the women leapt out of the passenger side. She wore a short-sleeved khaki shirt and olive green pants, a uniform complete with a utility belt holding a semiautomatic handgun and radio. Stef quickly located the insignia on her sleeve and recognized the logo of the California Fish and Game Department. A silver badge adorned the left side of her shirt. Her hair was short, curly and blonde. Her eyes were obscured by wraparound sunglasses. Stef realized she could be the woman who'd been kayaking with Jackie the first time she saw her.

"Fish and Game emergency!" she hollered. "Get in."

"What?" asked Jackie. "What's going on?"

"Sturgeon rescue operation," the warden explained. "Come on. We need you." She turned to Stef. "You too. It's Stef, right? Get in!"

Stef's mouth fell open, but the warden wasn't waiting for objections. She was already back in the van. Jackie shrugged and flashed a darling smile at Stef, then got in the backseat. Stef got in the other side behind the driver, a plump Asian woman about thirty years old wearing shorts and a T-shirt and a baseball cap over fine black hair. Jackie introduced her as Pat. The warden's name was Gail. They were a couple. As soon as the doors were shut, the van was in motion and back on the road.

"Now that you've got us captured," Jackie said, "how about details?"

Gail turned around in the passenger seat to face them. "Lots of overflow this spring on the Sacramento River. Which means a lot of fish went over the weirs into the overflow areas. Not a problem for most of them because they can get back using the fish ladders. But the sturgeon are too big. The water's gone down now and we've found a bunch of those suckers trapped in a shallow channel that's getting shallower every day. Another few days of warm weather and they'll die in there."

"Sturgeon?" Stef asked, recalling a photo from Rudy's Bait Shop of an old man beside a fish larger than he was. "Sorry, I don't know much about fish. Those are big, right?"

"They're big," Gail confirmed. "The largest freshwater fish in North America. You get caviar from sturgeon, so they're a highly prized game fish. We've got green and white sturgeon here. The green ones are a threatened species. We've got to get them out of the overflow pond and back in the river before it dries up."

"How big are we talking about?" Stef asked warily, hoping the monster in the photo was a rarity.

"Six, seven feet long," Gail said. "They can live hundreds of years. Really cool fish. You're lucky. A lot of people will never see one in the wild. Today, you're going to see plenty of 'em. Up close."

Stef turned to Jackie and whispered, "Lucky?" Then she turned back to Gail and asked, "Do they have teeth, like sharks?"

"They won't hurt you," Gail assured her. "Unless they knock you out slapping you with their tails. We're going to take 'em out, tag 'em, put in transmitters, then put 'em in the river. Jacks, you'll be on the tagging and transmitter crew. Pat and Stef, you'll be helping to catch 'em."

"I have to tell you," Stef admitted, "I've never used a fishing pole. I'm willing, but I'll need some help."

"Fishing pole?" Pat laughed, displaying a row of brilliant white teeth. "This operation's more low tech than that! You put a fishing pole in there and you could wait hours to catch one of those monsters. Even days. They probably aren't even feeding under these conditions."

"She's right," Gail said over her shoulder. "You don't need any special skills for this. Just physical strength." She lifted her sunglasses and peered intently at Stef, her expression full of flirtatiousness. "You look like you qualify." Gail glanced at Jackie and grinned.

She knows my name, Stef thought, *so Jackie's been talking*. No telling what she'd been saying.

"I don't understand," Stef said.

"We get 'em with our hands," Gail explained, then put her glasses back on and faced forward.

Stef widened her eyes in disbelief at Jackie, who smiled and said quietly, "Don't worry. It'll be fun."

"Have you done this before?" Stef asked.

"Once. A few years ago. It happens when we have higher than normal rainfall and the river overflows like it did this spring. Sorry about the crawdads. Some other time."

"Crawdads?" Gail asked.

"I was going to show her how to set out traps," Jackie explained.

Gail waved her hand dismissively. "You can do that anytime. Today we've got bigger fish to fry." She laughed. "Well, no frying going on today. We're gonna take 'em alive."

CHAPTER NINETEEN

When they arrived at the river, they met up with other volunteers and game wardens and got their assignments. Jackie helped set up a tagging station on the concrete weir that formed one side of the shallow waterway where the sturgeon were trapped. The pond was about thirty feet wide and three feet deep. Watching the water, Jackie could see the bony ridges of some of the fish cutting the surface. As Stef followed her team leader into the pond, she looked positively terrified. Jackie tried not to laugh. This wasn't the day she had planned at all, but it should prove to be interesting.

The procedure for catching the fish was for the volunteers to line up in two lines facing one another a hundred feet apart, then walk slowly toward each other holding a wide net, urging the fish ahead of them, like a cattle roundup, until they had corralled them into a smaller area. Then, when one of the fish went into the net, they would manhandle it to get it into a cloth sling and carry it to the operating area. After that, Jackie or the Fish and Game vet would cut a tiny incision in the fish, slip in the transmitter, sew it up and hand it over to a couple of strong volunteers who would carry it in the sling across the muddy terrain to the main channel of the river and let it loose. All of this had to be done as quickly as possible to minimize trauma to the fish. Fortunately, it was a warm day. Like the other volunteers, Jackie would be standing in water most of the time so the fish's gills could stay submerged during the operation.

Waiting for her first patient, she sat in a lawn chair on the road, watching the two rows of volunteers start toward one another with their nets. Stef was in the line to the right, walking in the thigh-high water. She looked serious and composed. Jackie was anxious to see how she'd act when confronted by one of those huge fish. Stef had been told how big they were, but until you actually saw one up close, you just didn't get it. As Stef's head jerked to the left, then to the right, Jackie figured she was getting a glimpse. The water was murky, so it was hard to see much more than the spines of the fish. The two lines of rescuers came gradually closer together. When they were forty feet apart, somebody yelled, "Got one!"

A flurry of activity followed that announcement on the side opposite Stef. The net was wrapped around the thrashing fish to hold it in place while two men tried to get a good grip on it, one up close to the head and one near the middle. They wrapped their arms around it as two other men held the ends of the narrow stretcher, waiting to receive it.

Jackie felt her pulse racing. She pulled on a pair of gloves to prepare and waded into the water. The team wrestled the fish for a couple minutes before they could get it into the stretcher, but once it was in and out of the water, it was immobilized. The men with the stretcher slogged through the water to bring the fish to Jackie. It was a medium-sized white sturgeon. The species was ancient, one of the oldest fishes in the world. They were covered with bony plates and looked prehistoric. She tried to imagine what they would look like to a first-timer like Stef.

They might scare some people, but she didn't think Stef scared too easily.

She made a quick incision, then inserted a small transmitter under the skin while Gail attached a tag to the fish's fin. Jackie sewed it up, then off went the fish across a grassy flood plain in its green stretcher, on its way to the river and freedom.

"Good job," Gail boomed. "One down!"

Jackie turned back to watch the teams in the water. There were two struggles ongoing now between man and fish. In one case, woman and fish. Stef had her arms around a big one. It was thrashing hard. The strength of the fish's writhing efforts knocked her down. She was briefly underwater, and then she was back on her feet and trying again. Jackie could hear her laughing as she and one of the men finally managed to shove that fish into a sling. Jackie was overjoyed to hear that laugh. She had never heard a real laugh from Stef before.

Stef glanced over to Jackie, smiling widely. Jackie gave her a thumbs-up.

The process continued as stretcher after stretcher came Jackie's way. Some of the fish were unbelievably huge. She knew they could be a hundred years old or more. She had one of the green ones under her scalpel this time, larger than most. Its gills opened and closed rhythmically as she worked as quickly as she could.

Though she had fished these rivers thousands of times, she had never caught or seen a sturgeon in the river before the first rescue operation she'd participated in. But she'd seen them brought in by other fishermen. She'd always thought it must be quite a thrill to hook a powerful fish like this. But wrestling them with nothing but your body, as the crew down below was doing, had to be even more exciting.

Just as she finished, another fish came over, Gail carrying the back end of the sling.

"Jacks," she said, "we've got a situation with this one."

They lowered the sling near her so she could look at the fish. Another green one. There was something protruding from its head. She touched it, feeling sharp metal.

"What the hell?" she said.

"Poachers," Gail explained. "These fish are sitting ducks in this shallow water."

Jackie balked at that metaphor, but let it slide. This wasn't the time for humor. "This looks like a metal file," she observed.

"They shove makeshift spears through their heads to kill them. This one must have broken off and got away."

Jackie shook her head at the brutality of the deed. "We'll have to take it out. Anybody got a pair of pliers? Meanwhile, keep her in the water."

While pliers were being located, Gail had one of her colleagues photograph the unfortunate fish. This was a crime and the photos were evidence. Pliers in hand, Jackie got a firm grip on the top of the metal shaft. She pulled on it, gently at first, but it didn't budge. She pulled harder until it started to move, straight up, steadily and smoothly. A four-inch shaft of metal, also evidence, gradually emerged. The fish jerked as it left its body.

"Damn!" Gail said, holding a plastic bag open to receive the file. "Will it live?"

"No way to know," Jackie said. "Since it survived till now, it may. Let's skip the transmitter on this one. She's been through enough. Take her to the river."

They whisked the fish away.

"Bastards!" Gail exclaimed, zipping the plastic bag shut.

When the drama over the injured fish had passed, Gail grabbed a bottle of water from the ice chest. "We're going to be here awhile," she said, unscrewing the cap. "We'll need to get some food out here."

"Let me call my mom," Jackie offered. "I'll bet she can get somebody in town to donate lunch."

Gail nodded. "I'll bet she can."

Between patients, Jackie made the call. Less than an hour later Ida Townsend arrived carrying a box of sandwiches to the staging area. She wore a floral print sleeveless blouse over the same pair of black and white striped shorts Jackie had seen her in the other day. Apparently, they were becoming a favorite and, unfortunately, not just to be worn in the privacy of her own home.

Adam followed behind her hugging a brown paper grocery sack that completely hid him from the knees up. Jackie took the bag from him and peered inside. It was full of snack bags of chips.

"Your father donated those," Ida said, letting the box drop on the table. "The sandwiches came from the Sunflower Café."

"Thanks, Mom. Everybody's working up a big appetite. But maybe not the best place for children. This is serious business."

"He wouldn't stop crying until I said he could come," Ida explained. "Adam, honey, run get that bag of jerky."

Adam ran back to the car while Jackie opened a bag of barbecued potato chips.

"You brought jerky?" she asked.

"Brought my new flavor." She lowered her voice to a near whisper. "It's got a cola-papaya marinade."

"Cola-papaya?"

"Among other things," Ida explained matter-of-factly. "Papaya has a natural enzyme that tenderizes meat."

"Tenderizes? I don't get it. You dry it so it's as tough as leather, so why tenderize it?"

"Jackie, you may know a lot about mange and hairballs, but who's the expert here on jerky?"

"You," Jackie conceded.

"That's right. Besides, Ida's World-Famous Beef Jerky is not as tough as leather. It's meaty and moist. You watch, this one's going to be a hit."

"Seems like the flavor you have already is a hit."

"Oh, sure, Ida's *original* flavor, but I'm expanding. You gotta be flexible and nimble in the business world. You can't rest on your laurels. My business plan calls for innovation."

"Business plan?" asked Jackie in disbelief.

Ida laid her index finger against her temple. "Out of the box, Jackie. Out of the box."

"Okay, Mom."

"Don't you tell anybody what's in it. Give them a chance to try it first. I'm thinking I can charge half price while we're in beta testing mode."

"Mom," Jackie commanded, "you're not charging these people."

Ida frowned. "All right, but if they like it and want to order some, I can take an order, can't I?"

Jackie shrugged, her mouth full of chips. When Adam returned with the bag, Ida took out a jar of jerky. "Watch Adam for a minute," she said. "I'm gonna pass these around."

"While you're doing that," Jackie called after her, "tell everybody there's food."

"Grandma said there's dinosaur fish," Adam said, looking up at Jackie with wide eyes.

"No wonder you wanted to come along."

"Where are they?"

"Out there." Jackie pointed to the muddy pond.

Just then Stef came stumbling up, soaking wet, her hair dripping down the sides of her face. She collapsed on the grass, lying on her back. Jackie came and sat beside her.

"This is so cool!" Stef said. "Those incredible fish! They're all muscle. It's such a rush. But, man, I'm exhausted."

Jackie reached for a bottle of water and unscrewed the top, handing it to Stef. "We've got some sandwiches. Take a break and get your strength back."

"I've done some crazy shit in my day, but this beats most of it. Catching giant fish with my bare hands." Stef lifted herself onto her side and chugged some water. "How are you doing?"

"My job isn't nearly as exhausting as yours. I think we've had fourteen so far, which is a large percentage of the total that come up this river to spawn each spring. This is important. We couldn't just leave them to die. There aren't enough of them to ignore any of them. Like Gail said, Fish and Game emergency."

Stef rolled on her back again. "I've got to say, I never considered there was such a thing as a Fish and Game emergency."

"Gail's always complaining people don't take her job seriously. They don't realize all the things game wardens do. She gets so steamed when people call her fish cop."

"Fish cop?" Stef smiled. "That's not so bad. Regular cops get a lot worse."

She'd said that like she was speaking from experience,

Jackie thought, tucking away a mental note. "Do you want a sandwich?"

Stef nodded.

"How about some jerky? My mom's giving out samples of her new flavor."

"Your mom?" Stef sat up.

Jackie realized Stef had no idea who her mother was. "Sorry. I sometimes buy into my mother's own delusions of grandeur and figure everybody knows who she is." Jackie pointed to her mother a few yards away where she was chatting with the volunteers and passing around her jar.

Stef looked startled. "Ida's World-Famous Beef Jerky? That's your mother?"

"Uh-huh."

"I'll be damned! You know I never heard of that jerky before I came here."

"You wouldn't. The 'world' in 'world-famous' means Stillwater Bay. It's a goal, not a fact. This is the only place she markets to...so far." Jackie grabbed a sandwich from the box and handed it to Stef.

"That's funny. Had me fooled." Stef unwrapped the sandwich and took an oversized bite. Then she looked up with an inquisitive expression. "So that means Rudy in the bait shop is your dad?"

Jackie nodded. "That's right. I heard you met him."

"Yeah. You and your parents live in the same town then."

"We do. And my paternal grandparents as well."

"Oh, right. Your grandfather was in the bait shop that day too."

"And my sister Rebecca and her husband. And my brother Ben and his wife. Ben and Rosa operate a food truck in town. It's a Brazilian charruscaria. That's a place that serves grilled meats. Maybe you've seen it. Parrots and flowers and lots of color."

Stef nodded, her mouth full. "I have seen it. That's your brother's? Wow. Your whole family lives here."

Jackie was about to answer when Adam came running up to her and whined, "I can't see any!"

"Stef, this is my nephew Adam. My sister's son."

"Hi, Adam," Stef said. "What's wrong?"

"I can't see the dinosaur fish," he complained, his forehead furrowed in frustration.

"Jacks!" called Gail from the water's edge, "they're bringing in another one."

"Gotta go," she said, patting Stef's knee. To Adam, she said, "Where's Grandma? I need her to get back here to watch you."

"I can watch him for a few minutes while I eat," Stef offered.

Jackie nodded and ran down to the tagging station just as another stretcher was brought up with an angry white sturgeon in it. As Gail clipped the tag on, Jackie heard a loud squeal from Adam. She quickly scanned the water's edge and located him riding atop Stef's shoulders. He's got a good view now, Jackie thought, making a small incision in the fish.

"I see one!" Adam yelled, pointing toward the water.

Stef held a sandwich in one hand and had the other firmly on Adam's leg, keeping him anchored. Further down the bank, her mother was peddling her jerky to the volunteers. Jackie turned her attention back to her patient, sewing him up with rapid stitches. A moment later, he was on his way to the river.

"Hey," Gail said quietly, jerking her head toward Stef. "Is that the lesbian lope?"

Jackie laughed. "That's it!"

Gail nodded. "Okay. I get it now. I walk like that?"

"Everyone has her own version, but, basically, yes."

Gail looked pleased with herself. She apparently approved of the lesbian lope.

"What's going on with her anyway?" she asked. "Last I heard, you thought she was an asshole. A few days later, you're on a date."

"You call this a date?"

"No, the crawdad thing. You were going to take her out to Disappointment Slough, right?"

"Right."

"So how'd you get from you're an asshole to let me show you my special fishing hole?"

"As you might expect, it had to do with a dog."

Gail laughed shortly, then glanced back at Stef. "She seems okay to me."

"Today, yes," Jackie said thoughtfully, "she does. She seems great."

She watched Stef carry Adam along the bank to a prime view of volunteers engaged in a vigorous wrestling match with a fish. Adam bounced up and down on her shoulders, squealing with delight. Jackie felt a sudden surge of fond feeling take her over as she watched Stef tilt her head back so she could look into Adam's face and grin at him. Jackie had never seen Stef so carefree and playful. She was caught up in the moment, simply enjoying herself. She'd forgotten herself for a while, forgotten whatever it was that seemed to weigh so heavily on her mind most of the time.

In that instant, amid the cries of fish wranglers and a young boy's laughter, under a hot afternoon sun, sweaty, dirty, tired and hungry, Jackie fell in love.

CHAPTER TWENTY

As the last couple of fish were being rounded up in the overflow channel, Stef and another of the women volunteered to walk the bank in either direction to look for signs of any more pockets of stranded sturgeon.

It had been a long day and everyone was tired, but Stef was invigorated by the change of pace. It felt good to be helping, to be active and involved in a community project, working alongside the others, especially Jackie. Though it was serious business, it was also fun. Maybe not so much for the fish. It had been even more fun when Jackie's nephew Adam had shown up. He had been so thrilled with everything that was happening. She smiled, remembering how he'd begged to ride one of the fish. Cute kid.

"Take some jerky with you," insisted Ida Townsend, shoving a nearly empty jar under her nose.

"Thanks," Stef had said, taking a piece. She chewed on it as she walked on a dirt road past muddy flats where small puddles of water stood, looking for deeper pools where the big fish could have retreated.

Ida Townsend was a funny woman. Intense and outgoing. She was also very short. It would be a surprise if she was even five feet tall. She had strong facial features—pointy nose and high forehead, a puckery mouth and narrow chin. Jackie didn't resemble her much except in personality. Both women were friendly and unabashedly familiar in manner. Jackie seemed a little more reserved and serious, but neither of them would ever be hugging the shadows in any social situation. Jackie's father, Rudy, Junior, was no wallflower either. Brash and opinionated, but likable. They both seemed like good-hearted people.

The jerky was good. A little sweet. A little tangy. She finished it and looked back to see the party of volunteers in the distance.

The Sacramento River lay to the north, edged by a tangled line of trees and bushes. To the south was farmland crisscrossed by streams and sloughs. She'd walked almost a mile when she decided to turn south on a dirt road, following a rivulet draining out of what looked to be a larger body of water further on, large enough to accommodate sturgeon.

As she walked, her mind kept returning to Jackie. A remarkable woman, really. The more Stef got to know her, the more remarkable she seemed. She was so together. She seemed to know what she wanted in every facet of life.

Stef briefly let herself consider the possibility of hanging around a while longer than planned. She had to move her boat by the end of July. That was the agreement, but she could rent a slip at the marina. She wondered if it would be possible to make a place for herself in Jackie's life. Was that such a crazy idea?

Maybe she could be a fish cop, she thought, amusing herself. But then she remembered the gun problem. Even a fish cop carried a gun and might have to use it once in a while. Just thinking about it made her go cold. Suddenly feeling frustrated, she shook the thought off and kept walking.

As she neared the pond she had spied, she could see a young man in the water. He wore a cowboy hat, cargo shorts and no shirt, and moved slowly through the water away from her, carrying a long pole. The water hit him mid-thigh. He paused and raised his pole, then slammed it hard into the water in front of him. Whatever he was aiming at, he must have missed because he pulled the spear out empty and continued to peer into the water.

Stef stopped walking, a chill running down her back. She pulled out her cell phone and called Jackie. "I may have found a poacher," she reported.

"Where?"

"I'm about a mile and a quarter southeast. Straight down the weir for a mile, then south. I think we need a fish cop over here."

"Okay. I'll send her right away. You stay away from him. Just wait for Gail."

Stef continued walking. She noticed as she neared that the man was large and well muscled. She dropped down next to the water as he turned her way, revealing a close-cropped full beard. He looked alarmed to see someone. She saw a sharp piece of metal tied to the end of his pole. Her gaze was diverted by the back ridge of a sturgeon breaking the surface a few yards away, the white body of a seven foot long fish gliding silently through the brown water. *The thing is, Jackie,* she thought, *if I stay away from him, he's going to kill a fish.*

"What're you after?" she asked casually.

"Frogs," he said, narrowing his eyes at her. "Frog giggin'."

"Are there frogs in this mud puddle?" She approached the edge of the pond.

"Biggest damned frogs you've ever seen," he replied, laughing.

"Catch any?" Stef asked.

"One so far."

It was then she spotted a Ford pickup on a dirt road at the edge of a cornfield about a hundred feet farther south.

"Is that your truck?" she asked.

He pushed the brim of his hat higher to get a better look at her. "What's it to ya?"

"I thought I'd go take a peek at that frog. I'd like to see a giant frog."

She started walking toward the pickup, which prompted the man to wade quickly over to the shore to cut her off. She stopped, facing his resolute expression. Now that he was closer, she could see the cold insolence in his eyes. She was thoroughly accustomed to creeps like this. For the first time in a while, she felt like she was back on home turf.

"Why don't you mind your own business, lady," he said, allowing the suggestion of a threat into his voice.

"I'm beginning to think this is my business," she said evenly. "I'd like to take a look at that frog."

She started to go around him and he grabbed her arm roughly and held her. "How do you figure my frog is your business?"

"Frogs aren't my business," she said, yanking her arm free. "But at least for today, sturgeon are."

"Sturgeon? I told you I was giggin' frogs."

She eyed his spear more closely, a butcher knife blade lashed to a wooden pole. "I've never seen a frog gig like that. They must be some gigantic frogs for a blade that big."

He sneered. "I told you they were."

She started toward the pickup again, but the poacher ran around in front of her and pointed his spear at her, causing her to stop abruptly.

"Stop!" he warned.

Stef raised her hands, but stood her ground defiantly. The blade of the spear was a foot away from her stomach.

"You a game warden?" asked the man.

"No. Just a concerned citizen worried about the safety of some very valuable fish."

"You should be more concerned about your own safety. I'll be on my way now."

He backed away slowly, keeping his narrow eyes and the spear trained on her. When he'd gotten twenty feet away, he turned and ran toward his truck. Stef ran after him. When he reached the vehicle, he tossed the spear in the back of the pickup. She tackled him and they both fell to the ground. She could immediately tell she was overpowered. He was just too strong for her. All she could do was slow him down and hope help arrived in time. They struggled, rolling over in the dirt until she managed to kick him off, sending him onto his back with a thud. She rolled away and got up on all fours, attempting to stand, but he was on her before she could get her balance. He jerked her to her feet, then flung her against the side of the truck. She hit hard and dropped to the ground, momentarily stunned. She recovered her breath just as the truck's engine started. She pulled out her knife and wedged it under the nearest tire, pushing the tip of the blade into the rubber, then rolled out of the way as the truck started to move. The tire blew and instantly went flat.

The truck clunked along for a few feet before stopping. Stef got to her feet as the man jumped out of the cab and slammed his door. He came around to see the destroyed tire, then he turned toward her with unmistakable fury.

"I'm gonna kill you," he breathed between his teeth.

She turned and ran down the center of the dirt road. He came after her. He was big and powerful, but he wasn't fast. However, she'd had an exhausting day, so she was faltering. When she looked over her shoulder, she saw him closing in. A few seconds later, his fingers got a brief hold on her shirt. With his next attempt, he threw both arms around her and brought her to the ground. He landed heavily on top of her, knocking the wind out of her.

She tried to wriggle free, but it was no use. He rolled her over and pushed her shoulders to the ground so she was flat on her back under him, then he clamped one of his huge hands over her throat and tightened it.

I'm going to die, she thought, squeezing her eyes shut as her windpipe was closed off.

A gunshot rang out. The brute on top of her released her throat. They both looked down the road to see a white van careening toward them, Gail hanging out the passenger window with her handgun drawn. The poacher got to his feet as the van slid to a halt. Gail jumped out, and the guy took off running back the way they'd come, back to his truck.

"Halt!" Gail commanded. "Fish and Game!"

The man kept running. Gail fired again, hitting the ground beside his feet. He skidded to a stop and put up his hands.

Jackie dashed over to Stef and helped her to her feet.

"You okay?" she asked, her voice panicked, her face full of concern.

She really cares about me, Stef realized.

"I'll be fine," she said, brushing dirt from her shirt. "You showed up just in time."

Down the road, Gail had handcuffed the poacher, who stood quietly resigned to his fate.

CHAPTER TWENTY-ONE

Gail dropped a large combination pizza on the table, then took her chair. Pat poured from a pitcher of beer, filling their glasses. The four of them sat in a noisy restaurant, the one pizza place in Stillwater Bay, all of them exhausted, dirty, smelling like fish, sunburned and, in Stef's case, bruised up by both fish and man. It had been a difficult but satisfying day. Jackie wrapped her fingers around the cold beer glass, waiting for the foam to subside before taking a drink.

Pat raised her glass and said, "To the sturgeon!"

They touched glasses.

"To Stef," Gail proposed, raising her glass again, "the sturgeon champion."

Stef glanced at Jackie who smiled proudly at her. There was a scrape on Stef's chin where she'd contacted the dirt road, but she seemed in good spirits and mostly unharmed.

"That guy had a box full of ice in his pickup bed," Gail said. "Already had one in there. He had to chop it in half to fit it in. Green one, so he's in big trouble." She picked up a slice of pizza. "There were three more in the pond there. Thanks to Stef, they're safe and sound swimming upriver tonight."

"Thanks for coming to my rescue," Stef said. "I swear that guy was going to kill me."

Gail nodded emphatically. "Yeah, you probably shouldn't have put yourself in that position. There's a lot of money involved for these guys. If they'll shove an ice pick through a magnificent fish like that, they're capable of doing the same to you."

Jackie put her hand on Stef's shoulder. "Why *did* you do that, Stef?"

"Risk my life for a fish?" she asked with a short laugh.

Jackie remained serious. "Yes."

Stef gazed at her, then gave a small shrug and turned her attention to her pizza. As usual, Jackie was frustrated with Stef's reticence. But in this case, maybe there was no obvious answer. Maybe she had acted without giving it much thought. The alternative, that she didn't value her life, was too cynical to believe.

"Especially without a weapon," Gail remarked.

"I had a weapon," Stef countered. "My knife. I could have taken him out with that, but I didn't want to kill the guy."

"And believe me," Jackie said, "I can vouch for her ability to do that."

Gail reached down to her bag on the floor, extracting the knife, which she laid on the table in two pieces. The blade was broken cleanly from the handle "One of the guys picked this up on the road. It did its job, but won't be of much use after this."

Stef touched the broken blade as Jackie leaned up against her and said, "Sorry."

"Well," Gail sighed, "some hundred-year-old fish can thank you for another hundred or so. Damn, I'm glad this day is over. Working on Saturday puts a dent in a girl's routine."

"What are you complaining about?" Pat groused. "This

is my first Saturday off in three months and look how I spent it."

"We've still got tomorrow morning," Gail said. She put her hand on Pat's arm. "You can sleep late. I might even bring you breakfast in bed."

Pat's expression softened into a grateful smile. "Now you're talking."

"They'll cancel classes over crawdad festival weekend, right?" Jackie asked. "So there's another weekend off."

Pat looked askance, her smile fading. "Working the festival for twelve hours a day. You call that a weekend off?"

"You work the festival?" Stef asked.

"We all do," Jackie answered.

"I volunteered to work security," Gail said, "but Hartley says they've got that covered. So I'm going to be Crusty the Crawdad this year, believe it or not."

Jackie laughed shortly. "Oh, my God!" She turned to Stef to explain. "The festival mascot."

Gail nodded. "I hope it isn't too hot. That costume is liable to bake me alive."

"What will you be doing?" Stef asked Jackie.

"Our little bluegrass band will be providing entertainment. Pat's our bass. My sister is guitar and my grandmother is fiddle."

"Your grandmother's in your band?"

"Yes. It started out as a family thing. We can all play something."

"Rehearsal tomorrow afternoon," Pat reminded Jackie. "Your house at two."

"Stef plays guitar," Jackie said.

"We should get together sometime to play," suggested Pat.

"Hey," said Jackie, "why not tomorrow? Bring your guitar and jam with us a little bit. Then we can go set that crawdad trap after rehearsal."

"Sure," added Pat encouragingly.

"I don't want to interfere," Stef said. "If you're rehearsing."

Stef's guarded expression confused Jackie. She had shut down again. Jackie's invitation seemed to make her uncomfortable.

"Come on," Jackie urged, taking hold of her arm. "It's just some friends having a good time. You can come after rehearsal, then, if you're more comfortable. It'll be just you and me."

Stef nodded and noticeably relaxed.

"I hope you'll come out to the festival too," Jackie said. "It's our big event, and it gives you a good feel for what this town's about. Not just crawdads."

"No, not just crawdads," Gail laughed. "But there's no denying fishing is the backbone of this community."

"Which puts you right in the heart of things," Stef noted.

"Exactly."

Pat raised her beer glass. "To fish cops everywhere!"

Gail smiled gratefully as they toasted.

"Speaking of cops," Pat said, jerking her head toward the pickup window.

Jackie looked to see Don Hartley, in uniform, collecting a take-out box. A divorced forty-four year old, Hartley was going home to a springer spaniel named Lady, a sweet dog who suffered from chronic ear infections. His pale, lined face set in its usual stern expression, Hartley passed near their table with a pizza box held in both hands.

"Hi, Don," Jackie called.

He looked their way, his eyes registering recognition. "Evening, ladies." He nodded, continuing toward the door.

"One of your local force?" Stef asked casually.

"Not really one *of*," said Jackie. "Just one. We have only one."

Stef stared unbelievingly. "One cop?"

"It's a small town," Gail said. "Can't afford more than one. We have a police chief too, but he's old and doesn't go out on patrol."

"He should retire," Pat muttered.

Stef looked blown away. "One cop," she repeated quietly. "Do you have a one-room schoolhouse too?"

"No," Jackie replied. "But when my dad went to school, they had two grades in every class. Even when I went, classes were very small. As far as I know, I was the only lesbian in my high school class. Pat was a year ahead of me, but she wasn't out yet. Nobody knew about me. I kept it to myself."

"Sounds lonely," Stef remarked, picking up an errant piece of sausage from her plate.

Jackie shrugged. "Yes, it was lonely. But college was a whole different story. The world opened up for me there. Veterinary school...as you can imagine, classes full of lesbians. I think I went a little crazy during those few years."

"Sowed some wild oats?" Stef asked.

"Acres and acres of them!" Jackie laughed. "But that's all way behind me. I'm not into fun and games anymore. Now I'm just looking for that one woman, you know. Somebody to be serious about." Jackie smiled uncertainly, avoiding looking at Stef.

"What about you?" Pat asked Stef. "How was it in your high school? Were you out?"

"Yes. It was a big school. There were other gay kids, and I didn't feel like I had to hide. I even took my girlfriend to the junior prom."

"No kidding?" Jackie remarked. "Did you wear a prom dress?"

Stef laughed. "What do you think?" She gave Jackie a meaningful look.

Jackie shook her head. "No."

"Right. A spiffy maroon tux."

"We went to very different high schools!"

After Gail and Pat dropped them off at Jackie's house and said goodbye, Jackie invited Stef in.

"I need to get home," she said, moving toward her bike. "Deuce has been alone all day, and I'm beat. A shower and sleep is about all I'm good for tonight."

Jackie nodded. She too was beat. "I'll see you tomorrow then. You can come by about four o'clock, after rehearsal."

"Okay," said Stef slowly, still clearly ambivalent.

Jackie followed her to her bike. "You were great today. Thanks for all your help."

She was sure she conveyed the look of a woman waiting for a kiss, but Stef pretended not to notice and merely nodded with an uneasy smile before slipping on her helmet and riding off.

Jackie didn't know what to think about this woman who held her cards so close to her chest. Almost everything about her remained a mystery. The one thing Jackie was sure of was how thoroughly Stef had invaded her consciousness. She couldn't stop thinking about her. Ever since that day Stef had kissed her, Jackie's mind had lingered on the way those few moments had stirred her up inside. She wanted to feel that again, but wanted Stef to feel it too. She didn't know if that was possible but she dreamed about it anyway, about being taken with passionate desperation by that troubled, fascinating woman who had captured her heart and mind.

CHAPTER TWENTY-TWO

Stef made sure she didn't arrive too early. She hoped everyone would be gone when she got there, but a red Honda Accord was parked in front of the house next to Jackie's pickup. As Stef took off her jacket and stored it in one of her saddlebags, Jackie came around the side of the house with another young woman carrying a guitar case. She was taller than Jackie, thin and shapeless, with blonde shoulder-length hair and pale, freckled cheeks. Their guitar player, Stef remembered, was Jackie's sister Rebecca.

"I'm not telling her," Rebecca said resentfully. "You call her and tell her yourself. She'll blame me if I tell her."

Jackie and Rebecca both saw Stef at the same time. Jackie's face broke into a wide smile.

"Stef!" Jackie called, rushing over to her and giving her a familiar hug. "This is my sister Rebecca."

"Hi," Rebecca said, holding out her hand to shake, then she turned to Jackie and said, "I've got to get home if I'm going to get Sean and Adam ready in time." She hugged Jackie goodbye. "See you Wednesday for another practice." She waved toward Stef. "Nice to meet you, Stef."

"I'm so glad you're here," Jackie said warmly. "Are you ready to go catch some mudbugs?"

"Sure."

"Just let me make a call first. I have to let my mother know I'm not coming to Sunday dinner."

Jackie ran into the house, and Stef leaned against the side of the pickup bed. Inside was a wire cage with a yellow nylon rope tied to its handle. The crawdad trap, she surmised. She found herself smiling at the idea of catching crawdads.

It seemed like every time lately she'd been with Jackie, she'd spent a lot of time smiling and a lot less time thinking about the personal drama that had consumed her thoughts for the last three months. In the last few days, particularly, whenever she had even a thought of Jackie, she could feel her lips turn up in an involuntary smile. Was it possible there was something significant going on here? Was it possible this kind of life— Jackie's life—might suit her? It was a strange idea to consider. This place, so small and personal, wasn't the kind of place she had ever considered calling home. Even thinking these thoughts made her nervous, but somewhere in the back of her mind, it also made her excited. It was like looking through an open door into a foreign, almost inconceivable, but wondrous and alluring land, feeling that all she needed to do was step through to be in the midst of it.

Tri-Tip appeared, rubbing against her legs. She reached down and scooped him up, petting him until he purred.

"Nothing wrong with you, is there?" she said. "Not that you care about anyway. Who needs four legs? We do just fine with two. You've got three, so you're already ahead."

She could see why some people wouldn't want a damaged animal, but for others, like Jackie, the damaged ones might be more appealing. Their need was greater. The greater the need, the more valuable the aid.

Jackie ran back out, breathless, and Stef put the cat down and got in the truck. Once they were on the road, she asked, "You were supposed to be at your parents' tonight?"

Jackie sputtered. "Naw. It's a standing thing. Every Sunday. Unless something else comes up."

Stef noticed a slight, clever smile on Jackie's lips. She understood that she was the something else that had come up. She relished that thought for a moment before asking, "How was practice?"

"Good. We've got a lively set lined up for the festival. Granny's a little off these days, but it doesn't matter. It's mostly for fun. Everybody in the family plays something and not always well. Even my father, who's tone-deaf. He plays a jug when he joins us."

"A jug?" Stef laughed. "What about Pat? How did she end up in your family band?"

"Her family and mine were neighbors when we were kids. Her grandfather was one of the original residents here. He came over from China and helped build the levees. I've known her all my life, and we were in band together in high school."

"And Gail? Is she from here too?"

"No. I met her five years ago when she and Pat got together. And that pretty much accounts for all the lesbians in Stillwater Bay." Jackie laughed self-consciously. "Unless you count the Kelly sisters."

"Kelly sisters?"

"Brenda and Malvia Kelly. An older couple. They moved here about ten years ago when they retired. Teachers, both of them. They're not really sisters."

"Glad to hear it."

"They got married in Canada and Brenda changed her last name to Kelly, so when they came here, at first people assumed they were sisters. They never bothered to correct anybody. Most everybody knows now they're a couple, but we all still call them the Kelly sisters. I guess we shouldn't, but it's an old habit. No point in changing, really, because we all know what it means."

"No other lesbians around?"

"A few, sure. Couples, mainly, and some very young ones. There's a tiny gay club in the high school now."

"So if I lived here and wanted to date a local girl, I may as well forget it."

Jackie looked at her with a goofy, surprised look. "There's me! I'm single."

"True. There's you. That's it, though. I'd have a choice of one."

"One's enough," Jackie stated without taking her eyes off the road. "If she's the right one."

Stef smiled to herself and realized she felt completely comfortable to be riding in Jackie's truck on the way to a crawdad fishing hole. The anticipation of what the evening had in store played on the fringes of her consciousness. Lingering tauntingly just out of reach. There was no mystery about Jackie's interest in romance. She'd been giving off every signal possible almost since the day they met. Stef had been receiving but resisting. This was so unexpected and potentially complicated. But tonight, she knew, they were on a date. She would let Jackie set the pace. Stef didn't want to plan anything or expect anything. She didn't want to know ahead of time how it would happen. She just wanted it, whatever it was, to happen on its own, in a natural and spontaneous way.

On their way out of town, they passed the marina on the left and Rudy's Bait Shop on the right.

"How long has your family had that place?" Stef asked.

"Forty-five years. Since it opened. My grandfather started it."

"You've got some serious roots in this town."

"I do. It was a great place to grow up. I think it's important to live with a sense of place. Everywhere we're driving through, each place reminds me of memories from my life. I could tell you a story about every one of them. Don't worry, I won't." Jackie turned to smile at her, a radiant smile full of innocence and undiluted joy.

In some ways, Jackie seemed naïve. She was a small-town girl who had no experience of the dark side of life. Or if she did, it didn't seem to have left a mark on her. She was cheerful and open and trusting. She seemed unscarred by life. Stef wasn't used to people like that. Where she came from, there were a lot of hard, cynical people. Maybe it was just the business she'd been in more than the city. You're bound to get around a different crowd selling bait than you did running down drug lords. Thinking about Rudy's Bait Shop and Jackie's idyllic life in this lazy Delta town, Stef was envious.

She leaned her head back against the headrest and decided to live in Jackie's world for a while, to enjoy it and let it envelop her. To live in the present, in a warm spring day in a beautiful natural setting with an incredible girl. How could anybody not enjoy that? Just a matter of pushing those other things out of her mind for a while.

When she opened her eyes, she turned to look at Jackie, who was looking straight ahead at the road. She was awfully cute. Her body exuded a warm glow of golden browns, from her tanned caramel-colored legs and arms to her hair with its tones of maple syrup, sleek and shining with amber highlights. Her eyes were the same—rich bronze depths punctuated with golden light.

She glanced at Stef and accused, "You're staring at me."

"Yep. Nice view."

All those hues of gold and brown turned a slight shade redder as Jackie self-consciously turned off the main road onto a two-lane country road. Stef didn't mind a bit that she'd embarrassed Jackie.

"I've been coming out here since I was four years old," Jackie said. "It was our family fishing hole. One of them. We had a few."

"You did a lot of fishing, I guess, being in that business."

"Sure. That's why my grandfather started it. Love of the sport, which he passed on to his kids and grandkids. You've really never been fishing?"

"No, never."

"Your dad didn't fish?"

"My dad wasn't around. He and my mom split up when I was little. He wasn't a part of our life after that. I have no idea if he liked to fish or not. My mother never liked the outdoors. We didn't go camping or anything like that. When we did go somewhere, it was the zoo or a museum or ice skating. Places where nature was thoroughly controlled. I think she's afraid of nature. It's so unpredictable."

Jackie laughed. "She's got a point. Nature is dangerous. When my sister and I were kids, we had a lot of close calls. We ran wild around here, really. We had a couple of friends who drowned. My best friend got thrown off her horse and into a cinder block wall. Killed instantly."

Stef winced. "That's tough. How old was she?"

"Nineteen. By then, we were in college together, both of us planning to be vets." Jackie looked ahead at the road, not at Stef. "Her name was Leslie. She was crazy about horses. She wanted to be a large animal vet. She was an experienced horsewoman. She'd been thrown lots of times before. It was such a sad, shocking thing for everyone. Her father had the horse put down. Leslie wouldn't have wanted that. He was just an inexperienced colt who got spooked. But her parents were thoroughly devastated and it was something they could do, some sort of response. You feel so helpless when something like that happens. In the blink of an eye, everything changes and there's nothing anyone can do about it."

Jackie's voice broke, revealing the emotion she clearly still felt over this tragedy. She quit speaking. Maybe she wasn't unscarred by life after all, Stef thought. Maybe she was just one of those people who could bounce back from hardship without letting it harden her. That was an admirable quality.

In the blink of an eye, Stef thought, looking out the window, *everything changes and there's nothing anyone can do about it.*

She reached over and laid a comforting hand on Jackie's shoulder. "Was she your girlfriend?"

"Only in my fantasies. She was straight. She was dating a boy at the time. They would have gotten married, had she lived. I was dating a boy too, actually, and was engaged to him for a while. But I was in love with Leslie. For years."

"Did you ever tell her?"

"Not exactly. The subject of lesbians came up now and then. Other lesbians. The idea seemed to disgust her, actually. I tried to kiss her once when we were sixteen."

"How'd that go?"

"She pushed me off. Told me to stop. I told her I was just kidding and she said, 'You'd better be.' I didn't try it again. I couldn't risk another move. I was afraid of losing her friendship. It was better than nothing. That's what I thought at the time anyway."

"I'm sorry you lost her."

Jackie glanced over with a thankful smile, then took Stef's hand in hers and held it between them on the seat. Stef closed her fingers over Jackie's, enjoying this spontaneous gesture of affection.

At the end of a cow pasture, they reached a levee and climbed the dirt road to the top where Jackie took her hand back to maneuver the sharp turn. They suddenly had a wide-open view of an expansive waterway flanked by the grassy interior slope of the levee and the occasional scrub oak. The water was grayish green and murky like most of the Delta sloughs. There was a fisherman in a small aluminum boat on the opposite bank in the shade of a tree. Other than that, the road and the water were deserted.

The truck bounced on the rutted road as Jackie took it slowly for less than a mile to a spot where a smaller slough forked off from the main channel. They pulled off at a wide dirt pull-out and parked.

Stef stepped out of the truck and stood on the bank of the slough, listening to a red-winged blackbird singing. The sky was clear except for some wisps of stringy clouds. On the other side of the levee were fields planted with rows of corn and occasional, well-spaced houses. There was a warm breeze and an odd odor, vaguely familiar, in the air.

"What's that smell?" Stef asked.

Jackie sniffed the air. "Anise. It grows wild around here."

Stef took a deep breath, recognizing the licorice aroma.

Jackie took the trap and a can of dog food out of the back of the truck.

"This is a nice spot," Stef said. "Hardly anybody around."

"By boat, we're quite a few miles from the river, more than you'd think based on how short a drive it was, so not a lot of boat traffic. There are a lot of spots like this in the backwaters of the Delta. Lots of others you can only reach by boat."

She started down a narrow dirt path to the water's edge, then punched several holes in the bottom of the dog food can with a can opener. "You don't want to open the can so they can get the food out. Just let them smell it."

"What do crawdads normally eat?" Stef asked. "In the wild where dog food and hot dogs don't normally show up?"

"They'll eat most things. Little fish, dead fish, worms, insects."

She put the dog food can in the cage, then Jackie waded a short distance into the water and lowered it behind a submerged log. She tied the cord to the log, then returned to shore.

"By tomorrow morning," she said, shading her eyes from the western sun with her hand, "that would be full of mudbugs if we left it overnight. Like twenty or thirty. That's all there is to it."

"Seems pretty straightforward," Stef said.

"We'll check it in a little while. We might catch a couple if they're close by and smell the bait." Jackie sat on a boulder and anchored her heels in the sand.

The fishing boat across the way suddenly roared to life and headed upstream. The sound of its motor gradually faded away.

"Tide's coming in," Jackie observed. "There's a full moon tonight so it'll be a spring tide."

"What's a spring tide?"

"That's the highest tide. Because of the full moon. It's the best time to catch fish."

"Why?"

"Fishing is about two things. Where and when. You learn with experience how to read the water and find where the fish hang out. But when is even more important. Like most things, being in the right place at the right time is often the key. Fish feed when the tide's moving in or out. The movement stirs things up, like shrimp and worms and whatever lives in the mud. During a spring tide, things get shook up more than usual and the fish get excited."

Stef laughed shortly. "Sorry. That struck me as funny, the

idea of excited fish. I guess there's more to fishing than I would have thought."

Jackie nodded. "Some people can talk your leg off about technique, the right equipment and all that. There are as many techniques as there are old fishermen. And women. Granny swears by the cows."

"Cows?"

"When the cows are up and eating grass, the fish are biting. When they're lying down being lazy, you won't catch anything."

"Is it true?"

"It's worked for her. Some people have a fishing pole for each type of fish they go after, all rigged up differently. But, you know, there still has to be a fish there to catch, and luck plays a part too. You don't have to know much to catch a fish." Jackie pointed to the west. "It was right down the road I caught my first fish. I was just a toddler and obviously knew nothing about it. My dad gave me his pole to hold while he went to the car to get a beer. When he came back, he just left me holding this huge fishing pole while he talked to my mom. After a while, I thought it felt funny, kind of jumpy, but I just sat there holding it like I'd been told to do. Finally, he looked at the pole and said, 'You got a strike!' He told me to reel. I tried. It took a long time, not because there was such a monster fish on the line, but just because I was awkward and didn't know what I was doing. I finally got it reeled in and there were two striped bass on the line, one on each hook. He always fished with two hooks, but normally people reel the thing in after the first hit, so they don't get two fish at once. I was so excited I threw the pole down and jumped around screaming. I don't remember it very well, but this story's been told to me many times."

Stef realized it was Jackie in the photo she'd seen on the bulletin board at the bait shop, the little girl proudly holding a line with two fish hooked.

"That's a cute story," Stef said.

"It never happened again in all the years since."

Jackie smiled warmly at her. She seemed anxious to show and thereby share her world with Stef. To welcome her into it, open-armed and unreserved, like the town itself. The atmosphere Stef had noticed since arriving in Stillwater Bay was one of familiar hospitality. The closest thing she had known to this unambiguous goodwill was from visiting her grandmother when she was little. She'd show up at the back door, uninvited, unexpected and usually disgruntled about something at home or school. Grandma Mattie's face would light up like she'd opened the door to Ed McMahon delivering a check from Publisher's Clearing House. "Oh, look at my little sweetheart! Soaking wet and grouchy to boot. You look like a half-drowned cat. Take off those muddy shoes and come on into the kitchen. I'm going to slice you a big old piece of chocolate cake!"

That was always her solution to Stef's troubles. A bowl of ice cream or blackberry cobbler or chocolate chip cookies and a glass of milk. Grandma Mattie served up love and dessert. And that was normally all that was needed. And all that was wanted. By the time that piece of cake was half eaten, they'd be sitting at the kitchen table laughing together over some funny story, all childhood misery forgotten.

Grandma Mattie had died when Stef was twelve and she'd never known such unquestioning warmth since. She had no doubt her mother loved her, but her mother's affection was understandably diffused with worry and pragmatism and was never totally unreserved like her grandmother's had been.

Not everyone in Stillwater Bay was open and friendly, but most of them were. They didn't seem to care who she was or what she'd done before. They automatically liked her, trusted her and accepted her with a kind of general belief that the world would do them no harm. Jackie was a product of that environment. Stef wondered if her invitation could possibly be as straightforward as it felt. Jackie would be so easy to escape into.

A flock of ducks flew overhead, quacking raucously on their way to their evening roost. A little black mud hen swam out of a clump of tules into their clearing, saw them, and abruptly spun about and hurried away. This was the scenery Stef had pledged herself to for the foreseeable future. How could this not bring her peace?

"It's hot," Jackie said, wiping the back of her hand across her forehead. "Do you know how to swim?"

"Sure. I'm guessing you learned by jumping in a river. I had swimming lessons."

"You'd be right about that." Jackie flashed a devious smile.

Without warning, she leapt to her feet and tore off her shirt, then shimmied out of her shorts and ran into the water in her underwear. She swam twenty feet out where she stayed, treading water, grinning a challenge. *She wants to play*, Stef thought with an unexpected sense of lightheartedness. She removed her watch and hat, laying them on the sandy shore, then rapidly stripped to her own underwear and jumped in. The cold slapped her, but as she swam out, the shock rapidly dissipated and it felt good.

Before she could reach Jackie, she swam away laughing. Stef gave chase, knowing she wanted to be caught, and a few minutes into this game, she got hold of Jackie's ankle and climbed up the length of her until she could lock one arm around her waist. Jackie screamed and giggled, her voice echoing across the water. She pushed with both hands against Stef's shoulders as they splashed through their mock struggle, but Stef held fast. She heard her own laugh like a foreign language she could barely comprehend. Before yesterday, it had been months since she'd heard this particular laugh, carefree and unrestrained.

With Jackie still trying to wriggle free, Stef pulled her closer and placed a couple of light kisses on her mouth. Jackie quieted and let herself be kissed properly as they drifted together, gently kicking to stay afloat. Still kissing, Stef stroked powerfully with her legs to move them closer to shore until she could feel the muddy bottom beneath her. She stood in water up to her shoulders, encircling Jackie in her arms and kissing her deeper, tasting again the sweet, soft warmth of Jackie's uninhibited desire.

The bare skin of her back and stomach felt velvety smooth in the water. Jackie wrapped her legs around Stef's waist, anchoring her nearly weightless body close. Stef ran her hands over Jackie's back, then around to the front where she caressed her through the lacy material of her bra. Jackie's murmur of pleasure verified she wanted to be touched like that so Stef squeezed harder and kissed Jackie deeper, tasting her eager mouth and tongue with growing urgency.

Stef's senses were soon overwhelmed with Jackie's body. She closed her eyes. There was nothing but Jackie. She no longer felt the water they were standing in. There was just Jackie's skin and arms and exploring mouth, so anxious and generous, and the delicate, distinctive aroma of anise wafting past them on the breeze.

Gradually, a foreign sound reached her ears. It wasn't a cow lowing or a bird singing or the soft moans of a woman whose body wanted desperately to give itself to her. It was unnatural and unwelcome. She released Jackie's mouth and looked down the length of the slough to see a motorboat heading their way. On it were two men and two women in swimming suits, talking and laughing. Their voices rose and fell on the air currents as they sped past.

Stef noticed it was getting dark. The sun had gone down and the sky was orange and purple on the western horizon. The moon had moved higher in the sky and shone brightly down on them. Waves from the passing boat splashed over their skin and Stef shivered, suddenly realizing she was cold.

"Come on," Jackie said, taking Stef's hand. "Let's pull in our trap and go back."

The trap contained three crawdads, two adults and one juvenile. Jackie lifted the largest one out between thumb and forefinger, careful to avoid the pinchers. After seeing something akin to affection in her face as she regarded the creature, Stef agreed to release them back into their habitat. With towels from the truck, they dried off their hair, then sat on the towels on the way back to town, underwear soaking through their shorts.

As she drove, Jackie frequently glanced Stef's way and smiled. Stef still had reservations about Jackie. She was a beautiful young woman and Stef wanted her badly. But she also seemed so pure of heart and Stef was worried about what Jackie wanted from her. Whatever it was, it was likely more than Stef was prepared to give.

"Do you want to go to dinner or something?" Jackie asked as they reached town. "Our Cajun place isn't bad. A little seafood étouffée or jambalaya?"

"I can't see myself going out to eat like this," Stef laughed, indicating her wet shorts. "It seems like every time I go anywhere with you, I end up all wet."

Jackie raised her eyebrows, then lowered her voice and said, "I'd say that was a good sign."

Stef snorted in appreciation.

"I have a better idea," Jackie said. "Let's pick up some eggs at the Quickie-Mart, and I'll cook you my famous mushroom and broccolini frittata."

Stef chuckled quietly. "Sounds...terrific."

After parking in front of the convenience store, Jackie leaned across the seat and kissed Stef purposely and suggestively. It was a kiss that promised a lot and there was no mistaking its message. Stef tried to recall how much food was in Deuce's dish, if he would be okay to be left alone for the night.

When Jackie pulled away, her eyes shone with joyful excitement. Stef couldn't help leaning over and giving her one more kiss before they got out of the truck.

CHAPTER TWENTY-THREE

Jackie was ecstatic over this turn of events. Tonight Stef was happy, even talkative. Whatever the reason for her earlier barriers against Jackie, they were down now and Jackie couldn't wait to take advantage of the warm welcome.

Mona was checking out a customer when they walked in. She waved in their direction. Their clothes were still damp, but no longer dripping and no longer clinging in the way that had allowed Jackie a stimulating view earlier of Stef's taut nipples poking against the fabric of her shirt.

"Do you want anything else?" Jackie asked, pulling a carton of eggs from the refrigerator case. "A bottle of wine, maybe?"

"Yeah, let's get some wine."

They walked to the back aisle where the liquor was kept as the customer up front left the building.

"Red or white?" Jackie asked.

"You're the chef." Stef smiled in that way she had, semi-reluctantly, her lips curling up on the left side.

Jackie had a feeling she wasn't going to be making dinner tonight, despite these preparations. Once she got Stef home, she anticipated a hot rush to get naked. That anticipation made her light-headed. After their leisurely kissing session, she couldn't wait to resume touching Stef. Her nerves were on edge with the thought of it. From the first time she saw her, this woman had lit her curiosity and awakened her sexual appetite. Standing next to her in the wine aisle, she moved closer so their hips touched and felt the shock wave flash through her body. It had been a long time since anything like this had happened to Jackie and she relished it.

She reached for a bottle of chardonnay as the bell on the door tinkled, signaling somebody coming into the store. She held the chardonnay up for Stef's approval as a ruckus from the front of the store drew their attention. Mona screamed. A man's voice rang out a muffled threat. Jackie dropped the egg carton, sending egg shells and yolk splattering all around her feet. Stef immediately bolted toward the trouble. Jackie stood where she was for a split second, too startled to move, then followed, coming around a product display to see two men in ski masks, one of them pointing a gun at Mona. Her hands were raised above her head. The gunman swung toward Stef and yelled, "Stop! Hands on your head!"

Stef skidded to a stop and immediately obeyed him, locking her fingers together on top of her head.

"You too!" the man commanded at the sight of Jackie. "Anybody else back there?"

"Nobody else," Stef said evenly. "Just take it easy. Tell us what you want. You have our full cooperation."

The man, who was short and stocky, chuckled tersely, then pointed the gun back at Mona. "You! Open the cash drawer. Then get over there with them."

Mona did as she was told. The three women stood in a row at the side of the store while the second robber went behind the checkstand to take the money. When he'd put it all in a bag, he grabbed two cartons of cigarettes and moved out from behind the counter.

Jackie felt her legs trembling. She realized she was terrified. Stef seemed oddly at ease and moved closer to her so their bodies were touching, offering her some subtle comfort.

The two men backed out of the store. When they hit the doorway, they turned and ran. Stef rushed to the door and watched them go, then she came back in. Mona had sunk to the floor, where she sat with her face in her hands. Jackie knelt beside her and put an arm around her shoulders.

"It's okay," she said. "They're gone."

"Do you have a silent alarm?" Stef asked.

"Yes," answered Mona in an unsteady voice. "I hit it, but it'll take a while before somebody shows up. Hartley's been off duty since five, so he'll have to come from home, which is over by Walnut Grove."

"These guys have hit up and down Main Street," Jackie explained. "After five, the place is wide open. They know they've got easy targets here."

"This has never happened before," Mona said, still sitting on the floor. "This town never used to have crime. Now all of a sudden, it's a freaking crime wave."

"It's the same guys," Jackie said. "That's what my dad thinks. Two young guys. Black ski masks. They take money, booze and cigarettes."

"How many times have they struck?" Stef asked.

"Three times before."

While they waited, Stef remained thoroughly serious and aloof. The playful woman who'd appeared earlier in the evening had retreated again. Jackie thought she even detected a little irritation when she tried to talk to Stef, hoping to jostle her into a more lighthearted mood.

By the time Don Hartley showed up, Mona was back behind the counter carrying on business. Jackie had cleaned up the eggs and Stef was standing outside, leaning against the wall of the building, eating a piece of Ida's World-Famous Beef Jerky.

Hartley, sporting a five o'clock shadow, arrived wearing his street clothes, a white T-shirt and jeans. No time to put on a uniform, he explained before taking their statements. His badge drooped from the T-shirt pocket. He talked to Mona first, then Jackie. They both gave a general description of the men, as much as they could considering the ski masks.

"They were both wearing dark pants," Jackie said. "Navy blue or black. Dark long-sleeved shirts and gloves. They were completely covered."

Don turned to Stef and asked her the same questions without enthusiasm.

"The gunman was five six," she reported. "He had a slight limp, left leg. Caucasian. His eyes were pale blue. He was left-handed. The gun was a Beretta nine millimeter semiautomatic."

Hartley, who had been slouching against the counter, slowly rose to an attentive stand as Stef spoke. He made notes with sudden enthusiasm.

"The other guy was Hispanic."

"How do you know that?" Hartley asked.

"His voice. Unless he was putting it on. His eyes were brown. He was right-handed. There's a tattoo on the inside of his right wrist. When he reached for the cigarettes, his sleeve rode up. About six letters, maybe a name. Both of them wore black chinos and black Nike sneakers. The white guy wore a dark gray pullover hoodie. The Hispanic guy's shirt was dark brown."

While Stef spoke, Jackie stood listening in amazement. Suddenly Stef was a completely different person, completely professional, devoid of sarcasm or disdain and no hint of emotion, positive or negative. This was the third personality Jackie had observed, all of them totally distinct. When Stef had finished her report, Hartley crooked his index finger at her and led her outside to speak to her privately. Jackie shook her head in frustration.

"She sure notices a lot!" Mona declared. "Even what kind of gun they had. How'd she know that? Is she some kind of gun expert or something?"

Jackie recalled Stef's earlier claim that she had no interest in guns. "I don't know," she said distractedly. "I don't really know what she is."

When Hartley returned, he went to talk to Mona. Stef walked over to Jackie and said, "Let's go."

"Should I get the eggs?" Jackie asked.

Stef shook her head. "Sorry, I don't feel much like dinner now. It's late. I think I'll just head home."

Observing Stef's solemn expression, Jackie realized there was no way to save this evening. On the way to the house, Stef sat in the passenger seat staring out the window. She said nothing and seemed to be in a world of her own. Despite her calm demeanor during the robbery and its aftermath, the incident had obviously disturbed her. That too seemed out of character. Stumbling into the middle of a robbery would be upsetting for most people, but Stef didn't seem like one of those people. She came off as, in her father's view, "somebody who could slit your throat without blinking."

Jackie had so many questions, but Stef's body language told her she shouldn't ask. Not tonight.

When they arrived at the house, Stef said goodbye with no mention of getting together again and no goodnight kiss. Perplexed and disappointed, Jackie watched her ride away.

CHAPTER TWENTY-FOUR

Monday morning before work, Jackie stopped by the bait shop to see her parents. Her father was out front talking to a local fisherman. He acknowledged Jackie with a short wave in her direction. She walked through to the bait room where her mother was feeding the fish in tanks. The shirt she wore was one Jackie had never seen before, a psychedelic tie-dyed T-shirt with the image of a marijuana leaf in a circle and the words "I Roll With Mary Jane."

"Mom!" Jackie objected, holding a hand out toward her shirt.

"What?"

"Your shirt!"

"Isn't it groovy?" Ida swished her hips side to side, modeling her attire.

"Groovy? It's...It's—" Jackie fumbled for a word to express her horror.

"Too big?" Ida suggested. "Maybe a little long. But I can hem it. I got this for fifty cents. Can you believe that?"

"Yes, I can." Jackie pointed accusingly at the lettering on the shirt. "Do you know what that means?"

"Of course. What do you think I am, square? I was cool before you were born, Miss Smarty-Pants."

"That's really inappropriate, especially for someone your age."

"Oh, hang loose, Jackie, baby. It's a bait shop, not a bank. No reason to be so uptight."

"But, Mom, it's—"

"And quit changing the subject."

"Huh? What subject?"

"The subject of where you were last night." Her mother's look was stern and accusing. "Because I already know where you weren't. You weren't having Sunday dinner with your family. When I asked Becca why you weren't there, she got all sassy with me and said, 'I am not my sister's keeper.'"

"I did call, Mom. I left a message."

"I know. Something better to do, you said."

"I did not say that," Jackie objected. "I said I had *something* to do, not something better."

"But it must have been something better, right, or you wouldn't have blown us off."

Jackie knew her mother was only partly serious, but she wasn't used to Jackie not showing up for Sunday dinner. Jackie's social life, apart from her family, was minimal and predictable. So an aberration like this would have been noted with interest. And no one was more interested in people's social lives than Ida Townsend. Especially when it came to her family members.

"It might have been a tiny bit better," Jackie admitted, kissing her mother's cheek. "I had an appointment I had to reschedule from Saturday because Gail dragged me out all day for the sturgeon rescue."

"I heard there was all kinds of excitement after we left."

Jackie was glad to see her mother's face light up with the new subject. "They said Gail arrested a poacher."

"Yes. He tried to strangle Stef."

"I heard that! Stef, she's the houseboat girl, right? Is she okay?"

"She's fine. It turned out okay, except for the one fish he'd already got."

Ida shook her head. "I don't know what this town is coming to. Saturday some jerk kills a sturgeon and nearly kills a woman, then Sunday night the Quickie-Mart gets robbed. Did you hear about that? That was last night about nine o'clock."

Jackie hesitated before answering, not wanting to upset her mother with the news that she had been present. "Yes, I heard about it. This wave of robberies is scary."

"Your father wants to keep a loaded gun here in the store. No! I said. Somebody'll get killed. And he says, that's right. Those bastards come in here to rob me, they'll get killed."

"That doesn't sound like a good idea," Jackie said.

"It's a terrible idea." Ida sprinkled fish food over the minnow tank. "But he says, what choice do we have?"

Jackie recalled Stef's calm and reasonable behavior from the night before. "Let them have the money."

Ida shrugged. "Yeah, but it burns me up. And you know how your father is. He's not going to let anybody pry a dime out of his dead fingers." She shook her head. "It's just got me so worried."

A couple of young men came into the store and hoisted a bag of ice onto the counter. Rudy broke off his conversation to wait on them.

"Can we get a pound of clams?" said one of them.

"Sure. Go ask Mrs. Townsend back there."

The boy sauntered back to the bait room. "Pound of clams, Mrs. Townsend."

She scurried to the tank and scooped up some clams, then poured ice over them while the boy waited. He was tall, Hispanic, good-looking, in his early twenties. He smiled at Jackie and said, "How ya doin'?"

"Good," she said. She felt oddly uncomfortable in his presence.

His friend, who was short and stocky with light blue eyes and sandy hair, picked up a six-pack of beer from the refrigerator case and set that beside the bag of ice. Then he grabbed two sandwiches from the food case. Jackie glanced at their feet and saw they were both wearing black Nike sneakers.

"Here you go, Eddie," said Ida, handing over the clams. "Good luck."

"Thanks." The boy winked at Jackie before returning to the check-out counter where Rudy rang him up.

"You going for stripers?" Rudy asked.

"Yeah."

"Where ya headed?"

"Whiskey Slough," said blue-eyes. "Got a sweet little spot there just crawling with them. Big ones." He held his hands fourteen or fifteen inches apart.

"If you land a whopper, come on back and show it to me."

"Sure thing," said the tall boy.

When they'd gone, Jackie asked her mother, "Do you know those two?"

"That's Joey Cahill and Eddie Delgado."

"Local boys?"

"Uh-huh. I think you know Eddie's mother. She's one of the cooks over at the high school."

"Oh, sure, Mrs. Delgado in the cafeteria."

"That's right. Nice family. I don't know the Cahills. They moved here a couple years ago into that new subdivision over by Walker Landing. Joey's been in here a few times, usually with Eddie. That's how I know him. Why do you ask?"

"Just wondered," Jackie said evasively. The fact that the two boys matched the general description of the Quickie-Mart robbers intrigued her, but was no reason to make assumptions. More importantly, it was no reason to say so to her mother. She knew from experience that an off-handed observation like that in the possession of Ida Townsend could run amok all over town.

"I gotta go, Mom," she said.

"You never told me where you were last night," Ida reminded her.

Jackie smiled. "I know."

She walked through the store, which was now empty except for her father. "Dad," she said, heading for the door, "please don't keep a gun here. That's very dangerous."

He sputtered in her direction without looking up.

"I'm serious," she said firmly, knowing that his failure to look her in the eye was a bad sign. She made a mental note to readdress the subject the next time she came in.

In the parking lot, she ran into Marcus Cole, a family friend and owner of Cole's Auto Repair. He wore blue work pants, a short-sleeved shirt, a baseball cap on backwards—his usual get-up. When he saw Jackie, he stopped short and smiled wide, his blue eyes shining, his face well creased. Marcus was in his forties, wiry and fidgety. Free time drove him crazy, so he kept his shop open seven days a week and worked there himself every one of them. The prospect of an entire weekend with no job to go to would have been torture to him.

"Hi there, Jackie," he said enthusiastically.

"Hi. Not working today?"

"No cars in the shop, but your mom's got a rough running engine, so I said I'd take a look."

"I remember her mentioning that."

"Probably just needs new plugs." He pulled off his cap and scratched his scalp through his thin brown hair. A pronounced indentation from the hat's plastic band ran across his forehead with a row of round red marks left by the adjustment tabs. Jackie was pretty sure that pattern was by now a permanent feature of his forehead. "She said she'll give me a ten-pound jar of Ida's World-Famous Beef Jerky if I fix it." He grinned like he'd hit the jackpot.

"I know you're a car guy," Jackie said, "but do you know anything about fixing boat engines?"

"Sure. I can fix anything with a motor. Lawn mowers, chainsaws, food processor. Boat motors are easy. You're not planning on putting a motor on your kayak, are you?" Marcus hooted at his joke.

"No. I have a friend with a houseboat and a dead engine."

"What kind of motor is it?"

"Uh, sorry, I don't—"

He waved a hand. "Doesn't matter. I can fix it. Just tell me where and when and I'll take care of it."

Jackie remembered Stef's financial situation. "I don't suppose you'd take a jar of Ida's World-Famous Beef Jerky for that, would you?"

"Oh, no, no. No need to pay me. It'll be fun. Boat motors are a kick. Besides, after what you did for our little Smokey, I can never thank you enough."

"That's really nice of you, Marcus. My friend doesn't have much money. How is Smokey these days?"

"Great. She's a fur ball of trouble, that little stinker. But she keeps Annie company when I'm at the shop. Annie prefers Smokey's company anyway, I'll bet."

Jackie laughed. "I'm glad she's doing well. I'll call you about the houseboat to set something up. Say hi to Annie for me."

"Will do." Marcus sauntered into the bait shop where Jackie heard her mother's loud and enthusiastic greeting. For a second, she flashed back to her mother's ridiculous shirt and wondered what Marcus, or anybody who came in the shop, would think about that.

As she drove to work, she remembered standing in Disappointment Slough in Stef's arms, lost to the sweetness of her embrace and the hunger of her kisses. Just thinking about it sent a surge of desire through her core. When she got to work, she called Stef's number, hoping to find her in a good mood, hoping she could arrange to get together again. But Stef's mood would remain unknown because she didn't answer and the phone went right to voice mail.

"Good morning," Jackie said. "It's Jackie. I hope you're feeling better today. I really enjoyed our evening together. Until the robbery, of course." She laughed nervously. "I'd like to see you again. Soon. Please call."

CHAPTER TWENTY-FIVE

Would Stef be happy to see her with another offer of unsolicited help? Marcus sat in the passenger seat beside Jackie, a skinny arm propped on the frame of the open window, his ball cap on backwards as usual, smiling distractedly at the countryside. Jackie hadn't heard from Stef for a few days and didn't know what to expect from her.

She was uneasy, but more hopeful about Stef now that they'd spent some time together and she had seen a more playful, friendly and amorous side of her personality. It wasn't just the romantic turn their relationship had taken that made Jackie optimistic. It was seeing Stef having fun. She had seemed so serious before and fundamentally sad, as though she had a great burden on her shoulders. One thing Jackie had figured out was that Stef was the kind of person who didn't ask for help, even when she was desperately in need of it. So if you wanted to help her, you just had to shove your way in. I'm fully capable of that, she thought with satisfaction.

When they arrived at the houseboat, Marcus looked it over, nodded approvingly. He obviously couldn't wait to get his hands in her guts. Stef stood on a stepladder at the stern with a can of paint and a paintbrush. Deuce came running toward the pickup, barking a friendly welcome. As Jackie got out of the truck, she noticed the blue trim of the boat had been brightened up considerably. Deuce stopped barking and came up to Jackie for a pat on the head. Too bad your owner isn't as eager to see me, she thought.

Stef stepped down from the ladder. Marcus strode over to her on his long legs and Jackie followed.

"Hi," Jackie said cheerfully. "This is Marcus. I've brought him to look at your engine. Unless you've got it going already."

Marcus shook Stef's hand.

"Hi, Marcus," she said. "I haven't got it going, no. I've been painting."

Jackie stood back and gazed appreciatively at the newly-painted trim. "Beautiful color," she said. "Really brightens it up. I didn't realize the old color was so faded."

"Meander Blue," Stef said.

"What?"

"The color. It's called Meander Blue."

Marcus already had the cowling open on the motor and was peering into it. He seemed to have forgotten about them.

"Jackie," Stef said quietly, "if I could afford a mechanic, I would have hired one already."

"He's not going to charge you. Not for labor. Just parts if you need any. He's doing me a favor."

"How old is this thing?" Marcus asked. "Seventies maybe, huh?"

"Seventy-five!" Stef answered. Then she lowered her voice again and addressed Jackie. "I don't know. I don't like owing people favors."

"He's doing it for me, for treating his cat, so why don't you cool it with the *I don't need nothing from nobody* attitude? It seems to me you can use a hand."

Stef looked taken aback at Jackie's tone, but she said nothing.

"Nice engine in its day," Marcus said. "Hundred and fifteen horsepower Johnson. I've seen a couple like this before. Does it fire up at all?"

"No," Stef said.

"Don't get mad if I ask the obvious," Marcus said. "But experience has taught me to start at the beginning. Is there gas in it?"

Stef laughed. "Yes. New gas. I've replaced the battery. New spark plugs and wires. There's spark on all the plugs now, which wasn't the case when I started."

"So maybe not an ignition problem. Maybe a fuel system problem. How long since this thing worked?"

"Three years. The last time she was in the water, it worked okay. That's what the previous owner told me. But since it's been here, it hasn't been used at all."

"Not good to let an engine sit like that. Do you have a water barrel for the prop so I can try to start it? Wouldn't want to burn it up in case it does kick over a few times."

Stef got a large plastic bucket, positioned it under the propeller, then filled it with a hose.

Marcus hovered over the engine with a spray can. "Carburetor cleaner," he explained. "Highly flammable. Give her something to burn."

He tried starting the engine. It sputtered, ran for three seconds, then died. Stef looked momentarily giddy at this brief burst of life, which was apparently more than she had expected.

"Yep," Marcus said, nodding. "Not getting any fuel."

"What's causing that?" Stef asked.

"Could be a lot of things. Fuel pump not working. Clogged fuel line or fuel filter. Carb gunk. I'm gonna pull the carburetors and check 'em out." He looked absolutely thrilled at the thought. "Is there someplace I can sit and spread the parts out?"

"There's a picnic table over by the grill. You can use that."

"Okay. I'll get to work."

"Can I help?" Stef asked.

"Naw. I like to work alone. You girls go do girl stuff. Go on. Git."

He sprinted back to the truck to get his tool box.

"He's good," Jackie assured Stef. "I know he seems kinda goofy."

"At this point, I'll take it. Come on in. I'll make some iced tea."

"I called the other day," Jackie said.

Stef looked embarrassed. "Yeah, I got the message."

They went inside and Stef filled a teakettle with water and put it on the stove. Apparently she didn't think any explanation was necessary for why she hadn't returned the call. Jackie sat on the built-in sofa in the living area and peered at a couple of photos on the wall. A middle-aged woman stood in a huddle of three young adults, two boys and a girl. The girl was clearly Stef at maybe twenty years old. The photo next to this was of an older woman, in her sixties, with white hair and a mere hint of a smile.

"This is your family?" Jackie asked.

"Uh-huh." Stef leaned against the kitchen counter, facing Jackie. "The one on the left is my maternal grandmother. Grandma Mattie. She's been gone awhile now. The other one is my mom and brothers, Jay and Bruce."

"Your mother's very tall. Where does she live?"

"Hayward. Same house I grew up in. Grandma Mattie lived in the next block, so whenever I was angry or sad or hungry I ran over there for comfort. I always thought of her as my refuge." A brief, distant smile passed across Stef's face. "Mostly from my brothers."

"It's always good to have a place to run to," Jackie conceded. "Does your mother still work?"

"Yes. She works in a doctor's office. General office stuff."

Jackie nodded. "What about you? What sort of work do you do?"

Stef hesitated, looking suddenly troubled. "I'm unemployed," she said, averting her eyes.

The teakettle let out a shrill whistle. Stef lifted it off the burner and poured the hot water into a glass pitcher, into which she dropped a tea infuser.

"That'll need to sit there awhile," she said, turning back to Jackie, who sat with her hands on either side of her, pushing down against the couch cushion.

Jackie wondered what unhappy thoughts she had triggered with her question. She stood and walked up to Stef, slipping her hands loosely around her waist, then kissed her tenderly on the mouth. She looked into those tragic hazel eyes, wishing she could see what lay beyond. Stef stood limply, seeming not to know how to respond. Jackie had expected more enthusiasm and wasn't sure what this ambivalence meant. It seemed that for every step forward with Stef, she slid two steps back.

"So why didn't you call me back?" Jackie asked, trying to sound more curious than accusing. "I thought we were going somewhere."

Stef attempted a smile and touched Jackie's cheek gently. "Maybe because I'm not sure where we're going. Maybe you're going somewhere I'm not. You said the other day you're looking for somebody to be serious about. I'm not that person, Jackie."

"How do you know? We've barely gotten started."

Stef look conflicted, as if she were arguing with herself. Jackie wished she could hear that argument, wished she could understand what ghosts haunted Stef's mind. She hoped this was the moment Stef opened up to her. But instead of talking, Stef pulled her close to kiss her, and Jackie gladly cooperated. They stood beside the kitchen counter in a close embrace, their kisses long and sensuous. Everywhere their bodies touched, Jackie's skin tingled with raw energy.

"Kissing you is incredible," Jackie breathed when they pulled apart.

Stef smiled. "It's not bad from my point of view either. Do you think this is what Marcus meant when he suggested we go do 'girl stuff'?"

"I doubt it, but I'll take this over painting your toenails any day."

Stef snorted. "You just try to paint my toenails and I'll—"

"Hey!" called Marcus near the kitchen window.

Stef and Jackie broke abruptly apart. Stef leaned toward the window and hollered out. "What's up?"

"There's a lot of crud. Floats are shot. We'll need new ones. Fuel filter too. Gummed up." He walked up the steps to the sliding glass door and peered through.

"That was fast," Stef remarked to Jackie. She slid the door open.

Marcus wiped his hands on a rag. "I'll need to get carburetor kits and rebuild the whole dang things. That should do the trick."

"Are you sure?" Stef asked.

"Sure as eggs is eggs."

"Will that be expensive?"

"Naw! Less than forty bucks for the kits. Just a bunch of gaskets, mainly, and then you got your fuel filter. A few bucks more. The thing is, parts for this classic won't be sitting on the shelf at Jim's Marina. I'll make some calls and see if I can find 'em. Might have to order 'em."

Stef nodded her understanding.

"Is there a head in this thing?" Marcus asked. "I'd like to wash up before we go."

Stef pointed. "Straight down the hall on the right."

Marcus held up his grease-covered hands. "You got anything to cut this grease?"

"There's a bar of lava soap in the drawer under the counter there," Stef said, indicating the shelf next to where Jackie stood. "Jackie, can you grab that?"

"This is a nice little place," Marcus announced, glancing around appreciatively. "Not bad at all."

Jackie pulled open a drawer. Lying face up inside was a five-by-seven framed photo of two uniformed police officers, a man and a woman. She lifted it out of the drawer, recognizing Stef's face, all smiles, leaning familiarly against a handsome Hispanic man with a thin mustache. He had his arm slung around her shoulders. Near the bottom of the picture was scrawled the message, "Next time, Hot Stuff!" Before Jackie could process what she was looking at, Stef seized the photo from her hand, saying, "The other drawer." Her voice was sharp. Jackie looked at her face as she shut the drawer on the photo and opened the one next to it to retrieve a bar of soap. Her expression was full of frustration. She was clearly unhappy that Jackie had stumbled on that photo.

Soap in hand, Marcus walked down the hall, whistling.

"You're a police officer," Jackie stated, suddenly comprehending how much sense that made.

Stef shook her head. "No, I'm not. Not anymore."

"But you were. That's you in that picture."

"I used to be a cop." Stef turned to the sink, avoiding Jackie's eyes.

"It looks like a recent photo," Jackie persisted. "How long ago did you quit?"

Stef turned back to face Jackie, her face full of conflict, as if she were battling an internal debate. She was so changed from a few minutes ago, as if she'd fallen from her soaring place in the sky, like a kite that had lost the wind. Jackie was sorry she'd stumbled onto something that was clearly painful, but she was encouraged to think she was on the verge of a discovery. Stef looked, for a fleeting, promising moment, like she was going to open up. But then, just as suddenly, she closed.

"I don't want to talk about it," she said softly. "It's all in the past."

Frustrated, Jackie was unable to let it go. "Did something happen? You can tell me. I'll understand."

"Look," Stef responded, an edge of anger in her voice, "I said I didn't want to talk about it."

"It's a little tight in there." Marcus was on his way back to the main cabin. "But gets the job done. I'll let you know when I find the parts. Then I'll get her going. Guaranteed. You'll see."

Stef nodded. "Thanks again, Marcus."

"You're welcome." He turned to Jackie. "I'm ready if you are."

Marcus led the way out and Jackie followed, feeling injured. She paused in the doorway to make a silent connection with Stef. She looked slightly apologetic, but Jackie understood the apology was for her harsh tone of voice, not for her refusal to let Jackie into her world.

"Bye," she said quietly, then followed Marcus to the truck.

CHAPTER TWENTY-SIX

Gail and Jackie sat down on the bench in front of the bait shop with their ice cream cones, concentrating on licking them down to cone level before they melted. It was morning, just starting to heat up, and they were passing time while deciding what to do with their day. As often happened on Saturday, Pat was working and Gail was on her own. They'd narrowed their choices down to kayaking or a movie, but Jackie, whose mood was dipping below normal, wasn't enthusiastic about either.

The bench they sat on was the front seat from her grandfather's 1957 Chevy Bel-Air. The rest of the car had gone to the junkyard years ago. Jackie had never seen it, but she had seen photos—a chunky looking turquoise and white classic with wide whitewall tires, convertible roof, chrome trim, and pronounced fins in the back, like a rocket ship. The seat was two-tone, turquoise panels surrounded by ivory trim. Grandpa came by and washed it on a regular basis, but the vinyl was cracked in several places and discolored by age.

"Maybe she's on the lam," Gail said between ice cream licks, continuing a conversation from earlier. "Running from the law."

"She *is* the law."

"She used to be the law. Maybe she was one of those dirty cops who got caught and made a break for it."

"I doubt that. I don't think she's a criminal."

"If there's no crime, why won't she talk?"

Jackie shrugged. "Something bad happened. Something that hurts too much to talk about."

Gail bit into her cone with a crunch. "Then maybe you shouldn't push her. I know it hurts your feelings that she won't tell you, but if it's that painful, maybe you should respect her need to keep it to herself. Maybe someday she'll tell you. In her own time."

"The thing is, I could help."

"Maybe. Maybe not. For a lot of things, the only cure is time."

Jackie sighed resignedly. "You're right. But I could at least make the time go easier. You saw how much she enjoyed that day out on the river."

"You're taking credit for that?" Gail raised an eyebrow.

"Not entirely. But the next day, out at Disappointment Slough, I'm taking credit for that. She seemed really happy. Maybe I could just help get her mind off it, that's all."

"Maybe you could, just by being with her. Make her laugh, distract her and try not to worry about the rest. It'll work itself out." She sucked liquefied ice cream from the base of her cone. "You too. Try to have fun. You definitely have her interested. She's tasted the bait. Now land the hook and reel her in."

Jackie looked askance at Gail before concentrating on her ice cream and silently considering her advice.

After popping the last of her cone in her mouth, Gail leaned against the back of the bench contentedly. "This thing," she asked, returning to the subject on both of their minds, "whatever her dark secret is, are you sure that isn't the attraction?"

"What do you mean?"

"You know how you are, Jacks. You can't resist a homeless mutt. The more messed up they are, the more you want to take them in and cuddle 'em up."

"That may be true of animals, but it isn't true of women. Loser women don't appeal to me at all. Besides, I don't think Stef's like that, a messed up mutt. I think she's just going through a rough period." Ice cream dripped on the wooden floorboards of the porch next to Jackie's feet. She finished her cone before continuing her train of thought. "Maybe she's like a champion horse with an injury. With a lot of care, she can be a champion again. She still has all the potential. She just needs someone to believe in her capacity to heal."

Gail sputtered sarcastically. "A champion horse? You're so confident she can be healed, even though you don't know what she needs to heal from."

"Does it matter?"

"Yes! What if she's a homicidal maniac or a drug addict or... she's got a fatal illness? Whatever it is, it's bad enough she can't tell you. You don't know anything about her, really, do you?"

Jackie frowned. Gail was right. It could be anything. But she hadn't even considered the idea of a fatal illness. What if Stef quit her job because she was dying? Floating along the tranquil waterways of the Delta might easily be someone's idea of a good way to use up her last few months alive.

About to lapse into despair, Jackie suddenly realized that was a ridiculous idea. Stef was strong and vibrant, the picture of health.

She punched Gail in the arm.

"Ouch!" Gail complained, grabbing the spot. "What was that for?"

"For trying to kill off my girlfriend."

Gail scowled her bewilderment before releasing her arm and sinking back into the car seat.

"You want to see what I got for my mother?" Jackie asked, not waiting for Gail's answer. She pulled a two-piece shorts outfit from her tote bag and held it up by its hanger. The shorts were yellow with white piping and the shirt was white with yellow sleeves and collar. A simple swirl design in yellow and green adorned the front of the shirt, an abstract floral motif.

"That's really cute!" Gail said. "Is it her birthday?"

"No. Just something I picked up for her. I thought I'd give it to her this morning, but she's not here, so I'll just leave it with Dad." She folded the outfit and tucked it back in her bag.

"I bet she likes it. It's a little more...coordinated than most of her things."

Jackie laughed. "That's the idea. As long as she thinks I didn't pay over a couple dollars, she'll like it."

They both came to attention when Rosa's Brazilian Churrascaria pulled into the parking lot and rolled up to their location. Rosa was in the passenger seat and Ben was at the wheel.

"Is Mom here?" he called.

"Not until later this afternoon," Jackie said.

"Good. We can catch the lunch crowd before she gets here."

"You're going to park here?" Jackie asked, astonished. "After what happened last time?"

Rosa leaned across Ben to answer. "This is where people expect us to be on Saturdays."

"But if Mom sees you—"

"You just said she wasn't here, didn't you?" Ben replied. "We'll be outta here by one o'clock."

The truck pulled over to the edge of the highway in the usual spot. Jackie shook her head.

"Do you think my family's weird?" she asked.

Gail snorted. "I don't know. No weirder than any other family, probably."

CHAPTER TWENTY-SEVEN

"Well, cut off my head and stuff me in a suitcase!" Stef called boisterously at the familiar figure stepping out of a beat-up Camaro in her driveway. "Look what the cat dragged in!"

Deuce was already jumping up Womack's legs for a greeting. Typical. A stranger drives up and that dog's all, "Hi! Come on in. Let me show you where the valuables are."

Womack hailed her with a wave and broad smile, then pulled a grocery sack out of his trunk. He approached on flip-flops, wearing tan shorts and a short-sleeved cotton shirt, sunglasses covering his eyes, his wavy black hair pushed back from his long face and his left arm almost a solid block of tattoos. He was tall and big. In a police uniform, he was an intimidating presence. But to those who knew him, he was a lighthearted, easygoing fella. The kind of guy you wanted at a party. He knew how to have fun, but he was also a solid cop, somebody you could rely on in a pinch. Stef hadn't seen Womack for months. She wondered briefly if he'd tried to kill any other cops lately with his lethal homemade pepper spread.

"Hey," he said enthusiastically. "Look at you!" He came up and gave her a one-armed hug, then reached for Deuce's head to give him a pat. "Molina's dog?"

"Yes. Name's Deuce."

"Deuce? Why not Ace? Hey, boy, you some kinda second-rate scout?"

"Molina's nickname was Ace," Stef explained. "In his previous life. Nobody called him that anymore except some of his old gang."

Womack laughed. "Okay, I get it. Ace...Deuce."

"How'd you find me?"

"I chatted up that cute little Debbie in payroll. I figured they had to know where you are to send you your check. Nobody can hide from Womack, right? But, hell, you're way off the beaten path, that's for sure." He flipped his glasses on top of his head and observed the houseboat thoughtfully. "So this is home sweet home, is it?"

"That's right."

"How about showing me around?"

She waved him toward the cabin door and led him inside where he set his bag on the counter. He pulled out a six-pack of Michelob. "Put these in the fridge, huh? And look what else I brought you." He took a quart jar from the bag. "My hot pepper spread! This is the real deal, the habanero version."

Stef held the jar in both hands and laughed. "Thanks! You know I love this stuff."

"Exactly! I can still see your face from that day. Hilarious! Sweat, tears, snot. Everything that could come out of your head was pouring out! Molina too. I'll never forget that."

"Me neither. I won't be eating this by the spoonful, though. It's going to last a while."

After a tour of the boat, they sat side by side in the two lawn chairs on the aft deck with cold bottles of beer. A half-dozen strips of Ida's World-Famous Beef Jerky lay on a paper towel on the table between them. Womack slung his feet up on the deck railing and leaned back and took a swallow of beer, then smacked his lips. A pair of ducks flew over, momentarily distracting him.

"What's this place like?" he asked. "Anything ever happen around here?"

"It has its moments. Actually, they're having a little crime wave here lately."

"Really? Maybe you can help them out."

"Naw. Not my job, not anymore. I'm leaving all that to you masochists. Besides, they've got a cop on the beat."

"A cop? You mean one cop?"

"Right. One cop."

Womack chuckled. "Really small town. I think I drove through it on the way out here. Right on the river there."

"That's it. Stillwater Bay."

"Have you met that one cop? Is he a Barney Fife sort of fella?"

"Actually, he seems very competent."

Stef didn't mind the small talk. She figured Womack had something on his mind, but she was in no hurry to talk about it. They were work friends, good ones, but hadn't socialized much on the outside, so his coming all the way out here to share a beer was extremely suspicious behavior.

"How do you like small-town living?" he asked.

"Hard to get used to. You can't walk into a store without seeing somebody you know, even after just a couple of weeks here."

"That's a small town all right. I grew up in a small town. They're okay. Pros and cons."

"Everybody's very friendly. And by friendly, I mean nosey. They're not the least bit afraid to ask everything they want to know. Where you from? What do you do for a living? Is there a Mister Byers? Do you sleep in the nude?"

Womack let out a loud croak. "No kidding." He sucked a swallow from his beer, then said, "Do you?"

She gave him an indulgent smile. "What'd you come out here for, you big goof?"

"Just wanted to see my girl," he replied, smiling his toothy smile. "See how she's doing." His smile gradually faded into a look of concern as his long face grew even longer. "How *are* you doing, Stef?"

"Fine. I'm doing fine." She could tell by the sober look on his face they were done with small talk.

"I heard you weren't coming back."

"That's right."

"That's a shame." He spoke without looking at her. His gaze was straight ahead at the pasture with its dry grass and the tree line beyond that marked the path of Duggan Creek. "The guys all miss you. The girls too." He glanced at her with a twinkle in his eyes. "Especially the girls."

Stef took a swallow of beer, and Womack ripped a hunk of jerky off with his teeth, chewing with deliberation.

"Did Shoemaker send you out here?" she asked.

He swallowed the jerky and said, "Not exactly. He mentioned I might want to pay you a visit, that's all."

"Check up on me. See if I've gone bonkers or something?"

"No, no. Nobody's worried about you. We all know you can take care of yourself. Everybody misses you, that's all."

"I miss you goons too, to be honest."

"We sure wish you'd come back."

"Anything interesting going on?"

"Same old, same old."

It was hard for Stef to broach a serious subject with a guy like Womack. Their relationship had always been on a different plane. But she was intensely curious about what the rumor mill had been spinning out.

"What did the guys say?" she asked.

Womack turned to catch her expression, narrowing one eye. "About?"

"About what happened," she said impatiently.

"It was terrible, that's what they said. What do you think?" He stuck another piece of jerky in his mouth.

"Sure, I know that, but I mean about me. Do they think I panicked? Or missed the mark? Or mistook Molina for the perp? They weren't there. They couldn't know how it was, so there must have been a lot of speculation."

Womack regarded her levelly, chewing. He put his beer on the table and took his feet off the railing so he could face her. "Stef, you know what the place is like when something like this happens. Of course there's a lot of buzz. There's a couple of jerks talking about something they don't know anything about. But anybody who's worked with you would never think you panicked. None of that shit matters. It's just talk. The only thing that matters is the facts and the outcome of the investigation. I, for one, knew all along you'd be exonerated, and I told everybody that too."

"Did you have a station pool going on that?" she asked cynically.

"No! It wasn't like that. Nobody took it lightly. If you think they blame you, that they think you screwed up, you're wrong. There was speculation. That's just natural when a tragedy happens and people don't have the facts. But once the verdict came down, it was over. Everybody accepts that decision and wants you back on the job. Especially me. I'd be happy to work with you any time. It was an accident and it wasn't your fault. It would have been the same with any one of us."

"Thanks," Stef said quietly.

"Is that why you won't come back?" Womack asked. "You think you don't have the support?"

She shook her head. "No. Actually, everybody's been great. No, it's nothing to do with that. I just wondered what they were saying. You're right. It's natural for people to speculate, since they weren't there and they can't see this fucking movie that keeps playing over and over in my head." She drained her beer and set it on the table. "Want another?"

"Sure."

As she pushed herself up from her chair, he let his hand rest over hers briefly. She wasn't used to a tender, serious-looking Womack like the sympathetic guy currently regarding her. It made her feel vulnerable and weak. Maybe that was the reason she couldn't go back, she considered. Everybody would be looking at her like that. It's one thing to be scarred on the inside where nobody could know about it. But everybody back there *did* know about it. Even if she could forget about it, which wasn't likely, they wouldn't. Seeing her, they'd be reminded. There was no way to go back to the way things used to be. And that was the only thing she wanted, to go back to the way things used to be.

She slapped Womack's hand away with a disapproving grunt. "Hey, you got any new pictures of that kid of yours? Last time we talked, you said she was starting little league."

He brightened. "Yeah! She's got an arm on her you wouldn't believe. I've got some shots of her right here on my phone." He reached into his pocket.

"I'll be right back with your refill and you can show me." She climbed down the stairway into the cabin to get the beer.

Unlike her former colleagues, strangers knew only what she let them know. But Stef wasn't sure she could hide her wounds even from strangers. They were still too raw. Jackie, for instance. Jackie knew there was something haunting her. Her eyes were full of sympathy, maybe even pity. It was unnerving and a little bit maddening. She didn't want to see that reflection of herself in anyone's eyes, especially not someone close to her. That was why she couldn't tell Jackie. Their relationship, if there could be a relationship, couldn't be a case of rescue. They had to be on a more equal footing. Maybe it was already too late for that, Stef surmised. Maybe Jackie only wanted to be with her because she thought of her as another three-legged cat.

She pulled two beers from the refrigerator, remembering the other day, the look on Jackie's face when she left. She had been hurt that Stef hadn't confided in her. What she didn't know was how tempted Stef had been to do so. Looking into Jackie's sincere, concerned face, she had wanted to tell her everything. She'd wanted to open herself up and pour herself out.

But it hadn't been the right time with Marcus just down the hall in the bathroom. Afterward, she was relieved she'd held back. Wanting to share herself with someone worried her. What sharing meant, more than anything else, was making herself vulnerable. That was the scary side of love, showing someone your Achilles' heel and then hoping they didn't shove a spear in it. No, that wasn't right. It wasn't *hoping*. It was trusting.

She twisted the caps off the bottles, thinking, *Jackie seems like one of the most trustworthy people I've ever met.*

CHAPTER TWENTY-EIGHT

Stef waited at the paint counter in the local hardware store as a quart of Meander Blue was mixed up. The kid behind the counter held the can out to show her the color, a bright blue with a subtle hint of green, the color of a tropical sea in shade.

"Look right?" he asked.

She nodded, leaning heavily against the counter.

He hammered on the lid, then put the can in the shaking machine. Over the hum of the machine, Stef heard two elderly women chatting nearby. She wasn't actually listening to them until she heard the name "Rudy Townsend." Then she stood at attention and listened with interest.

"He's in the hospital," said one of the women. "Taken over to Lodi Memorial a couple hours ago by ambulance."

"What happened?" asked the other woman.

"I don't know. Maybe a heart attack. Hank Turner was delivering the mail on their street when the ambulance arrived. He said the paramedics carried Rudy out on a stretcher with an oxygen mask on. Poor Ida was in hysterics."

The two women moved on to another topic as the clerk handed Stef's can of paint over the counter. Outside the store, she called Jackie's cell phone. No answer. She called the vet clinic. Niko answered and told her Jackie had left the office to attend to a family emergency.

"It's her father, right?" Stef asked.

"Right. They took him to the hospital."

"Have you heard anything?"

"No. Not yet."

Stef hung up, wondering what to do. She wanted to do something. This was a potentially devastating turn of events for Jackie. Her family was so close, so much a part of her everyday life. If she were to lose her father…

"Hey!" she barked at a man walking through the parking lot. He stopped abruptly, looking around as she stepped toward him. "Do you know where Lodi Memorial Hospital is?"

The man, around fifty years old, in Bermuda shorts and a T-shirt, peered at her through a pair of thick prescription glasses. "Yes," he said tentatively. "It's in Lodi."

"And where's that?"

"You don't know where Lodi is?"

"No."

He looked astonished, then pointed to the east. "It's over there."

"How about drawing me a map to the hospital?" she suggested, opening one of her saddlebags to get a pad and pen.

"Okay," the man agreed.

***

A half hour after leaving her office, in a state of high anxiety, Jackie burst into the hospital emergency room and asked for her father at the reception desk. Waiting for an answer, she caught sight of her mother in a nearby hallway, talking on her phone.

"Never mind," she told the receptionist. "There's my mother."

She rushed over to Ida, who interrupted her call to give her daughter a hug.

"I'll call you back," she said into her phone. "Jackie's here."

"Where's Dad?" Jackie demanded. "Is he okay? Becca said he had a heart attack."

Ida waved her hand and shook her head. "It wasn't a heart attack. He'll be fine. Nothing to worry about."

"What was it?" The casual expression on her mother's face allowed Jackie to relax considerably.

"The doctor said ana...ana." Ida frowned in frustration. "An allergic reaction."

"Anaphylaxis?"

"Yeah, yeah, that's it!"

Jackie breathed a deep sigh of relief. Not a heart attack. And he was going to be fine.

"We're just waiting for him to be released now so we can go home. I'm sorry you had to leave work and come all the way out here for nothing."

"It's okay. I'm just glad it wasn't serious." Over her initial panic, Jackie noticed her mother's outfit. It was the one she had given her, the tasteful white and yellow shorts set. "Mom, that outfit looks darling on you!"

"Your father said the same thing this morning before he collapsed. He said you should buy all my clothes. And I said, well, once in a while is okay, especially if she gets a good bargain like this, but I'd hate to give up my fun at the thrift store and the flea market."

Jackie smiled resignedly as her mother pulled down on the hem of her shirt to straighten it, admiring the design. When she looked up again, Jackie was alarmed to see tears in her eyes.

"Oh, Jackie," she sobbed. "I thought he was dying. He got all red and couldn't breathe. I was scared to death."

Jackie gave her mother a comforting hug, patting her back lightly. "It must have been horrible. What was it? A wasp? I know he's allergic to wasps."

Ida stopped crying abruptly and adopted an expression of

resentment that startled Jackie. "How was I supposed to know he was allergic to papayas?"

"Papayas? He ate a papaya?"

"Thirty years and he never said a word about being allergic to papayas."

"Oh!" Jackie exclaimed with sudden understanding. "The jerky?"

Her mother nodded, her mouth set defiantly. "I said, try this, it's my new stuff. And he eats it, all the while knowing he's allergic to papaya."

"Did he know there was papaya in it?"

"Of course he didn't know. That's my secret ingredient."

Jackie decided not to question her mother's logic at a time like this. "Can I see him?"

"He's right in there." She pointed to a door on the left. "I'm just taking a break to make some calls. Everybody's so worried, so I want to let them know he's okay."

Jackie nodded, then gave her mother another hug before slipping into the exam room where she found her father propped up in a bed connected to a monitor charting his vital signs. She glanced at the screen, reassured to see a regular, normal heartbeat and pulse. He wore a hospital gown, his legs and stockinged feet lying exposed on top of the sheets. Otherwise, he looked entirely normal. His color was good and he seemed fully alert. When she came in, he smiled and reached out for a hug.

"How do you feel?" she asked.

"Not bad. Still a little light-headed. Did you hear what happened?"

"I ran into Mom in the hall and she told me."

He scowled. "Did she tell you she tried to kill me?"

Jackie sat on the doctor's stool. "Not exactly. You shouldn't say that. You'll make her feel worse. And you'll start a rumor."

"It would serve her right. She's always starting rumors about everybody else."

Jackie couldn't argue that point and could even see the humor and justice of it, but she knew her mother felt awful already and didn't need to have it rubbed in.

"She thinks you should have told her about your papaya allergy."

"I haven't thought about that in nearly forty years. Once I ate a piece of dried papaya when I was a kid and broke out in hives. Nothing like what happened today."

"That happens sometimes with food allergies. The reaction isn't always the same."

"And who would ever guess there's papaya in beef jerky anyway?"

Jackie shrugged. "I'm guessing it won't be there next time."

"The doctor told her to get it out of the house."

Jackie patted his arm. "I'm glad you're okay. We had quite a scare."

He nodded thoughtfully, then said, "Better it was me than some stranger, though. Imagine if some stranger had died from a piece of that jerky. His family would have sued us for everything we're worth." He shook his head, then looked up wide-eyed. "We were damn lucky!"

Jackie suppressed a smile. "That's one way to look at it. I guess they won't be admitting you."

"No. I'll be going home any minute, as soon as they give me the thumbs-up."

A tentative rapping on the door drew their attention. Jackie recognized Stef's eyes peeking in through the little window.

"Stef!" She jumped from the chair, astonished, and opened the door.

"I don't want to intrude," said Stef. "I just wanted to see if your dad was okay. I ran into your sister, and she told me you were in here."

"Becca's here?" Jackie asked.

"Everybody's here," Rudy replied, waving cheerfully at Stef. "We should have chartered a damn bus. When your grandfather heard they were serving meatloaf in the cafeteria, he hightailed it down there. That man is crazy for meatloaf. He'd eat it every day of his life if he could." He shook his head, mystified.

"You look good, Mr. Townsend," Stef said.

"I'm fine, just fine. It'll take more than a papaya-laced piece of beef to kill me."

Stef threw Jackie a look of amused perplexity.

After the story was retold, Stef said, "Since everything's okay, I'll get back to the old boat."

"Will you wait for me?" Jackie asked. "I'll be out in just a minute."

Stef shrugged, looking self-conscious. "Sure." She stepped out of the room.

Jackie took hold of her father's hand. "Unless you need something, I'll be going too."

"Run along. Becca's driving us home." He squeezed and released her hand. "You and the pretty houseboat lady have gotten to know one another, have you?"

Jackie felt herself redden as his expression conveyed that he understood more than he would ever say. "I love you, Dad." She kissed him on the cheek and left the room.

Stef was in the hallway, leaning against a wall, tapping a rhythm on the shiny tiled floor with one boot heel. She stood up as Jackie appeared and gave her a familiar, affectionate smile. Jackie was so touched at Stef's presence she almost felt like crying. Even though the incident was over, she realized she was still suffering the emotional impact of believing she might lose her father.

"It was really thoughtful of you to come," Jackie said.

"Nobody seemed to know what had happened or how serious it was. I was worried about you."

Jackie looked steadily into Stef's eyes, realizing she was perfectly sincere. "Thank you." She took a deep, cleansing breath. "It was scary there for a while. I kept thinking, what if he died. What would we do? What would happen to my mother? I can't imagine one of them without the other."

Stef took Jackie's hand. "You don't have to. Everything's fine." She smiled reassuringly.

"You think I'm naïve," Jackie said.

Stef shook her head. "No."

"I mean, I know people die. It'll happen someday. I hope it isn't a total surprise, though. You hope you have a chance to prepare."

"You can't prepare," Stef said. "It's always a shock, no matter how or when it happens. But there are degrees of shock, I guess."

Jackie observed Stef silently. It seemed she'd seen a lot more of life...and death than Jackie had. "Your father died a few years ago, right?"

Stef nodded. "I barely knew him. It didn't impact me."

"As a police officer, you must have seen a lot of people die."

"It doesn't happen as often to each individual cop as you'd think, like on TV. It's rare, actually. And definitely not something you get used to. It's hard to see someone die, whether it's a stranger or...someone you love." Stef's solemn expression changed abruptly to a smile. "But neither of us has to see someone die today, do we?"

Jackie shook her head.

Just then, Rosa rounded the corner carrying a travel mug of coffee, wearing a lightweight running suit and sneakers.

"Oh, you're here too!" she remarked, then scrutinized Stef.

Jackie introduced them.

"How is he?" Rosa asked, nodding toward Rudy's room. She took a long pull on her mug.

"He's fine now. I've just seen him."

"Good, that's good." She nodded. "Earlier he wasn't looking so good. This is just what I was worried about, you know? Ida's World-Famous Jerky! What she's gonna be famous for is killing people off." Rosa was getting herself worked up, gesturing wildly with her free hand. "And she wants me to be a part of this? Can you imagine? I'd lose my business and we'd be ruined."

"This was kind of a freakish thing," Jackie pointed out.

"I hope she's learned her lesson, that's all."

"You mean you think this will make her drop the jerky?"

Rosa nodded emphatically. "After almost killing her husband, I hope so."

"I don't think so. She's just giving up the papaya thing, but I think she's fully committed to this business."

"*Dios mio! Que está, loca?*" Rosa rolled her eyes in disbelief.

"Rosa won't let my mother sell her jerky off her truck," Jackie explained to Stef.

"No!" Rosa agreed. "And after what happened here today, can you blame me?"

"It's not really the danger of poisoning somebody, is it," Jackie suggested, "that stops you from selling her jerky?"

Rosa frowned. "No," she admitted. "Like I told her, everything on my truck is authentic Brazilian food. What would happen if I started selling beef jerky and then, next thing you know, hot dogs and biscuits and gravy or whatever you or Becca or Rudy decided you wanted me to sell? My mama would be turning over in her grave."

"Your mother isn't dead."

Rosa shrugged. "But she would be if I turned my truck into a free-for-all. Do you understand?"

"Yes, I do," Jackie said. "But Mom doesn't. I don't think this problem is going away."

"I'm not doing this just to be mean," Rosa continued. "I love your mother, but if she asks me one more time to put that damned jerky on my truck, Ben and I are moving to San Diego."

"So they don't have jerky in Brazil?" asked Stef. "I mean, dried meat is sort of universal."

"No! Not like this with the teriyaki and killer papaya zinger, whatever she calls it." Rosa was about to continue when Ben appeared, approaching rapidly.

"There you are," he said. "We need to get back if we're going to catch the after-work crowd."

They said their goodbyes, then Jackie and Stef walked through the waiting room to the big double doors leading outside. Just inside the doors, Jackie's mother stood talking on her phone. She didn't look up as they passed. Jackie decided there was no reason to bother her. From the sound of her voice, she seemed fully recovered from her fright and no longer in need of comfort.

"You should have seen him," Ida bubbled. "He looked like one of those Chinese dragons in the New Year's parade, all red and puffed up."

Stef and Jackie emerged into the afternoon sunshine. "I need to call the office and tell Niko everything's okay," said Jackie, "but he's already canceled all my appointments for today, so it looks like I have the rest of the day off."

After all the starts and stops between them, she didn't know whether Stef would want to spend time with her or not, but she decided to take a chance, encouraged by the fact that Stef had dropped everything to run over here. "Do you have to get back right away?"

"Yeah, I should," said Stef. "But if you don't have anything else going on, I wouldn't mind a little company." She grinned, her eyes suggesting all sorts of mischief before she slipped on her sunglasses. Then she strode off through the parking lot toward her bike.

Jackie smiled to herself. Even when Stef was talkative, she thought, she wasn't exactly talkative.

Though Stef seemed very mellow and less guarded than usual, perhaps even willing to talk about herself, Jackie had resolved not to push her anymore, to take Gail's advice. When she was ready to ask for help, Jackie would be happy to give it. Until then, she'd try to respect her need for privacy and be content with getting to know her better. Apparently, the door was now wide open for that.

She realized she'd somehow won Stef over, somewhere along the way. She didn't seem to be resisting anymore.

Once they quit fighting, there's nothing left but to reel them in.

CHAPTER TWENTY-NINE

Stef and Jackie stood close together in the main cabin of the houseboat, kissing one another slowly and ardently. Deuce lay nearby on a throw rug, half asleep. Stef's mouth was incredible. Jackie didn't want to stop kissing her. Her lips were full and soft and expressive. Jackie's back was up against the wall as Stef's hands moved over her bare skin under her shirt. Her mouth grazed her ear, sending stimulating shivers through her.

Ten minutes before, Jackie had arrived to Stef's eager embrace. There had been no preliminaries and no conversation. They were both way past ready for this.

Stef kissed the exposed skin above her bra, while her fingers tantalized her through the cloth until her nipples were hard and sensitive. Jackie clenched the back of Stef's neck and closed her eyes. Stef slipped a hand under her bra, touching skin to skin, then lifted the bra to free Jackie's breasts and make them available to her mouth. Stef's breath came rapidly as she sucked hungrily, her arms holding Jackie tightly against her.

One of her hands moved up the back of her thigh, up inside the loose leg of her shorts, sliding over her thin underwear and gripping her firmly. Jackie pushed hard against the wall, her body tightening with expectancy as Stef tugged her shorts over her hips and let them sink to the floor around her ankles. Stef's fingers moved over the silken material of her panties, playing along the edges of the elastic, brushing her skin as lightly as a feather while her tongue and mouth continued to tease her elsewhere. Jackie threaded her fingers through Stef's thick hair, stiffening involuntarily as Stef's fingers brushed lightly over her most sensitive and anxious center, sending a charge of pleasure through her.

***

Jackie lay naked under Stef's unabashed gaze. She stood at the foot of the bed, smiling that crooked smile of hers for several seconds before she removed her clothes, piece by piece, unhurriedly, while Jackie watched from the bed. Stef's body was muscular, which she had already known, but it was a beautiful thing to see in all its glory, the smooth, powerful thighs, the long, graceful arms, the lean stomach under shameless, opalescent breasts with ruddy areolae, drawn up tight around a pair of hard centers. The last thing, the panties, fell away to reveal a taut rear end that made Jackie's fingertips ache.

Stef crawled on top of her, letting her stomach rest against Jackie's as she kissed her mouth deeply and breathlessly. Jackie locked her legs around Stef's back and moved against her, interleaving both pairs of lips together so they kissed one another in every way possible.

Stef made her way down across Jackie's body, kissing as she went until she lay between her legs, breathing hotly on her thigh, then kissing her there, circling the area provocatively.

Take me, Jackie thought, filled with yearning. *Take me now!*

Stef nuzzled her way in deeper and opened her mouth to offer her tongue. *Her tongue, her tongue, her tongue!* It was everywhere, warm, wet and uninhibited, snaking its way up, down and in.

"Oh! Oh!" Jackie cried out.

Stef answered with a soft, approving murmur.

So much potential for power and pleasure were gathering there, gathering on the tip of Stef's tongue, flowing like a flash flood in a canyon, surging wildly against its confines, desperate for a way out. Then, suddenly, when the exquisite agony seemed impossible to bear any longer, it burst free with an explosive force.

"Wow!" Jackie breathed in the benign aftermath. "That was fantastic."

Stef lifted her head to look across Jackie's stomach, an uncompromised smile on her face. "Yes, you were."

Jackie reached her arms toward Stef, who crawled up to fill them. They held one another quietly while Jackie let the warmth of this woman's love wash over her.

***

Stef knelt above Jackie, taking Jackie's fingers as deep as she could, hard thrusts that sent waves of pleasure shuddering through her body. She tossed her head back, neck muscles tight, emptying her mind, letting her body take over. All she could hear was the sound of her own labored breaths and the creaking frame of the bed. Jackie pressed the palm of her hand hard against her, creating friction as they moved up and down together, a harmonic duo.

Right there, right there! she breathed, her eyes shut tight, biting her bottom lip almost painfully hard.

As she came, silently, she became perfectly still, letting the wave roll deliciously over her.

***

Stef could see a half moon through the open window. It cast a cool, romantic light through the bedroom. She realized she'd fallen asleep, but didn't know for how long. Jackie was curled around her back, a hand on her hip, surrounding her like a warm cocoon. Stef wondered if she was awake. She could hear nothing but the sound of crickets outside.

This wasn't such a bad place, she thought, this peaceful Delta backwater. Jackie seemed to have a good life here and was eager to share it. As eager as she was to share herself. She was a beautiful, generous, loving woman. Like the town itself, she was a sheltering harbor, a place to take refuge in.

"Are you awake?" Jackie whispered.

"Yes."

Jackie kissed the back of her neck. "Are you hungry?"

"Ravenous." Stef turned over to face her. "Let me see what I can find."

***

Stef had thrown on a long T-shirt to run to the kitchen to make snacks. She returned with peanut butter and jelly sandwiches. Jackie took one and immediately took a huge bite.

"Oh, thank you!" she mumbled with her mouth full. "I was so hungry." She took another bite.

"You've been burning a lot of calories," Stef said, pushing a strand of hair away from Jackie's face.

Jackie nodded, reaching the halfway mark on the sandwich.

"Look what I found while I was in the kitchen," Stef said nonchalantly, waving a medium-sized zucchini.

Jackie nearly choked. She swallowed what was in her mouth, then burst out laughing. Stef grinned and raised her eyebrows suggestively, her fist wrapped around one end of the vegetable.

***

Jackie moved slowly across Stef's body, stroking her, kissing her, tasting her stomach, caressing her thighs. She moved closer, feeling the taut excitement of the woman's body as it lay in uneasy anticipation of her next move, wanting her with a throbbing eagerness.

She opened the woman's secret world with her hands, hearing

Stef's sharp, inhaled breath of expectation, and took as much of her into her mouth as she could, tasting her, smelling her, immersing herself into the rich wet beckoning center of her.

***

"Oh, my God!" Stef cried, her body lurching with a spasmodic jerk. "What are you doing?"

"This," Jackie cooed, her mouth next to Stef's ear. "I thought you might like it."

"Oh," Stef said more calmly, relaxing. "Oh, yes, I—"

"Did I hurt you?"

"No. It was just a surprise."

"Do you want me to stop?"

"Uh, I...I...oh." Stef uttered a low moan, letting her head rest against Jackie's shoulder.

"Stop?" Jackie asked again, rubbing her cheek lightly against Stef's.

"No!"

***

Jackie rolled on top of Stef, pinning her arms to the bed by the wrists and grinning down at her. Stef tried to buck her off, but Jackie held her position, her sweet, bashful breasts glowing like two round moons above Stef's face in the gray light of dawn, so close she could nearly touch them with her tongue.

"It's no use," said Jackie, "you can't escape."

"Alas," Stef said in a tragic, feminine voice, "I fear it's true. What will you do with me, you brute?"

"I'm going to make you do unspeakable things."

"Oh!" cried Stef in mock despair. "What things?"

"I said they were unspeakable."

Stef burst out laughing and Jackie followed suit. Deuce ran into the bedroom and jumped up between them, licking Stef's face, causing her to laugh even more.

***

Jackie sat at the swing-up table at the edge of Stef's kitchen, eating her scrambled eggs absentmindedly, staring across the narrow space between them at Stef's multicolored eyes and wide, nearly apologetic smile. As if she's afraid to show how happy she is, Jackie thought. She wore an oversized shirt over bare legs, her hair a mess. *She's so cute.*

"Thanks for breakfast," Jackie said, then took a long swallow of coffee. "I need to get going, though. I have to run home before work and change clothes."

"You can't wear the same thing two days in a row?" Stef sipped from the mug she held in both hands. "After all, you wear a smock over your clothes. And who are you worried about? It's just Niko, right?"

"Right. But you've forgotten I have a houseful of pets."

"I had forgotten," Stef said. The smile on her face was sleepy and dreamy. There was no sign of the tragic demons in her eyes this morning, and Jackie felt proudly responsible for that.

She reached over and took one of Stef's hands away from her mug. "It's going to be a hard day to get through."

"You're tired?"

"Yep. And I just know as soon as I'm out of sight, you're going to crawl back in bed and enjoy a long, leisurely morning of dozing."

Stef looked suddenly alert. She put her coffee down. "I completely forgot Marcus is coming today. He found a carburetor kit."

"That's great! Maybe by tonight you'll have a working engine."

"Wouldn't that be something! That's the last thing. When the engine's running, I'll be ready to launch." Stef's eyes shone with the thrill of that possibility.

"But you won't be taking off right away," Jackie said hopefully. "You don't have to leave until the end of July."

"That's the latest." Stef squeezed her fingers. "Don't worry. I won't be leaving tomorrow."

Jackie managed a short laugh, but she wasn't sure what Stef was promising. When it came down to it, she wasn't sure about anything. They'd had an incredible night together, but whether that implied anything further...

"When can I see you again?" Jackie asked.

"If you're not busy, come by after work today. I have a feeling I'm going to be celebrating. I wouldn't mind having somebody to celebrate with."

Jackie jumped out of her chair and threw her arms around Stef's neck, kissing her gratefully.

CHAPTER THIRTY

When Jackie drove up, she saw Stef filling the big bucket with a hose under the boat motor. Marcus's truck was parked in the driveway, but he was nowhere to be seen. She walked up to Stef, wanting to throw her arms around her, but unsure whether they had an audience.

"Where's Marcus?" she asked.

"Underneath. I asked him to check out the new pontoon, to make sure it's on right."

Just then Marcus walked out on all fours from under the boat. Seeing Jackie, he hollered, "You're just in time for the big moment!" He leapt up, slapped his hands together to dust them off, and walked over. "The pontoon is in there solid," he announced. "Good job. Both of 'em's sound. She'll float just fine. Nothing to worry about."

"Are you sure?" Stef asked.

"Sure as eggs is eggs. You could have a big old hole in the cabin floor and not sink. A little water would splash in, but as long as your pontoons aren't leaking, you're floating."

Stef looked relieved.

"Is the engine running?" Jackie asked.

"We're about to find out," Stef said.

"No reason she won't start now," Marcus said with assurance. "Electrical's good. Fuel system's good. All systems go. Just gotta put a little gas in here to wet her whistle." He poured a shot of gasoline from a plastic cup into the top of each carburetor, then lowered the prop into the bucket of water. "Go ahead and turn the key."

Stef held up both hands with fingers crossed, her teeth clenched in excitement, then ran inside to the helm. Deuce barked and ran after her. Jackie and Marcus stood back a few feet, waiting in silent tension.

The engine seemed to cough once before it roared to life and kept running, robust and smooth. The propeller whirled around furiously and splashed water out of the bucket. Stef bounded off the deck of the boat, yelling, "Woo hoo!" and ran over to watch the prop spin, beaming with happiness. She threw her arms around Marcus, giving him a powerful hug, then did the same to Jackie.

Marcus shut off the engine and lowered the cover into place. "There you go!" he said with finality.

"Thank you so much!" Stef gushed. "I want to pay you for your time. You spent the whole afternoon out here."

"You don't have to do that," he said, waving a hand. "You already gave me the twenty-six dollars for the kit. That'll do."

Marcus gathered his tools together while Stef and Jackie stood staring at the engine, feeling as if a feat of magic had occurred.

"I feel I practically owe that man my life," Stef said at last.

"Don't worry about it. He had a great time."

"He seemed to." She sighed deeply. "I can really picture it now, you know? Being on the water."

"There are still things to do, though, right?"

"Plenty of things to do," Stef confirmed. "New carpet, new curtains. I want to refinish some of the wood surfaces inside and...yeah, there are projects to keep me busy for a while. But the most important thing is done, getting her seaworthy."

Marcus waved from his truck, indicating he was leaving. They both waved back and Stef hollered, "Thank you!"

"Wow," Stef said. "I can hardly believe it. And there's one other bit of good news. I've settled on a name."

"What is it?"

"Mudbug."

Jackie hesitated, completely surprised. "I like it!" she finally said.

"Good. I thought you would."

Marcus's truck was just clearing the end of the driveway. Jackie wasted no time putting her arms around Stef and drawing her into a long, passionate kiss.

"I missed you all day long," Jackie said. "I kept thinking, what am I doing neutering cats when I could be kissing Stef?"

Stef laughed. "Marcus was here all afternoon, so it was just as well you were neutering cats. And don't get any ideas about calling in sick tomorrow because I won't be here."

"Oh? Where are you going?"

"Visiting a friend," Stef answered vaguely.

Jackie warned herself to suppress the urge to push for more information, but Stef's continuing reticence put her on edge. Maybe I'm more like my mother than I thought, she decided. People whose secrets I don't know drive me nuts. But, no, that wasn't true. It was just Stef's secrets that drove her nuts.

"I've got band practice tomorrow night," Jackie said. "So I guess I won't see you tomorrow at all."

"Then we should make the most of tonight, shouldn't we?"

"Uh-huh," Jackie murmured, moving in for another kiss.

CHAPTER THIRTY-ONE

"Looking good, Stef," said Roberto as he sat across the table from her and immediately slouched down in his chair.

"Thanks for adding me to your visitor list," she said.

He jerked his chin up in acknowledgment, then glanced around the room at the other visiting groups. There were five other occupied tables, all with women who were most likely wives or girlfriends. At one table, a little girl sat on her mother's lap across from a young man who smiled at her with adoration. Some of these women, Stef knew, were here every weekend. Visiting the prison was as much a part of their routine as grocery shopping.

Roberto's orange jumpsuit fit his muscular body snugly. His hair was shaved, and he had a crude spiderweb tattoo on his neck that hadn't been there when he had started his prison term three years ago. His mouth was set in an attitude of world-weariness, and his eyes settled into a dull gaze that seemed to look right past her. There was a deep scar across the left side of his face that started above his eyebrow, cut through it, hopped his eye, and dug in deeper on his cheek. A memento of the fight that had left another man dead. Just to the left of that scar, under his eye, was a tattooed tear, a symbol of his having taken a life. Stef was familiar with the symbol, ironically an icon of grief, but often worn as an emblem of pride among gang members: *I killed a dude. I'm in here for a real crime. I'm somebody. Respect me.*

Roberto's eyes were the same as his brother's, dark brown with thick eyelashes, but the laughter Stef had often seen in his brother's eyes was absent in Roberto's. This man's eyes were lazy and vacant.

The last time she'd seen Roberto Molina was at his sentencing. Before that, she'd seen him around now and then. He and his brother Joe hadn't hung out together much, not since Joe became a police officer, but they kept in touch. Whenever Roberto was in trouble, any kind of trouble, he always turned up at his older brother's door, knowing that was one place he'd be welcome.

Stef had always been struck by the way they looked alike but seemed so different. It was all in the attitude. Sometimes she had even thought of Joe as the good one and Roberto as the bad one, which she knew was a huge oversimplification. It was just that given similar circumstances, Joe had somehow crawled out of the muck and Roberto had sunk lower. It had always been Joe Molina's greatest regret and sorrow that he hadn't been able to help his brother out of the downward spiral of gang activity and crime. He had helped Roberto with money, set him up with jobs, even let him stay at his apartment for weeks at a time. The money had disappeared with nothing to show for it. The jobs had lasted a pitifully short time. And when Roberto stayed at his place, Joe's valuables tended to disappear.

In trying to save his brother, Molina had always felt he was fighting against a swift and relentless current. Ultimately, he believed he had failed when Roberto killed a rival gang member and was found guilty of murder. But even then, Joe hadn't given up on him. He just went into a different phase, waiting for his brother to serve his time and come back to the world. Meanwhile, Joe had encouraged him to learn job skills like fixing computers and to stay out of trouble.

Molina had visited Roberto regularly. Inevitably, after those visits, he came back sad and disheartened. He kept going, hoping to see a glimmer of his little brother, that quiet little kid who used to grab his hand for comfort in the middle of the night. But that was a long time ago. If that little kid was in there, he was buried deep. But Molina apparently saw something he recognized once in a while, because he kept going.

Stef had never visited Roberto before. She had called him once, after the shooting, to say how sorry she was, how much she would miss his brother and what a great guy he had been. Roberto had said very little during that call. He had still been in shock. So had she.

"You look pretty good yourself, Roberto," Stef said. "Healthy and strong."

"Been working out," he said proudly.

His demeanor was marked by indifference, but the way he kept glancing around, at the surveillance cameras, the correctional officers and the other prisoners, suggested he was nervous.

"Do you want a cup of coffee?" Stef offered, noticing the vending machine. "Or a soda?"

He shook his head.

"Did you get the package I sent?" she asked.

"Yeah."

Stef too was uncomfortable, in a way she'd never been in a prison before. "I thought you might like to have a few things of your brother's."

"Yeah. Cool." His expression was blank, as if he didn't care that she was here or about anything she had to say. Not quite hostile, just uninterested.

His attitude diffused her urge to apologize again, to pour out the grief and regret she felt for what she had done. At least during that painful phone call, he had seemed to be listening and to be feeling something. She hoped he would relax and let her in.

"Are you still taking those computer classes?" she asked.

"Naw. That shit's really boring. I signed up for cooking. I thought it might be fun. Not that they're gonna teach you how to make anything decent in here. Nothing like Oysters Rockefeller or whatever."

"What have you learned to make?"

"I'm not in yet. There's a waiting list. Everybody wants that one. Gives you a chance to poison your enemies, you know?" He stared soberly for a second before laughing. "That's a joke, in case you didn't know."

"I knew."

A moment of silence passed between them as Stef considered what else they could talk about.

"So what are you doing here, Officer Byers?" Roberto said her name sneeringly, especially the "officer" part. It was most likely a habit, how he pronounced every law officer's title, and not a tone reserved for her. In the past, he had been grudgingly polite to her, she assumed for his brother's sake, as he was typically on his best behavior when she saw him because he was asking for help from Joe. But she had always known Roberto was full of contempt for cops, his enemy, he believed. As long as he was a criminal, that was true. That attitude had created a complicated relationship for the Molina brothers.

"I was hoping you could give me some information," she said, deciding to dispense with small talk.

"About what?"

"Do you remember Mrs. Avila, the landlady at the apartment house where you lived when you were in grade school?"

"That bitch?" He wrinkled up his face in disgust. "What about her?"

"Can you tell me her first name?"

He shook his head. "Mrs. Avila, that's all I know. Crazy old bitch. Stuck her nose in everything. Never gave anybody a break. She was a selfish old—" He glanced around to locate the officer walking the floor of the visiting room.

"Your brother didn't think so," Stef said. "He actually wanted to thank her for looking out for you two boys. For making sure you went to school regularly, among other things."

"Joe never saw anything bad in nobody. He couldn't see people how they really are. Hell, he even thought I was good. And look at you. That dude thought you were something! You arrest him and he wants to kiss your ass for it like he's your personal bitch or something. He wanted to be a cop just to prove to you he wasn't scum. What a dope, falling for a lesbo."

"That was just a kid's crush," Stef said uncomfortably. "He got over it years ago."

"Whatever you say, Stef." He rolled his eyes. "You still into girls?"

"What about Mrs. Avila?" she asked, ignoring the question. "Was she married?"

He laughed sarcastically. "Who would have her? Old man on the third floor used to screw her to get a few bucks off his rent. First of the month, she'd take a bottle of gin and go upstairs. I guess he had to get drunk to do it."

"But you called her Mrs. Avila, not Miss."

"I don't know. Maybe she was married before."

"Did she have kids?"

"None that I ever saw. Why are you looking for her anyway?"

"Like I said, your brother wanted to thank her. He never got around to it."

"So now it's your job?"

"It's not a job. It's just something I want to do for him, if she's still alive."

"Isn't that sweet?" His lips curled into a sarcastic snarl. "You want to do everything you can for him, don't you? Like taking care of his dog. How about getting his brother out of this place? Got any strings you can pull, Officer Byers? Old Ace would probably really appreciate that. Don't you think?"

Stef observed him silently. He probably thought using his brother's old gang nickname would annoy her. She'd known this wouldn't be the most pleasant visit she'd ever had with a convict, but she'd thought Roberto might like having a visitor, someone he knew who maybe wasn't a friend, but clearly wasn't an enemy, and someone who he might reasonably believe had his interests at heart, since she had been so close to his brother. If he would show any indication he was glad she'd come to see him, she was ready to respond warmly to it. For his brother's sake, if nothing else, but also because of her deep sorrow over the part she had played in his loss.

This is what Molina had meant when he said he kept searching for his brother in there. Stef was doing the same thing, but it was Joe Molina she was searching for, not a younger Roberto. The family resemblance made it seem possible, even probable, that there were other similar traits she might glimpse. Like a familiar smile or expression or speech pattern. His voice actually did remind her of her friend, but it was distorted by the words and delivery.

If he was glad to have a visitor, he disguised it well.

"Any chance you remember the address of that apartment house?" she asked.

"Sure. Two thirty-six Lincoln Avenue." A scant smile appeared on his lips, not the usual sarcastic one, but a real smile. "When I was five and first went to kindergarten, Mrs. Avila made me memorize the address. She'd quiz me on it. If she saw me sitting on the stairs, she'd say, 'What's your address, Roberto Molina?' And I'd say, 'Two thirty-six Lincoln Avenue!' like a damn soldier to his drill sergeant. She'd laugh and rub my head. That's one address I don't think I'll ever forget." His smile, which had widened during the story, faded. "Bitch!"

Stef wrote the address in her notebook. "Thanks. I should be able to track her down with that."

"When you find her, what're you going to tell her?"

"I think Joe would want me to tell her how things turned out."

"You mean that he's dead?"

"No. Well, yes, but—" Stef averted her eyes from his hard gaze. "I meant that he became something. That he was a good guy."

"You gonna tell her about me too?" He laughed derisively.

"I will, if she asks, but I mainly want to tell her what Joe told me, that he was grateful to her."

Roberto shook his head. "What a sap! You too. Like she cares. Like she's even gonna remember us, two sorry-ass kids who lived in her stinking building for a few years. So she made me memorize my address and stuck us on a school bus." He lowered his voice so the patrolling officer wouldn't hear. "Big fucking deal. It's not like it cost her anything. It's not like she was our grandma or something. It's not like she loved us, for Christ's sake." He looked like he wanted to spit. "Nobody ever loved me. Not even my own mother."

From what she'd heard, Stef thought it was possible that was true. "Your brother loved you."

Roberto looked her in the eye. "Yeah, he did. A sap, like I said. He was stupid. He thought he could fix me. After all the shit I put him through—" He swallowed hard, his Adam's apple jumping in response, and went silent, staring down at the table.

"Is there anything you need?" Stef asked. "Anything I can send you?"

He looked at her as if he were trying to figure something out. "Like what?"

"Whatever you want. I know your brother used to send you packages. So maybe there's something he sent you that—"

Roberto laughed shortly, his expression full of contempt. "What is all this? You want to take Joe's place? Is that it? You're not my relative. You were never even my friend."

"I was your brother's friend. I know he worried about you. And I know you don't have anybody else now."

"Damn straight," Roberto said, sitting up and glaring at her defiantly. "I got nobody because you murdered my brother."

Stef stiffened. "It was an accident. You know that."

"Whatever." He fell back against the back of his chair. "My lawyer said I could sue you," he announced. "For killing Joe. How about that?"

"Are you going to?" she asked calmly, suppressing all the churning emotion that this situation was causing.

"I might. Why should I be stuck in here for snuffing some motherfucking gangbanger while you're walking around free after killing a fine, upstanding citizen like my brother?"

Stef was determined not to lose her composure. "I don't think your brother would want you to do that."

"Don't tell me what my brother'd want!" Roberto was truly

angry now, his dark eyes flashing. His voice remained quiet, but it was emphatic. "You don't know anything about it. You think you knew him, but you didn't. I knew him! We were the same, Joe and I. You think he was better. I know what you think of me. I can see it in your eyes." With his increasing rage, he let his voice rise to normal levels. "You don't give a fuck about me. You think I'm piss in the gutter, but he didn't think that. He knew me. He cared about me. He's the only person in the world who cared about me!" Roberto's eyes watered with gathering tears. It was the first time Stef had ever seen any hint of honest emotion from him. "And you murdered him!"

Stef noticed one of the officers start toward them, attracted by Roberto's raised voice.

"You know how sorry I am for what happened," she said quietly. "I would give anything to undo it. I loved him too! If there's anything I can do for you..."

"I don't want anything from you! You can go to hell!" He sprung up from his chair and the officer arrived to take hold of his arm.

"You're no better than me," Roberto spat. "You're a murderer!"

Stef stood. "Take care of yourself, Roberto," she said, then addressed the officer. "We're done."

She strode to the door and didn't look back as Roberto got in his last dig. "And don't come back, you fucking murderer!"

After processing out, she left the building, emerging into brilliant sunshine. It always felt like a narrow escape to Stef, leaving a prison. She didn't like going to them. A small, irrational part of her always feared something would go wrong, some mistake would be made and they wouldn't let her out. This time especially she had felt uneasy on the way in.

When she got to her bike and pulled her keys out, she saw her hand was shaking. She swallowed the urge to cry, then sat on the seat vaguely watching a line of men in orange jumpsuits running single-file in the yard nearby.

This had been a mistake, she realized. She hadn't expected Roberto to be so angry. Why had she been so naïve? Of course he was angry. How could he be anything but angry? The only person he'd had in the world was gone. And she was responsible. Why had she expected him to commiserate with her, to unite in shared grief? He could rarely legitimately blame someone else for his troubles. At last he had somebody to blame for something. He wanted revenge. He wanted her to be punished. He resented that she was "walking around free."

As if, she thought bitterly.

CHAPTER THIRTY-TWO

The setting sun, surrounded by wispy pink and orange clouds, dipped into the golden surface of Disappointment Slough. The water lapped gently against the sand at Stef's feet. There was a breeze bending the slender tule stalks toward the water. Deuce walked along the shore, his nose down, preoccupied with empty clam shells discarded by fishermen.

She sat on a rock, her arms folded over her knees, staring absentmindedly at the water. She wasn't sure why she'd come here. Back when she was a kid, on a night like this, she'd have run over to Grandma Mattie's house and banged on the back door, confident of a comforting welcome, a therapeutic piece of cake and a funny story. But back then her problems—an argument with a friend, a bad grade on a report card—were so much smaller. They could be conquered with a slice of cake. What would Grandma Mattie do now? she wondered. What weapons would she have against so great a sorrow?

She picked up a stick and drew lines in the wet sand, arbitrary lines, until she found herself forming initials: S.B. + J.T. She traced the shape of a heart around them, inwardly chiding herself for being silly and sentimental.

She wondered for a moment at the name of this place: Disappointment Slough. She should have asked Jackie about that.

It was beautiful here. So peaceful. Nobody in sight. Not a sound to suggest there were other people in the world. Across the slough on the other shore, three ducks bobbed silently on the surface. Stef's mood was in direct contrast with her surroundings—dark and troubled.

Since yesterday's visit to the prison, she'd been nearly paralyzed with regret and despair. During the last couple of weeks, she had mistakenly thought that things were getting better, that she was on the road to recovery. She'd been enjoying herself, getting to know new people, even allowing herself the possibility of a new romance. She'd been beginning to tuck her nightmare into the background. She had even been considering staying here, surprising herself with so many new possibilities. She'd never expected to meet anyone like Jackie, here or anywhere.

But all of that optimism was just a fragile membrane of foolish hope, because it had taken Roberto Molina just fifteen minutes to shatter it completely. It wasn't his fault. He was just a hurt and angry young man lashing out at the only person he could. His accusations were harsh, but no more than she had often made against herself. The incident had reminded her that it would take a lot of time to put this tragedy behind her, that there were still months of heartache to work through until she could feel anything good about herself again. A few days of fun couldn't change that.

She noticed the moon on the eastern horizon, poking through the bluish branches of an oak tree. It was a half moon. No spring tide tonight. She was reminded of her conversation with Jackie that other night, the last time she was here. To catch fish, it had to be both the right time and the right place. Like most things, timing was everything. Like S.B. + J.T. Maybe it was the right place, but it wasn't the right time. Not for Stef. A broken heart isn't much to offer someone, especially not someone so full of love as Jackie.

She reached down with the stick and rubbed across her design until it was completely gone.

***

It was Deuce barking that alerted Stef to the vehicle coming up the driveway. She looked out the window and recognized Jackie's pickup. She was both happy and sad to see her.

As she opened the sliding glass door, Jackie got out of her truck, carrying something under her arm, and walked rapidly over to the bottom of the stairs where Stef greeted her with a hug.

"Hi," Jackie said, smiling with her usual unabashed cheerfulness. "What are you up to?"

"Just cleaning up the dinner dishes," Stef replied. "I didn't know you were coming out."

"No, it wasn't planned, but I have something for you and this weekend will be totally taken over by the crawdad festival, so I wanted to drop it by tonight."

"Oh, right, the crawdad festival. The whole town's getting ready for that."

"Sure. It's our big event. I hope you'll come."

"I might. What'd you bring me?"

Jackie presented her with a hinged wooden box, which she opened to reveal a Fairbairn-Sykes combat knife just like her grandfather's, cradled in a purple velvet lining. The blade gleamed in the sunlight like it was brand new. Astonished, she looked up to see Jackie smiling triumphantly at her.

"Where did you get this?" Stef asked, lifting the knife from the box.

"eBay. I know it's not the same as one that belonged to a relative."

"No, it's great. I can't believe you did this." Stef felt overwhelmed. She took a deep breath and set the knife back in the box. "Thank you. It's wonderful."

Jackie looked satisfied. Stef hated so much what she was about to say, and the gift made it that much harder.

"Did you get the name painted on?" Jackie asked, running to the rear of the boat to look.

Stef followed and the two of them stood admiring the blue lettering in its swirly script that spelled out the word *Mudbug*.

"It's perfect!" Jackie declared. "Now it's really yours, isn't it?"

"Mine and in working condition." Stef had a hard time looking Jackie in the eye as she said, "Jackie, I know we talked earlier about how I didn't have to leave until the end of July."

Jackie's smile faded as she read Stef's tone and face.

"But I've decided to go sooner, now that there's nothing to prevent it."

Jackie's mouth fell open. "But what about the carpet and curtains and all that stuff you wanted to replace?"

"None of that's going to stop me from cruising down the river. I can do those things anytime."

"I don't understand. Are you going to get a slip at the marina?"

Stef gazed into Jackie's eyes, seeing all the pain that was about to erupt. "No, Jackie," she answered gently. "There's no point paying for a slip when I'm going to be living on the boat. I can just drop anchor anyplace out there. I'll be moving around. That was always the plan."

"I know that's what you said before, but I thought maybe…"

Stef touched Jackie's cheek, lightly stroking. "My plans haven't changed."

"But there's no reason you can't stay a little longer."

Stef shook her head, struggling with her resolve. She pulled Jackie close and kissed her impulsively. Her lips were so eager and so exciting. She was afraid that if Jackie kept asking her to stay, she would.

Pulling back, Stef said, "Thank you for everything. You're a very special person, and I'm so grateful to have known you."

"You're saying goodbye to me?" Jackie looked utterly shocked.

"I wish I could spend more time with you. I really do."

"You can, Stef. There's nothing stopping you. Just stick around for a while. We can spend every day and every night together and figure this out. See if we might have a future together."

Stef shook her head. "We don't have a future together. And the more time we spend together, the harder it will be on you when I go. I don't want to hurt you any more than I obviously am."

"I don't understand."

"I'm sorry. I can't explain. I just have to go."

Jackie looked helpless. "Let me go with you!" she blurted.

Stef shook her head, recognizing this as a move of desperation. "No. I need to be alone. Besides, that's ridiculous."

By her body language, Jackie seemed to reluctantly agree. "There must be some compromise," she said quietly. "You could stop by on weekends or something."

"If you get any more tangled up with me, I'd cause you nothing but grief. I know you don't understand it, but you're so much better off without me."

Jackie looked confused and hurt. Any second she would start crying.

"Jackie, please just go and leave me alone. I'm really sorry."

"Stef," Jackie pleaded, her eyes moist, "I love you."

Stef winced at the phrase. "How can you? You don't even know me."

"It's true I don't know much about you. But I know how I feel. I have to be with you."

They stood facing each other for a few seconds without speaking. Stef didn't know what to say. She had nothing to offer. No words of comfort.

"I guess," Jackie said quietly, "you don't feel that way about me." She laughed with a tinge of bitterness. "If you did, you wouldn't want to leave, obviously. If you felt even remotely like I do, you'd light a fire under this goddamned boat and say good riddance and you'd come home with me and never leave." Jackie's voice broke as she started to cry.

Stef put the box down on the deck and pulled Jackie into a tight embrace, stroking her hair. "I'm so sorry. I wish I could explain. I do care about you, Jackie, but I can't live the life you imagine for us. I've been through some things I need to deal with...on my own. I can't drag you into all that. I can't drag any woman into that. It wouldn't be fair to you."

"Maybe I could help you," Jackie sobbed, her head tucked under Stef's chin.

"You're always wanting to help me." Stef smiled. "But this time you can't."

"Will you come back...when you've worked it all out?"

"I don't know." Stef lifted Jackie's chin so they were looking at one another. "We need to say goodbye now. Go home and forget about me."

"I won't forget about you. Ever."

Jackie's cheeks glistened with her tears. Stef wiped one away and kissed the spot where it had been. Then she kissed Jackie's mouth one more time, holding onto the kiss with the thought that she had never felt so much tenderness toward anyone before. She needed to get away as soon as she could, before she allowed herself to stay and ended up destroying the sweet, optimistic nature that made Jackie so appealing.

When Jackie left, she was no longer crying. Stef hoped she had already begun replacing her sorrow with resentment or anger or some other negative emotion that would allow her to quickly get over this hurt. What Jackie couldn't know was that Stef too would have a really hard time getting over it.

CHAPTER THIRTY-THREE

Jackie sat on her couch with Tri-Tip in her lap, watching the evening news on TV, or trying to watch the news, but her mind kept wandering to Stef. It had been that way all day. She couldn't focus on anything else. Even Niko had asked her what was wrong, thinking she was sick and should go home. Especially when his joke of the day failed to get more than an eye roll from her. "A duck, a giraffe and a penguin walk into a vet's office and the vet says, 'What is this? A joke?'"

When the doorbell rang, she picked up the cat and set him on the floor, then opened the door to a sight that made her stumble back in astonishment. On her porch stood a six foot tall figure in a bright red, plush costume that looked like a giant lobster, complete with antennae and huge pinchers waving menacingly like something out of an old B movie. As Jackie recovered herself, she noticed two human eyes looking out from holes in the lobster costume.

"Oh, hi, Gail," she said without enthusiasm.

Gail came in and pulled off the head of the costume. "They sprang for a new costume this year. About time, huh? How do you like it?"

"Cool. But it looks like a lobster."

"Once you get over a foot tall, what's the difference, really? Besides, do you actually think there's a crawdad costume to be had anywhere in the world?"

Jackie shrugged. "I guess not."

"You don't seem very chipper this evening."

"Sorry. I'm sure you'll be a big hit with all the kids." Jackie fell back onto the couch.

Gail sat beside her, the red material of her costume bunching up around her. "I can see you've been crying. Your eyes are swollen. What's wrong?"

Jackie sighed. "Stef."

"I figured." Gail nodded knowingly. "Did you have a fight or something?"

"No. We said goodbye. She's leaving Stillwater. For good, I guess."

"Sorry to hear that. Spit the hook and got away, huh." Gail patted her knee with a big red claw. "Is she gone, then?"

"Not yet. I tried to talk her into staying, but I guess I didn't make as big an impression on her as I thought."

"Maybe you shouldn't give up. Just because she slipped the hook once doesn't mean she can't be hooked. Just put on a fresh piece of bait and try again."

Jackie forced a smile. "I don't think there's any point. She doesn't want me. I'm not going to beg her. Actually, I did beg her and it didn't do any good."

"Then it's probably for the best."

"I just don't understand her. I never have. From the day we met, she's been pushing me away. If I was a little more insecure, I'd think she just doesn't like me. But I can see in her eyes she does."

"Not to mention her mouth and hands and—"

"Uh-huh, all that stuff. So why is she so anxious to get away and be by herself?"

"Scared of commitments," suggested Gail. "Or just plain antisocial."

Jackie turned to face Gail, whose head looked oddly small sticking out of her giant lobster costume.

"She likes to be alone," Gail said. "There are people like that. Not everybody's so comfortable around people as you are. It's obvious you want to bring her home, marry her, have her kids and be buried side by side in the same cemetery plot. You probably scared her off with that whole scene."

"I never said a word about kids...or marriage."

"You know what I mean. Domestic bliss. She wants no part of that. She's a hermit." Gail laid the back of her hand across her forehead dramatically. "I vant to be alone."

Greta Garbo in a lobster outfit, a very peculiar image.

Jackie smiled weakly. "She seems very sure of what she wants. And she doesn't want me."

"I knew she was bad news from the beginning. Didn't I say so the first time we laid eyes on her? Stay away from that one, I said. She's bad news."

"No, you didn't!"

"Well, I should have. Women like that—beautiful, sexy, hot—" Gail took a deep breath. "They'll always break your heart. They think they're all that. She's full of herself. She can't see that you're the best thing that ever came her way."

Jackie knew Gail was just trying to make her feel better, but it wasn't working.

Gail gave her a hug, then stood. "Plenty of fish in the sea, Jacks. You'll be better off with one who feels lucky to have you. The one that jumps in your boat, now, that's the one you want to take home."

Jackie frowned. She wasn't in the mood for Gail's fishy metaphors.

"It's a good thing you'll be busy this weekend," Gail said. "Take your mind off it. Pat played your whole set for me last night. It's a good show. You know you'll feel good once you're out there strumming on your old banjo." Gail put the lobster head back on. "I'll see you out there tomorrow. I'll be the one in red."

CHAPTER THIRTY-FOUR

The guy with the boat trailer was coming Sunday afternoon to move *Mudbug* to the marina. Stef spent most of Sunday morning packing and making sure everything was stowed securely. She worked steadily, trying to keep her mind off Jackie. By noon, she had the situation under control, so she decided to drop by the crawdad festival for a while and see what all the fuss was about. In the back of her mind, she also thought she might get to see Jackie one more time and found she couldn't resist the possibility.

The festival was crowded, hot and loud. The town was drastically transformed from its usual well-tempered self into a raucous celebration. She made her way down a jam-packed Main Street, weaving through the crowd, looking at an occasional trinket for sale at the craft booths, heading vaguely for the steamy white tent at the end of the street. She passed dozens of people with red and white paper boxes piled with bright orange crustaceans and lemon wedges.

When at last she reached the crawdad tent, she got her own box of mudbugs, boiled with bay seasoning, Cajun spices and lemon. There were half a dozen of them, piled on top of each other, a tangled mass of hard-shelled legs, pinchers and antennae. There was something oddly thrilling about eating something that could easily stand in for an alien monster in a *Godzilla* movie. Blown up to scale, of course.

After eating, Stef followed the strains of bluegrass music to the park where a small stage was surrounded by a crowd of people sitting on the grass.

The band belted out something that sounded like a Highland reel. They were all smiling and bouncing on their feet. The one old lady, who Stef assumed was Jackie's grandmother, wore a cotton blouse and ankle-length, mauve-colored skirt. She was the fiddler and was going at it with enthusiasm. Pat wore a white boater over her dark hair and a simple outfit of jeans and short-sleeved shirt. Rebecca wore denim cutoffs and a low-cut blouse, tucked in. She looked like *Lil Abner's* Daisy Mae, which was no doubt the look she was going for: hillbilly bombshell. Stef let her gaze rest on Jackie in a cute embroidered vest worn open over a white short-sleeved shirt. She picked her banjo at a rapid tempo, one foot tapping out the beat on the wooden floorboards. She looked overheated, but also lovely with the tint of pink on her cheeks.

When the song ended, the crowd clapped. Stef joined in, standing far enough back that she didn't think she'd be noticed. Jackie spoke breathlessly into the microphone. "Now we're going to do a Zydeco number for all you mudbug-lovin' river rats. This is called, 'The One That Got Away.'"

Jackie looked in Stef's direction, giving her the momentary feeling she'd been recognized, but a split second later she was looking at her instrument and picking out a tune, oblivious to Stef's presence. It was another happy song, despite the title. Some of the people standing nearby stomped the grass in tune with the music.

Stef saw Officer Hartley in uniform on the sidewalk at the edge of the park. Stillwater Bay's one cop. What was that like, Stef wondered, to be the only cop. Or the only vet? Where she came from, there were dozens of everything. Sometimes hundreds. Everything was more personal here. It was a little scary. But obviously the intimacy had a positive side. For those who were a part of it. Like Jackie.

Hartley noticed Stef and nodded a greeting across the lawn to her. She returned the gesture.

She listened to the band for a few minutes, trying to decide whether to make herself known to Jackie or not. They had already said goodbye, and it wasn't fair to put Jackie in that position here, to rain on her parade. Today she was happy. Better to let her enjoy herself. Still, it was hard not to walk up there and be the recipient of that beatific smile and all the goodwill that backed it up. Very hard. It was hard not to walk into Jackie's arms and stay there forever.

She headed out of the park and back into the throng of festival-goers, turning to look one more time at Jackie, the last time, she knew. The song concluded and Granny took a deep bow for her fiddle solo. Jackie slipped an arm around her grandmother's shoulders, then pointed with her index finger at her sister, a signal to have her deliver a breakdown of her own. Stef stood still, transfixed by Jackie's joyful face, committing this scene to memory. *A happy woman surrounded by people she loves playing happy tunes.* She smiled to herself, then turned and made her way through the crowd and into a side street, heading back to where she'd parked.

She'll have a good life without me, Stef concluded. A wonderful, happy life. Stef had nothing to offer her. In some ways, she thought, she was worse than nothing. If she stayed, she'd end up sucking the life out of that sweet, happy woman with all her gloom and guilt. If she ever doubted that, all she had to do was remember what Erin had said to explain why she was leaving.

I know you're hurting, Stef, and I feel for you. I really do. But you've shut me out completely, and I don't know what to do for you. I don't know how to help you. Whenever I try, you get angry, like I'm invading your territory. I don't want to live in the world of your grief. It's too dark and too sad. I feel like I'm drowning here trying to keep you afloat, and all you're doing is fighting me. This is apparently something you need and want to go through alone, so I'm going to let you do that. I need to get on with my own life.

CHAPTER THIRTY-FIVE

By one o'clock, Jackie called a break. The band was more than ready. She put down her banjo and stretched her arms over her head.

"I'm hungry," she declared. "Maybe I'll wander down the street and see if I can find something interesting."

"Everybody be back here by two o'clock," Pat instructed, sprawling in her chair. "If you see my honey out there, remind her to keep drinking water. I don't want her to get dehydrated in that stupid costume."

Jackie left the park in search of food, weaving her way through the crowd until she noticed a tall red plush head towering over everyone else. She made her way toward it, finding Crusty the Crawdad standing under the awning of the Sunflower Café with a large soda cup in one claw and an empty food carton in the other.

"Hi," she said as Jackie approached.

"How are you doing?" Jackie peered through the face hole at Gail.

"Not bad. It's very hot, so I'm spending my time in the shade whenever possible. How's it going on your end?"

"Good. I'm on a lunch break."

"You should try this crawdad jambalaya. It's terrific."

"You're eating crawdads?"

"Sure. Isn't everybody?"

"But you're Crusty the Crawdad. That's so cannibalistic."

Gail laughed. "I didn't even think of that."

"I'm not looking for anything with crawdads in it. This huge cloud of dank fishiness has been hanging over the park all day. It's getting to me. I may never eat a crawdad again as long as I live."

Gail tossed her empty carton in a trash can. "How are you feeling today? Any happier?"

"You were right. It's impossible to be sad playing that music. But as soon as I walked away from it, all I could think about was Stef and how I miss her and wish I could see her again."

Gail looked sympathetic. "Then you'd better eat your lunch and get back to playing the music."

A small boy came running up and flung himself at Crusty, wrapping his arms around her legs. She put a claw around his shoulders while his mother took a photo. Jackie waved and walked on, looking for something unrelated to fish.

She spied a red, blue and yellow trailer. *Corn dog!*

When she had her food, a big hot golden brown corn dog slathered with plain yellow mustard, she sat on the grass in the shade of a tree to eat, watching the people walk by. There were so many strangers in town, she saw nobody she knew. About halfway through her meal, she did recognize a couple of boys: Eddie Delgado and Joey Cahill. They were wearing shorts, T-shirts and black Nike sneakers. She watched them for a few minutes, noting the tattoo on Eddie's interior forearm. It was a word she couldn't read from her position, but clearly a line of letters in a blocky font. The boys were in good spirits, joking, shoving one another playfully. They moved on as she pulled the last bite of her corn dog off its stick.

"Hi, there, Jackie."

She looked up to see Don Hartley, looking overheated. Sweat clung to his forehead and the hair on his forearms sparkled with perspiration.

He knelt down to get closer to eye level. "I heard you playing a while ago. Nice job."

"Thanks. We're having a blast. How's your day going? Any trouble?"

"Not really. A couple drunk and disorderly. To be expected."

Jackie took a swallow of her soda, then said, "Any progress on the robberies?"

He shook his head.

"I don't want to jump to conclusions, but there are a couple of local boys who match the description Stef gave you."

"Oh?"

"Yeah. It may just be a coincidence. A lot of young men might fit that description."

"Maybe. So who is it?" He took a small notebook from his pocket.

"Eddie Delgado and Joey Cahill."

He wrote the names down. "Local boys, you said?"

"Cahill hasn't lived here long, but Eddie grew up here. As far as I know, they've done nothing wrong."

"Don't worry. I'll be discreet. I can look them up tomorrow and ask a few questions. Thanks." He put the notebook away. "Officer Byers has a good eye for detail. Good training."

Jackie was startled. "You knew she was a police officer?"

"Yeah. She told me."

Jackie remembered him taking Stef outside to talk privately that night at the Quickie-Mart. "She's not a cop anymore."

"I know. She resigned."

"Did she tell you that?"

"No. She didn't tell me much, other than her name and her department. In fact, she was so evasive, I got suspicious and checked her out."

"Really?" Jackie set her drink down between her legs. "Is she in some kind of trouble? Did she do something wrong?"

He shook his head and picked absentmindedly at the grass beside his boot. "No. She didn't do anything wrong."

Jackie realized he knew something. "What'd you find out?"

He looked up to meet her eyes. "Maybe you should ask her about that."

"I have! She wouldn't talk to me about it."

He regarded her with a somber expression. "I'm not surprised. Some things are just hard to talk about."

"Something happened to her, didn't it?" Jackie asked. "Can you tell me?"

"I shouldn't say anything, but you could Google it and find dozens of articles, newspaper stories and all that." He took an audible breath. "Seeing as how it's public information, I may as well be the one to tell you."

"You may as well because now I'm going to Google it for sure."

"Yeah, I figured. Okay." He rearranged himself to relieve the pressure on his right knee. "Back in March, she and another officer, Joe Molina, were chasing a suspect on foot. Molina cuffed him while Byers covered him. Some guy jumped her. Came out of nowhere. He tried to take her gun and they struggled. The gun went off, still in her possession. Molina was struck in the head by the bullet. It killed him instantly."

Jackie gasped, feeling like a huge weight had landed on her chest. "Oh, my God! That's horrible!"

Hartley nodded soberly. "Yes. Horrible. There was an investigation. That's routine in a case like this. She was exonerated. No charges were filed. Then she resigned. Her resignation was processed the day after the investigation concluded."

"Why'd she resign if she was exonerated?"

"I don't know."

Jackie shook her head, then took a deep breath, trying to let these new details sink in. "Thank you for telling me," she said quietly.

"Like I said, it's all out there." Don shook his head.

"Newspaper stories don't begin to tell it, though. Losing one of your own is tough under any circumstances, but losing him like that…it's got to be a nightmare. My heart goes out to her. It's nice she came out to the festival today to have a little fun."

"What? Stef is here?"

"I saw her a while ago in the park."

"The park? You mean where we were playing?"

"Right. She was there, listening to you play."

Jackie was stunned. "I didn't see her."

"Well, you were kinda busy." Hartley bounced up. "Thanks for the tip about the boys. I'll let you know what I find out."

She nodded, preoccupied with the story she'd just heard. She tried to reassess everything she knew about Stef in the context of this new information. She must blame herself for what happened. Oh, God! Jackie thought with sudden realization. It was the man in the photo, the handsome young officer with his arm around her.

Tears sprang to her eyes. She had cried so much in the last few days, but only for herself. This time, she was crying for Stef. For all the grief and guilt and loneliness she must be feeling. Suddenly every wary expression on her face, every troubled look in her eyes made sense. But what didn't make sense was why she couldn't tell Jackie. She wasn't in trouble and the story was already widely known, according to Hartley.

Jackie wiped the tears away and sat staring at the ice in her soda cup. She gradually began to understand. Stef was running away from everything that reminded her, from everyone who knew. She didn't want the story to follow her. She didn't want anyone to know because, like Hartley, they would feel sorry for her.

She was afraid Jackie would find her pitiable, would want to coddle and take care of her, as Gail had said, like a wounded mutt. It was easy to see Stef had far too much pride to be able to bear that sort of treatment. She was incapable even of asking for help when she needed it. Like now. Everybody needed help sometime. It didn't mean you were weak or that anybody would think less of you. Sometimes problems were just too big for one person.

More than ever, Jackie wanted to go to Stef and try to comfort her. Stef clearly thought she needed to go away, to be alone and let herself heal. That's what injured animals do. They withdraw into isolation to nurse themselves. It's an instinctive response to injury. But it isn't always the best solution.

She thought of Niko's endless jokes that almost always started off, "A dog/cat/bird/giraffe walks into a vet's office." But the thing is, in real life, animals don't walk into a vet's office. They have to be dragged in against their will. Some people were like that too.

Jackie looked at her phone to see it was nearly two o'clock. She had to get back to the group. But she was desperate to go to Stef now that she knew her reason for running away.

It was okay, she told herself. Stef had been at the festival, so she hadn't left town yet. She might even still be here. Jackie tried to reassure herself as she reluctantly returned to the park, searching the crowd for Stef as she did so.

CHAPTER THIRTY-SIX

The joy of finally getting her boat in the water was diminished by not having Jackie there to see it. She was the one person Stef wanted to share this with. Instead, she was sharing it with a taciturn, burly man who unceremoniously loaded and hauled *Mudbug* on a truck trailer to the boat launch ramp. He backed down the ramp until the trailer was in the water. Stef stood on the dock, nervously observing the process of freeing the boat from the trailer. No longer held in place, she rose up. Suddenly, she was afloat! Stef whooped and punched the air with her fist, marveling at the beautiful blue and white craft floating placidly beside the dock. She was elated. Even the sullen truck driver smiled, seeing her joy.

Stef and Deuce went aboard. She took the helm and turned the key. The engine started right up. "Thank you, Marcus!" she declared, listening with satisfaction to the steady hum of the engine.

She shifted into reverse and eased the boat back from the ramp into the wide river, gauging how the craft responded to the throttle. Marcus had given her a few tips about how to pilot a houseboat, reassuring her that because this one was small, it would be more like a regular boat than the really big ones. They, he claimed, were more like driving a tank or a spaceship, a description that made him laugh because he had driven neither. But *Mudbug*, he said, would run light and responsive, and she should get the hang of it in no time.

She maneuvered slowly over to a slip where she could park, so slowly it nearly hurt. She hoped he was right, that she'd soon get the hang of it. There was plenty of open water to practice in in the days to come. When the boat was securely moored and Deuce was locked in the cabin, Stef disembarked and stood on the dock looking at *Mudbug*, waiting for her to sink.

When ten minutes had gone by and the boat was still afloat, she decided it was safe to leave for a few minutes. She walked off the dock to the street. She wanted to get to Rudy's Bait Shop before it closed, to get her fishing license. If you live on the water, you may as well fish, she reasoned. Especially with all that gear in the hold.

Both Rudy and Ida were in the shop tonight. Ida was sweeping in the bait room, wearing wacky pink shorts with yellow ducks on them. Rudy rolled a display rack in from the outside, getting ready to lock up.

"Hi, again," he greeted her. "Stef, right?"

"Right. I'd like a fishing license. Do you have time for that?"

"Yeah, all right. We're about to close up, but that'll just take a minute. Such a busy day today. Festival day. Everybody comes in wanting to see the live crawdads." He pointed to the tank by the door. "Like it's an aquarium in here. But that's okay because they buy things while they're here."

"It's gotten awfully quiet out there now. The festival must be over."

"Over at seven. Yep, it was a good day." Rudy went behind

the counter. "My crawdads there are the only ones in captivity that lived through this day, that's for sure."

Stef laughed.

Rudy pulled a form out from below the counter and set it on top, along with an ink pen. "But nobody out there was eating local crawdads anyway today. All those mudbugs at the festival were shipped in here from Louisiana."

"Really?" Stef asked. "Why?"

"They need too many of 'em. No way we can supply this shindig. Not set up for it. When the festival first started, we served local ones, but not anymore. They've got commercial operations there in Louisiana, so they ship us a frozen ton of them, and we serve 'em up like we just caught 'em in the backyard. Nobody knows the difference. Now, that's not for telling around. Just between us locals. So don't tell anybody."

"Listen to him," Ida huffed. "Don't tell anybody. Hasn't he been telling everybody who came in here all day long? My Lord!"

"We'll get you set up with a license," Rudy said, ignoring his wife. "I'll give you a list of all the rules. What you can keep, what you gotta throw back."

"I wouldn't want to break any rules," Stef said, filling in the form. "By the way, can you tell me how Disappointment Slough got its name?"

"Sure. Bad luck fishing hole, that's how. Back in the day. But I've never understood that. It's always been one of my favorite spots."

"I should have guessed it had to do with fish."

"Most things around here do." Rudy's eyes twinkled.

"As you can see, I'm going to try my hand at it."

"If you're going for cats," Rudy said, "you wanna use a heavy sinker to keep you on the bottom. That's where they are. They're scavengers, bottom feeders. You know how to clean a fish?"

"I've got YouTube." Stef signed the form and handed it to him.

"YouTube?" he asked. "What's that?"

"A website where people put videos of how to do everything. You want to know how to cook a roast, go to YouTube. Want to know how to milk a sheep, go to YouTube."

Ida stopped sweeping and stepped into the main room. "I'd like to know how to get my husband to put up the vertical blinds I bought six months ago."

Rudy frowned.

"I don't think YouTube can help with that." Stef laughed.

Rudy put on reading glasses and perused her form. "What's this address? Hayward? You need a current address. You want to put Baylor Road on this."

"That's my mother's address. As of this afternoon, I don't live on Baylor Road anymore, so that's all I've got."

Rudy looked over his glasses at her. "Where you living?" he asked suspiciously.

"On my boat. On the river."

"No! You got her running?" His eyes opened wide, pushing his wild eyebrows further up on his forehead.

"See for yourself." She indicated the window. "There she is, the blue and white one next to the marina office."

Both Ida and Rudy rushed to the window and looked down the street.

"Look at that!" Rudy declared. "Well, I'll be a—"

Ida nodded appreciatively at Stef while Rudy returned to his place at the counter.

"My husband thought it was impossible," Ida confided. "He thought because you're a woman, you wouldn't be able to fix that boat."

"I did not!" Rudy objected forcefully. "It had nothing to do with her being a woman. It had to do with her knowing nothing about boats."

"I had YouTube," Stef explained, unoffended. "And I had help."

"There, you see," Rudy said, glaring at his wife. "She had help."

"Still," Ida returned, "she deserves a lot of credit. She did a wonderful job." She narrowed her eyes at Rudy. "For a woman!"

He sighed in exasperation and shook his head, then laminated the license and handed it over. Stef gave him her credit card and slid the license into her wallet.

"Now you're legal," he declared.

She looked from one to the other of them. Jackie's parents, she reminded herself, wanting to give them both a hug. But they didn't know about her. Besides, she wasn't part of the family no matter how you looked at it. She'd had a brief affair with their daughter. Then broken up with her and broke her heart. Like they'd want to hug her for that! More likely they'd want to slap her.

"See ya," she said breezily, then left the shop and walked swiftly across the street toward the marina. As she started to put her wallet away, she noticed the pocket where she kept her credit card was empty. She stopped walking and opened the wallet. The card wasn't there. Rudy had forgotten to give it back to her.

She turned around and headed back toward the bait shop. The door was now shut, but she knew they hadn't had time to leave yet, so she ran across the street and shoved open the door, saying, "Hey, I forgot my—"

She froze. Two men in ski masks, long pants, long-sleeved shirts and black sneakers stood in the shop. One of them, blue eyes peering out of the holes of the mask, had a semiautomatic Beretta trained on Rudy. He was behind the counter, his hands in the air. The other man, apparently unarmed, had an arm locked around Ida's waist. She looked petrified. Her broom lay on the floor nearby. They were the same two who had held up the Quickie-Mart, Stef was positive. As she entered the store, the gunman swung toward her. She immediately put her hands on her head without waiting to be told.

"Get over there with her!" the gunman ordered, aiming his gun at her head, holding it at arm's length in his left hand.

"Okay," she said, her voice calm but her heart pounding wildly.

She slowly skirted him, watching the barrel of the gun follow her. He stood facing her, his back to Rudy. The other man pulled Ida toward the bait room. She remained stiff, like a mannequin, her feet dragging along the floor, but she was small enough that she created no problem for the man.

As Stef slid past the gunman, she saw Rudy reach down behind the counter, a look of grim determination on his face. When his hand reappeared, he was holding a small revolver.

No, no, no! Stef thought, panic-stricken. *What the fuck are you doing?* She broke out in a cold sweat and could feel the tension in her throat. She tried to communicate with Rudy wordlessly, to make him put the gun away before anybody else saw it.

Too late. Ida suddenly let out a shriek of terror, her eyes on her husband. The man dragging her let go and she fell to the floor.

"He's got a gun!" he yelled.

The gunman swung around to confront Rudy just as he pulled the trigger. The bullet grazed the robber's torso. He spun, losing his grip on the Beretta. It skidded across the floor. The other guy lunged toward Rudy, who stood immobilized, still pointing the revolver at the dead air where he'd fired. He was in shock.

The boy grabbed Rudy's arm and tried to take the gun from him, startling him back to the present. Rudy held on as they struggled, banging back and forth between the counter and wall. Stef felt dizzy and clammy, like she was about to faint. She instinctively reached for her knife, then realized the replacement Jackie had given her was still in its box.

The injured man, recovered from the surprise of being shot, moved along the floor toward his gun, which lay against a wall ten feet away. Stef realized she couldn't let him rearm himself. She dove past him for the gun. He grabbed her legs, pulling her back along the slick floor, putting the gun out of her reach. She clawed at the floor, but couldn't move forward. He released her legs and tried to climb over the top of her to get to the gun. She pulled an elbow back hard to catch him in the stomach. He groaned and fell off her. She rolled over and shoved him away. Then she went for the gun again and caught it securely in her right hand. Her heart beat furiously. On some level she knew this was the first time she'd touched a gun since that horrible day that had defined her whole life since, and that she'd vowed never to touch one again, had thought she was incapable of it. On another level, the one in charge, she didn't have time to think about any of that.

She rolled back over just as Blue Eyes was about to pounce on her again, but with the gun barrel aimed at his face, he stopped abruptly. With her situation under control, Stef looked over to see what had happened to Rudy. His assailant had wrenched the revolver away from him and kicked him backward into the edge of the counter. Ida screamed again as the man aimed the gun at Rudy's head.

"Shoot him!" yelled Blue Eyes.

"Dude," objected the other man, "it's Mr. Townsend." He sounded young. A scared young man. Obviously not a stranger to the bait shop.

"I don't care who the fuck he is. He shot me! Pop him."

Sitting on the floor, still aiming at Blue Eyes, Stef realized Rudy was in mortal danger. She carefully rose to her feet, watching both men closely. The one holding the revolver on Rudy trembled noticeably. Whether he would shoot or not, she couldn't tell. That's not the kind of chance you can take in police work. *If I guess wrong...*

"Do it!" yelled Blue Eyes, looking defiantly at Stef, clearly believing she wouldn't use her gun even if she knew how.

If she moved toward Rudy, this guy would be all over her, she knew. She had to keep them both in front of her. There was no way to stop the other boy except by shooting him. She had had so many nightmares in which she willed herself not to squeeze the trigger. Not to let her finger contract. Now she thought maybe she'd succeeded, that she had paralyzed herself so she wasn't able to shoot a gun at all, even now when a man's life was at stake. A brief wave of dizziness wafted over her.

She could see the boy struggling with his conscience and his need to obey his friend. He raised the gun and aimed more purposely at Rudy, whose back was against the counter. He bent back over it, trying to get farther from the gun. Ida screamed again, crying, "No, no!" The gunman swung her way, momentarily deflecting his aim away from Rudy. Stef took the opportunity of his forward-facing body to aim for his shoulder. She fired. As the slug hit its mark, the boy stumbled backward, dropped the gun, and slammed into the wall, crying out in pain. At that same instant, Stef kicked the other boy under the chin, sending him flying backward to land against one of the display shelves, knocking it over and scattering merchandise across the floor. To the sound of breaking glass, she sprang to the counter and leapt over it. She grabbed Rudy's gun, then shoved him past the injured boy groaning on the floor.

"Get over there with your wife and stay there," she commanded.

He scurried off, and she backed a few feet away from the boy writhing at her feet. Both guns in hand, she trained the Beretta on Blue Eyes as he gradually recovered from the kick and sat up. She put the safety on the revolver and slipped it into her pocket. Then she threw her cell phone to Rudy.

"Call 9-1-1," she said. "Tell them to send an ambulance."

She pulled the boy on the floor to his feet. His shirt was soaked with blood. His hand was clamped over his shoulder. It too was covered with blood, but it didn't look like he was bleeding enough to bleed out. She pulled him around to the open area of the store and pulled off his ski mask. He was just a kid, early twenties.

"Eddie!" Ida gasped. "Eddie Delgado?"

"Sit there," Stef ordered, pointing with the gun.

Eddie sat next to his friend and started to sob, still holding his shoulder.

"Ida," Stef instructed, "can you find a clean cloth he can put over that wound?"

"Eddie," Ida said sternly, struggling to her feet and clearly no longer afraid, "how could you? And I suppose that's your friend Joey, isn't it?"

The other boy, who knew there was no escape, took off his ski mask, slapped Eddie over the head with it, then threw it on the floor into a spreading puddle of sticky pink liquid that smelled overwhelmingly of fish. Stef backed away from the boys and knelt near Jackie's parents. Rudy was on the phone with the emergency dispatcher, explaining the situation, his voice slightly out of control with anxiety.

Stef took a deliberate deep breath and wondered if she'd been breathing at all for the last few minutes. She kept the gun in hand, aware that she had done just what needed to be done. She hadn't choked and she hadn't killed anyone.

Ida opened a package of cotton rags and handed one to Stef, who tossed it to Eddie. "Apply pressure," she said.

They waited, the defeated boys on one side of the room next to the toppled shelving unit, the fortunate victims on the other. Rudy and Ida stood together, leaning against each other. Stef resisted the urge to lecture Rudy. He'd learned his lesson the hard way. For once, he had nothing to say. He stood quietly, his arm around his wife.

Finally, they heard a siren. A patrol car came screaming into the parking lot out front, throwing gravel against the window as it skidded to a stop. Stef breathed a huge sigh of relief as Officer Hartley stepped into the shop, gun drawn, his badge drooping from the front of a Def Leppard T-shirt. As he crossed the threshold, he reeled back, covering his nose with one hand and screwing up his face in disgust. "What the hell!" he choked.

"Salmon eggs," Rudy explained flatly.

Hartley shook his head and blinked, then surveyed the scene as Stef approached.

"Looks like everything's under control here," he said with a nod toward Stef. He stood in front of the boys, looking down at them with his mouth set in an expression of dismay.

"Eddie Delgado and Joey Cahill," he said, not the least bit surprised to see them.

"You know them?" Stef asked.

"Never met, no, but I got their names earlier today from Jackie. She recognized them from your description. Ironic, isn't it, that they hit her parents' store the same night?"

At the mention of Jackie's name, Stef's heart skipped a beat.

Another siren sounded, approaching their location.

"That'll be the ambulance," Ida said, addressing Eddie. "You'll be okay. Don't worry. I'll call your mother and tell her where you are. Tell them to take you to Lodi Memorial. That's a good hospital. All my kids were born there, and I wouldn't go anywhere else."

Eddie said nothing, looking confused and miserable. The thought of Ida calling his mother didn't seem to comfort him. Stef glanced at Rudy, who rolled his eyes at his wife. She appeared completely recovered from any distress over the robbery. An ambulance pulled off the highway and halted out front, lights flashing.

Hartley turned to Stef. "Thanks for the help here." He gestured toward the gun in her hand. "Looks like this could have ended a lot worse ways."

Stef nodded shortly and surrendered both handguns to him, happy to get rid of them, but also understanding that a momentous event had just occurred. So momentous, in fact, that she knew if she thought about it much longer, she'd start sobbing from the sheer emotional impact of what she had just accomplished.

Hartley looked at her levelly and said, "I don't claim to know what you've been through, Byers, but when you're ready to get back to work, give me a call. We might have a position opening up soon. It's not a bad beat. Might seem a little quiet for somebody with your experience, but I figure you might be ready for a little quiet."

She nodded. "I hope you have a little more quiet yourself with those two out of the way."

After hearing the details of what had happened from Rudy and Ida and arresting the boys, Hartley took Cahill out in cuffs. Delgado was taken in the ambulance. Rudy and Ida stood near the checkout counter. Stef stepped carefully around the broken glass on the floor.

"You forgot to give my credit card back," she told Rudy.

He looked surprised, then located the card beside the computer.

"Thank you so much for saving our lives," Ida said, taking Stef's hand in both of hers. "My husband's a dimwit. If it wasn't for you... Oh, I hate to think..."

Stef leaned down to hug her. "You're welcome."

Ida opened the jar of jerky on the counter and held it toward Stef with a solemn expression. It was her all-purpose offering. Stef took a piece. Then she passed through the doorway into a remarkable Delta sunset. The sky was deep blue and pink with a tinge of melon orange. What a rejuvenating sight!

She walked across the street where *Mudbug* still floated in her berth, ready to take her on a journey. Deuce stood at the cabin's glass door, watching her approach. She laughed at the sight and suddenly realized she felt great. The urge to cry had passed and in its place was an equally intense feeling of triumph. She punched the air with her fist and said, "Yes!" then hastened her pace toward her new adventure.

CHAPTER THIRTY-SEVEN

By five o'clock, Jackie was convinced seven o'clock would never come. And if it did, she wasn't sure she'd still be alive. But it did and she was. When they turned off the equipment and packed up to go home, everybody was ready to collapse into puddles of their own sweat. Pat appeared at her side with an extra glass of champagne, looking like a wet mop.

"Congratulations," she said, handing the glass to Jackie. "We made it through another year."

Jackie clinked her glass against Pat's and took a healthy swallow. "Yes, we did! It looked like a good one too."

"Best ever by preliminary estimates." Pat pressed her champagne glass against her cheek. "Just got a call from Gail. She's home already and has the hot tub running. I'm going to go soak in it until I turn into a prune. Want to join us?"

"Tempting, but I have something I need to do."

Jackie rushed home to shower and change, and was feeling revived by the time she was back in her car and driving out to Baylor Road. She was convinced she could help Stef if only she could push her way past her thick defenses. She'd be more aggressive this time and wouldn't slink away when Stef told her to get lost. Stef needed her help, even if she wouldn't admit it. She knew Stef cared about her. And that gave her an advantage. This time, she wouldn't take no for an answer.

Turning up Stef's driveway, she was confronted with a sight that astonished her. Her heart leapt into her throat and her foot eased off the gas pedal.

The houseboat was gone!

She parked and walked over to the spot where it had stood. The blocks it had rested on were still there. The hookups for electricity and water were still there. The picnic table and grill were still there. But *Mudbug*, Stef, Deuce and all their stuff were gone.

It seemed incomprehensible that it shouldn't be here like it always had been. It was as if it had just vanished into thin air. But the fact was, it was a boat. It belonged on water and Stef had always intended to move it to water. Jackie just hadn't expected it to happen so fast. Least of all, she hadn't expected it to happen now when she had a new plan to put into action. It had been at least eight hours since Hartley saw Stef at the festival. For all Jackie knew, *Mudbug* could have already been at the marina even then. Maybe her visit to the festival had been Stef's last look at Stillwater Bay—and at Jackie—before she sailed away.

She sat at the picnic table in the slant light of the setting sun, disappointed and bereft. It was so cold and empty here all of a sudden. Though it was a warm spring evening, she shivered at the vacant space in front of her.

She was gone. She was really gone.

CHAPTER THIRTY-EIGHT

It was not until the following morning that Jackie heard about the robbery when her sister called asking if she knew any details. The story had spread through town already, and Becca had heard about it when she dropped Adam off at school. As soon as she got off the phone, Jackie rushed to the bait shop to find the door propped open and both her parents inside. Her mother was squatting and picking broken glass off the floor, and her father was in the bait room adding sardines to one of the tanks. Other than the mess on the floor and the overwhelming smell of fish in the shop, everything looked the same as usual.

"You were robbed?" Jackie stopped just inside the door to avoid stepping in glass.

Her mother looked up at her and squinted. "Nope. We weren't robbed."

"They didn't get a penny," her father boasted from the back room.

"Thanks to that young woman," Ida added. "No thanks to your fool of a father."

"Young woman?" Jackie asked. She knelt down to help her mother pick up the rest of the glass. Sticky salmon eggs stuck to several of the larger pieces.

"That woman who bought old Compton's houseboat." Her mother stood. "The cop."

"She isn't a cop," Rudy intervened.

"Don Hartley said—"

"He said she used to be a cop. He was here just a minute ago checking on us. He said that's why she was such a good shot. Because she used to be a cop."

"She shot somebody?" Jackie was alarmed and frustrated with her parents for not telling her instantly what she wanted to know, but it was clear they were talking about Stef.

"She shot Eddie Delgado," Ida said, carrying her dustpan full of glass to the trash can.

"Oh, my God!"

"In the shoulder," Rudy added, stepping into the room. "He'll be okay. Hartley said they got the bullet out and there shouldn't be any complications. He'll heal up okay. It was a very precise type of shot, he said. She knew what she was doing, that girl."

Jackie breathed a sigh of relief to hear that Stef hadn't killed somebody. Somebody else.

"It's a good thing somebody knew what she was doing," Ida remarked. "Your father shot Joey Cahill."

"What?" Jackie was alarmed. "Dad shot Joey Cahill?"

Ida waved dismissively. "Just nicked him. Your father couldn't hit the side of a barn at ten feet. If it wasn't for that policewoman, we'd all be dead. I'm sure of it."

"Why didn't you call me?" Jackie demanded.

"There was nothing for you to do. By the time everybody left, we just wanted to go to bed. We were exhausted. Just left the whole mess here and went home."

"It was an exciting night," Rudy added. "How'd you find out about it?"

"Everybody in town is talking about it. I got three calls on my way over here from people wanting to know what happened. Becca called me first thing. That's where I first heard about it. And I'm like, what? Why didn't we know about this? She's coming over as soon as she can get somebody to fill in at work. She called your house earlier and got no answer."

"That's because we came over here early to clean up," Ida explained. "I'll mop up the rest."

She walked to the back room to get a mop and Jackie noticed for the first time that she was wearing the tasteful new yellow and white top Jackie had bought her with a pair of stretch polyester hot pink shorts. Why would she do that? Jackie wondered. Rudy installed himself on his stool behind the counter. Jackie sent a text to her sister saying, "Nobody hurt. Everything under control. No hurry about coming over."

"We were so lucky," Ida said, returning with the mop, "that we had a police officer right here in the store when the heist went down."

"She's not a police officer," Rudy grumbled. "I just told you that."

"You should have seen her," Ida continued, undaunted. "She was a regular Jackie Chan."

"Jackie Chan?" her father complained. "What are you talking about? Did you see any kung fu fighting in here last night? I didn't see any."

Ida shrugged. "Well, then, Angie Dickinson."

"Who's Angie Dickinson?" Jackie asked.

"A policewoman," Rudy said. "Back in the seventies. She had blonde hair and went undercover a lot as a hooker. I never liked her as much as I did Columbo. Remember him?"

"Oh, yeah," Ida said, pushing the mop across the bright pink stain. "Columbo. He was good."

"With that raincoat and his wonky eye." Rudy shook his head and smiled, then hiked up one shoulder, partially closed one eye, raised one finger and muttered, "Pardon me, sir... Just one more thing, ma'am... Just one more tiny question if you don't mind."

"I see I'll have to go down to the police station," Jackie said.

"Obviously, you two aren't going to tell me what happened here last night."

"What happened," her father said, "is that two kids came in here and held us up."

"Eddie Delgado and Joey Cahill," Ida added. "It was late, around eight o'clock, way after closing time, but your father insisted on staying open until the festival was over on the chance he might sell one more overpriced T-shirt. The ones with the big red crawdads on them, those were the most popular, as we expected."

"Then what happened?" Jackie demanded, anxious to get back on topic. "After the boys came in, what happened?"

"They asked for all the money," her father explained. "Before I could even open the drawer, your ex-cop comes in and surprises them. Made them trigger happy."

"That's not what made them trigger happy," Ida contradicted. "Everything was fine until your damned fool father pulls a gun on them. Then everybody went crazy. Eddie was about to shoot your father in the head when that girl…" She turned to Rudy. "What's her name?"

"Her name's Stef," Jackie offered.

"Stef? No, I don't think so."

"Yes!" Rudy stated. "Her name's Stef Byers. It says so right here on her fishing license application." He looked to Jackie for confirmation and she nodded.

"She was phenomenal," Ida said, "whatever her name was. Just like Jackie Chan." Ida held the mop handle in both hands in front of her like a martial arts weapon. Rudy shook his head.

"Stef wasn't hurt?" Jackie asked.

"Not a scratch. She rounded up both those boys and sat 'em right over here to wait for the paddy wagon."

"It sounds like she really was phenomenal."

"And cool as a cucumber the whole time."

"Where is she now?"

"She took off last night," Rudy said. "Said she was getting underway as soon as she left here. Miles away by now."

"She didn't say where, I guess. Where she was headed?"

Rudy shook his head.

Jackie felt frustrated with herself. If only she'd come out to the marina last night after finding Stef gone. She might have caught her. It would never have occurred to her that she might even be at the bait shop getting a fishing license. Instead, she had gone home and spent a miserable, tear-filled evening alone.

"You can give her a call," suggested her father, his expression sympathetic.

Jackie realized she must not be doing a good job hiding her disappointment. "I'll do that."

Rudy approached her and put his arm around her shoulders. "She'll have to come back."

"She will?"

"She's a witness. More than a witness even. She'll have to come back for the trial."

"Oh, sure, I guess she will." That was something, Jackie thought, but a trial could take months to happen and might not ever happen, depending on the pleas. "But that would be in Sacramento, not here."

He nodded and gave her an encouraging pat on the back. Jackie noticed her mother standing nearby with a look of suspicion on her face.

"What's going on?" she asked. "Something's going on. Why are you sulking and your father trying to cheer you up?"

Rudy grinned gleefully and scuttled back to his place behind the counter. "Maybe you don't know everything that goes on in this town," he crowed. "Maybe not even when it's about your own daughter."

"Suppose you tell me," she suggested indignantly.

Jackie decided to leave them to their game, knowing her mother would get what she wanted in the end. She walked outside and called Stef's number. After three rings, it went to voice mail. "You've reached Stef Byers. Leave a message." Momentarily stunned by the sound of Stef's voice, Jackie hesitated before shutting her phone. If she was going to leave a message, she needed to decide what to say. She might only get one chance, if that, if Stef would listen to her message at all. She slumped into the Bel-Air car seat and stared across the road to a row of colorful boats docked at the marina, going over possibilities in her mind. Nothing seemed right. Nothing she could think of was any different from what she'd already told Stef.

I love you. I want you. Please, please come back to me.

But none of that had changed her mind before.

Or she could try something like, "I know what happened to Joe Molina and I'm so, so sorry. I felt sick when I heard about it and just wanted to hold you and comfort you and take care of you like…uh, something other than a wounded puppy." Obviously, that wouldn't work, nor would anything Stef could interpret as pity. So what could she say that would make a difference?

When her phone rang, she snapped it open and answered, "Hello!" thinking Stef had seen her number and was calling her back. But it was Niko, saying, "Are you coming in? Your nine o' clock is here. Mrs. Peterson and Max."

"Oh, damn! Sorry. I'm over here at the bait shop. It got robbed last night."

"I heard. Are your folks all right?"

"They're fine. They seem elated, in fact. Can you ask Mrs. Peterson to wait? I'll be there in ten minutes."

"Sure." Jackie was about to hang up when Niko said, "A leopard walks into a vet's office and says, 'Doc, I'm tired of this look. Can you change my spots?' The vet says, 'No.'"

Jackie let out a spontaneous squawk of delight. "That's a good one."

"Thanks. I know you haven't been very happy lately, so I figure if I can still get a laugh out of you, things can't be too bad."

Jackie smiled to herself. "I'll see you in a few minutes."

CHAPTER THIRTY-NINE

Stef parked her bike on the street in front of a small white house with wood siding and a patchy lawn. She'd memorized the address Womack had given her. Once he'd gotten her legal name from property records for the old Lincoln Avenue apartment house, tracking Luisa Avila down had been relatively simple.

The neighborhood seemed respectable but poor. Across the street a young man worked under a jacked-up car. A little girl rode a tricycle on the sidewalk two houses away. An elderly man next door paused on his way to his mailbox to peer at Stef and her motorcycle. She smiled his way and he shuffled off. It was weekday quiet up and down the street.

This had been Stef's first destination after leaving Stillwater Bay, piloting *Mudbug* up the Sacramento River, through Suisun Bay, and on to the Carquinez Strait to the Bay Area town of

Martinez. All large waterways, so plenty of room to get familiar with *Mudbug's* quirks. She was starting to get the hang of steering that tub. When she was done here, she'd go back to the heart of the Delta and explore some of the smaller channels, lose herself in remote locations where no roads penetrated.

The windows and front door of the house were open, leaving only a screen door covering the doorway. Her helmet tucked under her arm, she walked up a short sidewalk to the porch and was about to ring the bell when a woman's voice greeted her from the dim interior.

"Hi, hi," she said enthusiastically. "Come in."

Stef opened the screen door and stepped inside. The room was small and stuffy, furnished with old-fashioned chairs and tables. The walls were cluttered with knickknacks and photos. It was a much lived-in looking space. The woman who had called to her sat in a recliner across the room, facing the door where she could see anybody approach.

"Hi," said Stef, stepping over to the recliner. "I'm Stef Byers." She shook the woman's hand.

Luisa Avila was not as old as Stef had expected. Molina had described her as old when he was a kid of twelve, which was fifteen years ago. She looked to be in her mid-fifties, which would have made her just about forty at the time. She was large, as he and his brother remembered, close to three hundred pounds, wearing a loose kaftan-like dress. Her legs were up on the recliner's footrest, her broad-ankled feet clad in fuzzy pink slippers. She had a wide nose, eyes obscured behind thick glasses and mostly dark gray, puffy hair.

"Sit down," she said, motioning toward the chair next to her.

Stef sat. "Thank you for seeing me."

"So what's this all about? You said on the phone José Molina's dead. He was so young. What did he die of?"

"He was twenty-seven," Stef reported. "He was killed in the line of duty. He was a police officer."

"Was he?" Mrs. Avila nodded approvingly. "Good for him! Made something of himself after all. I always thought that boy could do something with himself if he tried. No thanks to that slut of a mother."

"That's why I'm here, because of how you took an interest in him. He remembered the way you made sure he went to school. He and his brother. He used to tell me about it. He wanted to thank you, but he never got around to it."

"So you want to thank me for him?"

"Right. And tell you it made a difference, what you did. He thought his life might have been wasted without your intervention."

"I didn't do much. Didn't have the means. I didn't have much myself in those days."

"But you did make them go to school and that was the important thing."

"That's what I thought. They could get out of that place and be around other kids and teachers, have a normal day, make friends and learn a few things. That building was no place for kids. I know I owned the place, but it wasn't for me to tell people how to live if they paid the rent. That place was a real dump." She shook her head in dismay. "I was so glad to finally unload it."

Stef nodded politely and glanced around, feeling anxious. She'd said what she came to say, but knew it would be rude to leave so quickly. Like most people, Stef assumed Mrs. Avila would find things of her own to talk about since she had a guest willing to listen.

"Were you his friend?" she asked.

Stef nodded.

"Girlfriend?"

"No. We worked together."

"You a police officer too?"

Stef hesitated, then quickly decided she didn't need to explain. "Yes."

"So he turned out pretty good?"

"Yeah, he was a good guy. Good cop."

"What happened to the little guy, his brother, Roberto?"

"He's in prison."

"Kill somebody, did he?"

"Yes."

"Not surprised. That little shit had a mean look when he was just a tiny kid. He was just hard through and through. Not really his fault, I guess. Considering. Was he in a gang?"

"Uh-huh. Norteños."

Mrs. Avila shook her head. "What about José?"

"He was Norteño too. He got out when he was twenty-one, when he decided to join the force."

"He was lucky, then. Smart. Smarter than his little brother. Too bad José got killed. Gunned down by one of those Norteños maybe? They don't like it when you change sides."

Stef shifted self-consciously in her chair. "No. The suspects we were after weren't gang members."

Mrs. Avila observed her silently while Stef wondered how to politely excuse herself. She had expected Mrs. Avila to chatter at her about her cat or her garden or tell her old stories, but she was just asking questions about Molina. Uncomfortable questions.

"You're not very talkative, are you?" Mrs. Avila noted. "You went to all this trouble to find me to tell me about José Molina, but you don't have much to say."

"I just wanted to tell you he was grateful to you. That's all. Because he wanted to tell you himself."

"If he had come, I guess I'd get to see for myself what kind of a man he turned into. I always liked him. That's why I stuck my nose in. He was a little charmer. I bet he was a good-looking man."

"Oh," Stef said, realizing she could at least satisfy that bit of Mrs. Avila's curiosity. "I can show you." She took out her wallet and slipped out a photo of Molina in uniform.

Mrs. Avila smiled at the picture, holding it close to her face. "Yep, a regular lady-killer, that one." She looked up to catch Stef's eye. "You're sure you and José weren't—"

Stef shook her head. "No. Just friends."

Mrs. Avila gazed steadily at her, her mouth shut tightly. "Why'd you come here?"

"I told you, to let you know he appreciated what you did."

"Uh-huh." She sounded skeptical. She had a direct and unnerving way about her. Stef had expected a pleasant, chatty old woman. Instead, she felt she was being probed, and she was starting to get irritated.

"Really," Stef said coolly, "that's it. And now that I've delivered the message." She pushed herself up from the deep cushion of the chair, anxious to leave.

"But I mean, why you? You're not a relative, not his girlfriend. You're a colleague."

"We were close. Close friends. He was like a brother to me."

"Yes, yes." Mrs. Avila nodded understandingly. "Brothers in arms. Like soldiers on a battlefield. What department was he with?"

"Oakland."

She chuckled. "Now that's a battlefield, for sure. You too, right? Oakland?"

"Right." Stef stood awkwardly in front of the chair, wondering if she was leaving or staying.

"Being his close friend, like a sister and all, you must have known him pretty well. What was he like?" She handed the photo back to Stef.

"What was he like?" Stef paused, wondering how to answer, thinking that was a hard question to answer about anybody, to try to give a sense of a person to someone who hadn't known him. She sat back down and focused on the photo. "He was obviously a handsome man. And he knew it."

Mrs. Avila laughed shortly. "Lady-killer, like I said."

"He usually did have a girlfriend," Stef confirmed. "But he hadn't yet found anyone permanent. He always knew she was just around the corner, though. He wasn't disillusioned or anything. Always optimistic. He had a wonderful sense of humor and laughed a lot. He had a relaxed, easy laugh, the kind of laugh that could make some really bad stuff seem not worth worrying about."

Stef paused, wondering what sorts of things Mrs. Avila wanted to hear, but she offered no help. She merely waited for Stef to continue.

"He was very confident in his abilities. He never considered failure. And he was super competitive. On the gun range, he always had to get the best score. Or if we were playing a trivia game, which we did sometimes to pass the time, he'd get so frustrated if he didn't win. One time, we had this hot chile challenge. Just a spur-of-the-moment thing." Stef laughed. "We both nearly killed ourselves. He took every challenge seriously. But he didn't get mad if he lost. He didn't have a temper. He was a good sport. He played soccer. He loved the game. Played in a city league. He'd come in on Mondays sometimes during the soccer season with bruises all over him. He played hard. He coached a girls' team too. I went to a couple of games. He'd get so excited when they made a goal. He'd jump around and pump the air with his fist, run in place and hoot. It was so entertaining that after every goal the whole team, and even the opposing team, watched him dance before they got into position." She laughed and looked up to see a smile on Mrs. Avila's lips. "Those girls adored him, every last one of them. They all came to his funeral, in their soccer uniforms, and gave him a really nice tribute."

Stef waited to hear if Mrs. Avila had any comment, but she was immobile except for the blinking of her eyes, small and indistinct through the lenses of her glasses.

Stef noticed a shelf of dusty glass figurines on the wall behind her. All birds. A green and blue hummingbird. A red cardinal. Yellow canary. A clear, graceful stork or crane, wings outstretched, framing a long, undulating neck.

She swallowed, noting how dry her throat had become. She quit looking at Mrs. Avila and looked down instead at the photo between her fingers. "He had a strong sense of responsibility," she continued. "A good thing for a cop. He wanted to protect people. The slogan, *to serve and to protect*, was always up front with him. He was very compassionate, equally toward everyone. He had a hard time keeping his heart out of his work. We busted this guy one time for running a meth lab in his apartment. The guy had a son about fourteen. The whole time we were there, arresting the guy, securing the scene, this boy was sobbing until Child Protective Services came and took him away." Stef shook her head, remembering. "Molina was really worried about that boy. He followed up on him, found out he was turned over to an aunt. Then he went and signed up with Big Brothers just so he could be that kid's big brother and help him out. He stayed in Big Brothers even after that. He was good with kids. So patient.

They liked him. They respected him too. He knew how to talk to kids." Stef felt a lump in her throat. "I always told him he was going to be the most fantastic father."

She heard her voice falter and realized she could no longer speak. Her eyes stung as the image in her hand began to blur. She fought to force down the emotion.

"Oh, honey," Mrs. Avila said, pushing down her footrest.

Stef put a hand to her face, unable to stop her tears from falling. Mrs. Avila rose from her chair and came to hug Stef in her ample arms, which was embarrassing and comforting at the same time, but also liberating in that it encouraged her to cry more freely.

"I'm sorry," she managed. "I don't know what's wrong with me."

"Here," Mrs. Avila said, pushing a box of tissues toward her. "What's wrong with you is you miss your friend, that's what."

Stef put the picture of Molina on the table, took a tissue and wiped her eyes, but she couldn't stop sobbing.

"You go ahead and have a cry," Mrs. Avila said, patting her on the back. "I'll go get you a glass of water. How about some tea? Would you like that?"

Stef nodded without looking up.

"Okay. We'll have tea. You get it all out now. Then we'll have a nice long talk."

Stef took advantage of the older woman's absence to allow herself something she almost never did allow, unrestrained tears. As she sat by herself in the dim, dusty room, she knew that when Mrs. Avila returned with the tea, she would tell her everything. She would tell her how Molina died and how her life had been shattered as a result. She'd tell her about how Roberto had accused her of murdering his brother and how right that had sounded to her. She'd tell her about the nightmares and her sense of helpless despair, of her flattened spirit and the feeling that there was no place for her in the world anymore. She might even tell her about Jackie, a woman who wanted nothing more than to give her perfect love, but how incapable of accepting it she felt, how her own imperfect and damaged heart was unfit to receive a gift so pure.

She could tell she was about to do that, reveal all of her buried pain to this stranger she had nothing in common with, whom she'd never see again, this stranger who no doubt had problems of her own, losses and regrets of her own. But Stef didn't care about any of that. And she knew Mrs. Avila wouldn't bring any of it up. Somehow she just knew that. She would listen with unselfish, objective compassion. She would listen, but she would offer no judgment and no advice, for which Stef would be grateful.

She wiped her eyes and tried to compose herself as she heard the shrill whistle of a teakettle from the kitchen.

CHAPTER FORTY

She could hear a siren somewhere in the distance.

As she turned the corner into an alley between brick apartment buildings, she saw Needham running up ahead. Molina fired again, aiming low, grazing Needham's leg. He went down with a cry of pain, and Molina was on him fast, slamming him facedown in the street, a knee in his back. Stef stood back covering him as Molina pulled out his cuffs.

Out of nowhere, somebody jumped her, knocking her sideways. She lost her balance, falling to the ground. Her attacker fell on top of her. She pushed his face back as hard as she could with her left hand while her right held fast to her gun. His hand clamped around her right wrist, then his fingers grabbed hers, trying to pry them off her gun as she managed to get her index finger on the trigger, struggling to aim the gun at him before he could tear it from her grasp.

She looked to the side to see if Molina was coming to her aid. He was running toward her. He fired his gun, startling the assailant just long enough for Stef to turn her gun toward his chest. His grip on her wrist retightened and he slammed her arm down hard on the ground just as she squeezed the trigger. The gun went off like a thunderclap, deafening her. Complete silence followed.

She watched the bullet coursing toward Molina, floating straight and slow, so slow she could have picked it out of the air if she'd been standing beside it. Molina didn't see it. She tried to yell at him, but her tongue was like stone. The bullet sailed into his forehead. He looked confused, reeling backward. Blood ran down his face, into his eyes, dripping from the end of his nose. His gun fell from his hand, hitting the ground noiselessly. He fell to his knees.

Stef's gun went off two more times without making a sound. Though the face of the man looming over her convulsed in agony, his eyes shut tight, his mouth open as if he were crying out, she heard nothing. He rolled off her into the street, clutching his abdomen, curled into the fetal position.

Molina lay in the alley, his eyes staring at her with mild confusion. She could suddenly hear again, the sound of traffic, sirens closing fast. She ran to Molina and knelt beside him, cradling his head in her arms.

"Hang on, Joe," she urged. "You're gonna make it."

He smiled ironically. "I'm not," he choked. "But you are. You're gonna make it, Stephanie."

She caressed his cool cheek. "You never called me Stephanie before. Why are you calling me Stephanie?"

"It's your name. It's a nice name. You should use it. It makes you seem softer."

"Why would I wanna seem softer?"

He smiled gently and whispered. "Give somebody a chance to love you." He closed his eyes, still smiling serenely. She sat with his head in her lap, looking down at him. He looked so young and innocent, like a small boy who'd fallen asleep in his mother's arms. There was a round black mark on his forehead, but no blood. His face was clean and smooth and tranquil.

"Stef," she heard behind her. She turned her head to look.

Jackie stood there in a white smock holding a hypodermic needle.

"What are you doing here?" Stef asked, panicked. "You're not supposed to be here."

"I need to give you a shot," Jackie said, taking hold of her arm.

"What is it?"

"Telazol."

"That's what you gave Deuce."

"Right." Jackie pushed the needle through her skin. "It'll help with the pain."

***

Stef awoke to Deuce licking her hand. As she lay in bed staring at the ceiling, she realized she'd never had that particular version of this nightmare before. It hadn't been as bad as most of them. She wasn't sweating. Her pulse rate was normal.

She ran her hand over Deuce's head, listening to the waves lapping at the sides of the hull through the open window. She lay there for several minutes, trying to clear her mind.

Finally, she rolled onto her side to face Deuce. "What should we do today?"

He wagged his tail and hopped on his front paws with the joy of being spoken to.

"We could go swimming. You'd love that, wouldn't you? We could go fishing."

Deuce barked in an attempt to hold up his end of the conversation. Stef got up and stretched, went through her morning routine to the gentle rocking of the craft, checking in the bathroom mirror to see if yesterday's crying jag had left any evidence. She looked okay. Once she got away from Mrs. Avila, it was all over. But what a strange afternoon that had been.

She made coffee and fed Deuce, then took her place at

the helm. After one nearly full day of travel, she was gaining confidence as the skipper of *Mudbug*. She was ready to try some of the out-of-the-way avenues. She consulted the map she'd bought from Rudy to choose a destination. Whenever she looked at that map, her eyes drifted involuntarily to Stillwater Bay, that little inlet by the Sacramento River that never seemed very far away from any Delta destination. She had to make an effort to look away. She had a feeling that if she threw her knife at this map, it would land right there every time.

"Let's head into Steamboat Slough," she told Deuce. "It's just up the way. Maybe we can catch us a big old striper for lunch. If not, according to the map, there's a store a little further on at Snug Harbor. The store might be a safer bet anyway."

The morning was mild and the sun lit up the trees on the shoreline with a bright, slanted light that made them glow all colors of green. Along the north shore were several houses built on stilts to bring them up to levee height, giving the residents a view of the river. Stretching ahead, there were no houses on either bank. Just a wide open path.

When you stop somewhere, Marcus had advised, put her in a place where you can just pull straight out. The easiest thing is to go forward. Until it's second nature, avoid tight turns. So far, she'd been able to do that.

Stef put her coffee mug in the cup holder and shifted into gear. Just off the port bow, she thought she saw an animal pop up a rounded head, then dive back under. Sea lion? Sea otter? Did sea otters come this far inland? Jackie would know that, she thought. Then she mentally berated herself for thinking again about Jackie. She couldn't get Jackie off her mind, either her conscious or subconscious minds, apparently. She wanted to go back to Stillwater Bay and sweep Jackie into her arms and never stop kissing her. The hardest thing about resisting that urge was knowing how joyfully Jackie would welcome her back. In time, that wouldn't be true, but right now, Stef had no doubt.

A mile into Steamboat Slough, Stef chose a spot to pull to the side, out of the way of ski boats, and try her luck at fishing. She'd already picked out a pole from Compton's old equipment, so she baited a hook and tossed the line overboard, leaning the pole against the deck railing. Then she sat next to it with her guitar, Deuce lying beside her, and strummed a few soulful tunes.

Her mind drifted to the near disaster of Sunday night. If she hadn't returned to the bait shop, what would have happened? Rudy and his gun could have gotten him killed. Could have gotten them both killed. That Joey Cahill seemed like a tough little shit. He wouldn't have thought twice about it. She shuddered at the possibility. Fortunately, she had been there. Nobody was killed. Even Eddie would be okay. Stef remembered how good she felt after that incident. It reminded her of how she used to feel, a few months ago, when her life was on track and what she did mattered.

Thank you for saving our lives, Ida had said.

Today she was thinking about lives lost and lives saved. She'd saved lives before. Probably a lot of lives she'd never even know about. And taken a couple. That was the risk, the reality of protecting the public. Lives were at risk. Your own life was at risk. You knew it and you lived with it. Molina had known it. They used to talk about it. You trusted your life to your partner. She knew there were times he had saved her life. And she had saved his. Except the last time.

Not everybody could live with the idea that their life was on the line every day. To do that, you had to believe you'd be okay, like Molina with his *I'm indestructible* routine. Otherwise, you'd be too afraid to act. Fear was deadly to a cop. In the thick of the action, she'd never been afraid. Like the other night. She hadn't been thinking that she might be shot. Only that Jackie's parents were in danger. Every move she made was designed to protect them. She hadn't really thought about it at the time, but it came with the job. Protect the public. That was the job, plain and simple. Though she wasn't a cop anymore, the training and experience wouldn't go away overnight.

Molina hadn't really thought he was indestructible. "If I get killed," he'd said on more than one occasion. He'd finish that thought with some practical request, like making her promise to take Deuce. Those conversations usually occurred over a beer in a bar. When he got really serious, he'd call her "Stef." Most of the time he called her "Byers." Never "Stephanie." Only her mother called her that. It was yet another odd thing about this morning's version of her usual nightmare.

A ski boat sped past on the starboard side, jostling Stef to attention. The fishing pole still stood motionless. She realized she had no idea how long it was supposed to take to catch a fish.

"What kind of music do you think fish like?" she asked Deuce. "Maybe hillbilly music? I could play a little 'Cotton-Eyed Joe.'"

She played one verse, but the music reminded her so much of Jackie and her banjo, she stopped playing and put the guitar aside. Her mind returned to the odd events of the day before, of how they had informed her conscious thoughts and even her dreams ever since.

Mrs. Avila, as expected, had listened and said very little. One thing she did say, though, had stayed with Stef. "You haven't really given this Jackie a chance, have you? You decided what was best for her. You didn't let her decide."

"Because I know how I am now," Stef had said. "She's so sweet and happy. I don't want to drag her down."

"Did you ever think she might be strong enough to pull you up?"

Stef had been thinking about that ever since, about how she might have answered Mrs. Avila's question.

Jackie *was* strong. She knew who she was. She knew what she wanted. She was smart and resourceful. In the midst of a crisis, she was sensible and effective. Yet somehow Stef had been thinking of her as someone who needed to be protected from the big, bad world. The benign environment of an insular Delta town had made her seem unequipped for the harsh realities of life. As if she would crumble when presented with a serious challenge. But there was no evidence of that. In fact, it was Stef who had crumbled under pressure. It was Stef who had lost her way and her sense of self.

She looked across the shimmering water, feeling the heat of the rising sun on her back. "Is this what life on the river is going to be like?" she asked herself. "Having my mind wander all day, playing reruns and eating away at itself? Not to mention talking to myself."

She heard her phone vibrate against the wooden table beside her chair. She picked it up, thinking it might be her mother, but the name flashing on the display was "Jackie." She froze, then nearly answered, but decided to wait for a message, a heartfelt message she could easily imagine: *I miss you, Stef. Please come back. Give us a chance. I love you so much.*

When the message was done recording, she immediately called into voice mail, anxious to hear Jackie's voice. But her words were totally unexpected.

"A guy goes to a hospital to visit his buddy who's just gotten back from a hunting trip that went horribly wrong. The buddy asks how it happened. The hunter says he ran into an angry female bear with cubs. The bear attacked him. The hunter's dog fought off the bear, dragged the man to a safe location, then ran for help. 'Wow, that's a smart dog!' the buddy says. 'Oh, he's not so smart,' replies the hunter. 'He came back with a vet.'"

Stef stared at her phone in confusion. She heard Jackie's voice again as the message continued.

"Did you laugh?" she asked. "I hope you did. I'll make you laugh every day, even if I have to resort to stupid jokes. And that's how we'll do it."

Stef stared at her phone again, stunned for a second, then she burst out laughing. Deuce approached her chair and she reached over to acknowledge him with a pat. "That Jackie is a pretty special girl, isn't she? She's a keeper, don't you think?"

Still smiling, she stood up and reeled in her line, finding a bare hook at the end.

"Hey! I wonder how long it's been like that? The heck with this!" She leaned the rod against the side of the cabin. "What do you say we chart a course for home, boy, and get ourselves a big old slice of chocolate cake? Or at least a few strips of Ida's World-Famous Beef Jerky."

Deuce wagged his tail in response, looking up at her expectantly.

CHAPTER FORTY-ONE

As Jackie pulled up in front of the bait shop, she was surprised to see Rosa's Churrascaria at the edge of the parking lot in its usual spot. The food truck wasn't usually here on a Wednesday. They did better lunch business downtown on weekdays. She waved to Ben, and he acknowledged her with a nod as he handed an order through the window. Maybe she'd grab a lunch plate before she went back to the office, she decided.

She walked into the shop where her father sat at the checkstand reading the newspaper, his reading glasses halfway down his nose. He looked up at the sound of the chime and smiled.

"Hi, Dad," she said. "What's Rosa doing here on a Wednesday?"

Suddenly her mother appeared from the back room, cradling a jar of jerky in her arms and wearing a pair of denim cut-offs with frayed legs and red paisley patches sewn in an apparent random pattern. "They're here?" she asked, her face lit up with excitement. She scurried toward the door, leaving Jackie bewildered and alarmed.

"Mom!" Jackie called, running out after her, fearing a rerun of the earlier battle of parking lot dominion. Or worse, she thought, recalling Rosa's threat to move to San Diego.

Ida ignored her and continued toward the truck. She reached up and placed her jar on the edge of the gleaming stainless steel counter under the customer window. Nobody was there at the moment, and Jackie realized she had time to swoop in and correct her mother's folly before it was detected. She sprang toward the truck and snatched the jar off the counter.

"What are you doing?" her mother asked with a frown.

Ida grabbed for the jar, clamping her hands on either side of it. Jackie held on and a tug of war ensued just as Rosa appeared, coming around the back of the truck. Realizing it was too late, Jackie let go of the jar and allowed it to retreat into the protective embrace of her mother.

"Is that it?" Rosa asked, seeming strangely unruffled.

Ida threw one last look of consternation at Jackie before opening the jar and tipping it toward Rosa. She reached in and took a piece, then bit it and chewed for several seconds, a look of serious concentration on her face. Jackie realized she had no idea what was going on here.

"Yes, yes," Rosa pronounced thoughtfully. "I think you've got it now. The white peppercorn makes all the difference. Cumin level is just right. Nice and smoky."

Ida broke out in a smile of satisfaction and offered the jar to Jackie, who took a strip of jerky and tasted a bite while Rosa ate some more of her sample. This wasn't the usual flavor. Nor was it the papaya fiasco.

"What is this?" Jackie asked.

"*Tempero baiano*," Rosa answered. "A classic Brazilian spice mix. You've tasted it before on our shrimp. My version anyway. This is Ida's version."

"Is it a go?" Ida asked hopefully.

Rosa nodded and held up a thumb, the last of her jerky in her mouth. Ida slid her jar onto one side of the shelf as Ben appeared in the window and took a piece for himself.

"It's authentic!" pronounced Rosa. She reached out to shake Ida's hand, sealing their apparent new business arrangement. "But, remember, Ida, if sales are flat after three months, it comes off."

"Oh, no worries," Ida said, with a carefree wave of her hand. She started back toward the door of the shop. "That'll bring so many customers to your taco truck, you'll have to buy another truck."

Rosa opened her mouth to retort, but Ida had her back to them and was already on her way inside. Rosa turned to Jackie and shrugged in resignation.

"It's pretty good," Jackie said.

"It's fantastic," Ben interjected. "Fantastic that we found a compromise, I mean, but the jerky's not bad either."

"No, not bad," Rosa conceded. "It was your friend's idea, Jackie. What she said got me thinking about a Brazilian version, and Ida was all for it."

Jackie finished the jerky, then returned to the shop. Her mother was out of sight in the back room.

"Any word from Stef?" Rudy asked.

Jackie shook her head.

"Sorry." He folded his paper and took off his reading glasses. "Your mother's started this big campaign to shower her with fame and fortune. In Stillwater style, that is. She's been spreading the word all over town about Stef's brave deeds. How she brought down a sturgeon poacher and caught the notorious Stillwater Bay robbers and saved our lives. She's turned her into a living legend. A real hero."

"I'm not surprised. Mom just loves to talk, and now she has something interesting to talk about."

"That's not the whole of it, though. She's trying to create a sort of siren song to lure Stef back. She's got the mayor convinced that Stef deserves a medal. And the key to the city."

"She's doing that for me?" Jackie asked, incredulous.

He nodded. "She's even convinced Chief Schuller it's time to retire. He's putting in his paperwork this week and putting

Hartley forward as his successor. By August, the town will be ready to hire its new cop."

"Stef?"

"If your mother has done her job well, there won't be a single citizen who won't be rallying for Officer Byers to fill that vacancy. And you already know that Hartley is down with it."

Startled, Jackie shook her head, well aware that if her mother set her mind to something, she was a force to be reckoned with. "But Stef doesn't know anything about all this. And even if she did, I'm not sure it would do any good. I don't think she wants to be a cop anymore."

"Don't be too sure. Too bad you didn't see her in here Sunday night. That woman was born to that job like a fish is born to water."

Jackie sighed dejectedly. "It's nice that you and Mom are trying to help, but it's not going to do any good. Nobody knows where she is and I haven't heard a word from her."

Ida came out of the back pushing a hand truck loaded with six-packs of beer. "You talking about Officer Stef?"

"Yes." Jackie opened the door of the refrigerator case.

"We'll find her, you'll see," Ida said, loading the beer on wire racks. "I'm going to ask Hartley to put out an APB. We'll have Fish and Game officers combing every river and slough from here to San Francisco until they find her and drag her butt back here."

"Is that so?" Jackie asked sarcastically. "And once you get her back here, are you also going to tie her up and hold a shotgun to her head until she agrees to marry me?"

"If that's what it takes to make my little girl happy," Ida said, dropping in the last carton of beer.

Jackie heard her father gasp. She spun around to see a tall woman silhouetted in the doorway by the bright afternoon sun. *Stef!* Her heart leapt. Deuce stood behind her, his golden coat all aglow.

"That won't be necessary," Stef said evenly.

"Stef!" Jackie cried, overjoyed to see her. "You came back!"

Stef stepped inside and smiled affectionately at Jackie. "Yeah. I've got a bone to pick with your father." She winked at Jackie,

then turned to Rudy, who looked immediately antagonistic. She held up a plastic card. "I want to complain about this fishing license you sold me."

"What's the matter with it? It's legal. Did some warden tell you something was wrong with it? He's full of baloney." Rudy slid off his stool and came around the counter. "Let me see the ticket. I'm gonna call Fish and Game and complain."

"No, I didn't get a ticket," Stef said. "It just doesn't work."

"What do you mean?" Rudy frowned and put his hands on his hips.

"I mean it doesn't work. I had my pole in the water for two hours and nothing happened. Not a single bite. I'm going to starve out there."

Rudy threw up his hands. "And you're gonna blame me for that?"

Stef grinned at Jackie, who was beside herself with happiness.

"Dad, she's just kidding."

"Oh," he said, looking uncertain.

"Is there somebody around here who knows how to fish?" Stef asked. "Maybe I could use a lesson. I might have to stick around a while until I figure it out. It might take a really long time, even. I'm a slow learner. I might have to take up permanent residence, get a job, register to vote and all that stuff until I learn how to fend for myself out there."

"Well," said Rudy thoughtfully, his hand on his chin, "I know a guy..."

"You dope!" Ida jeered, jerking her head toward Jackie.

Jackie ran to Stef and flung her arms around her, then kissed her for a good minute while her parents stood by, neither of them making a sound.

"Permanent residence?" Jackie asked when the kiss finally ended. "Are you serious?"

Stef nodded. "It seems like this town kinda needs me. Besides, I don't think I'm cut out to be a river rat. But *Mudbug* might be a lot of fun on weekends. How would you like to explore the Delta with me?"

Tears welled up in Jackie's eyes. She thought she could see

something in Stef's eyes too. Not tears, but a depth of feeling she'd never seen before, an open, questing look full of love and trust. No more barriers.

"Mom," she said without taking her eyes off Stef, "how about getting us some sardines? I've gotta teach this woman how to catch a fish."

"If anybody can, Jackie," Ida declared, "it's you."

Stef nodded her agreement and held Jackie's face tenderly in her hands. "She's right. If anybody can teach me, it's you."

Stef kissed her mouth gently, then held her close, filling Jackie's heart with hope and happiness.

It'll be okay, Jackie thought. *You'll see. We'll be okay...together.*